MW00975092

Up To No Good

Marsha Cornelius

HICKORY FLAT BOOKS

Up To No Good

Copyright 2016 by Marsha Cornelius

First trade paperback edition December 2016

Cover design by aresjun@gmail.com

Manufactured in the United States of America

ISBN: 978-0-692-88477-5

Also by Marsha (M. R.) Cornelius

H10N1
The Ups and Downs of Being Dead
Losing It All
Habits Kick Back
A Tale of Moral Corruption

CHAPTER ONE

At first, I think it's a huge grub all bloated and draped over some dead leaves. As the three of us get closer, I see it's a used condom on the side of the road. Ellie's dog Oscar strains against his leash to get a sniff, his white, kinky-haired snout twitching.

"Ewww. That's gross," Ellie says.

"I don't believe it," Sarah says, bending at the waist to get a closer look. I think she's just showing off her tight glutes since she started that intense 90-minute workout on YouTube. She straightens and looks my way. "Rachel saw one a couple days ago over on Twin Branches, didn't you?"

I nod in agreement. But also because a little voice in the back of my head warns me that if I don't do something with my own butt soon I'll be requesting one of those extender seat belts on future airplane flights.

The three of us have been walking on Saturdays for a few years now so I'm kind of used to Sarah's gorgeous body. I've even soothed my jealousy with the standards: *Some women are just born beautiful. She's got an amazing metabolism.*

Lately, I've added a new rationalization; she's five years younger than me. *She'll be struggling too when she gets to be* . . . I can't even bring myself to think . . . *forty.*

Ellie drags Oscar away before he tries to eat the damn thing. "Who would decide to have sex right in front of the Richardson's house?"

Her question diverts me from depressing thoughts of my approaching birthday.

"Probably kids who can't do it at home," I say. "Teenagers who let their lust run rampant last night."

I envision a high school boy with rumpled hair, a pretty girl with perky breasts, wrangling in the back seat of a car. Then the girl morphs into a trim, sexy me and the teenage boy turns into a faceless man with a bodybuilder's bare chest and shaggy hair. We are entwined in each other's arms. Soft music plays on the car radio as he kisses my neck; a gentle breeze blows through the open window as his fingers ruffle through my hair. Then as he slowly skims his fingers across my breast—

"That's pretty desperate, in November," Sarah says.

My face flushes.

"It's been really warm the last week or so," I stammer. "Maybe the Indian summer roused primal urges."

"And they're going to have sex on every street in the subdivision?" Ellie asks.

How many streets would that be exactly? And how many different positions? The faceless man's hand roams up along my inner thigh. His breathing grows heavy as I run my fingers through the thatch of hair on his rock-hard abs. A perimenopausal flush ignites in my belly and heads south.

Sarah snorts. "Maybe it was Stan Richardson. He's got a girlfriend on the side and she texted him to meet her out front."

Ellie giggles, too. "I don't see how Stan could reach around that gut of his to get a condom on."

The vision of naked Stan Richardson replaces my bare-chested lover who unfortunately gets incinerated by my pseudo-hot flash and is reduced to ash.

"Maybe Marcy has had it with Stan and she's got herself a boy toy," Sarah says.

We all glance at the Richardsons' house. It's one of three basic designs in our starter-home subdivision. Like thousands of others, Brian and I bought into the American dream of owning a home in suburbia. Unfortunately it was right before the economy tanked so like most of our neighbors, we're living in a house that's currently worth less than our mortgage. It makes for lively conversation at community gatherings, particularly among the men. They hate getting caught with their financial underwear around their ankles.

Brian and I chose the floor plan of our house because it had a separate formal dining room. Don't ask me why that was important. I guess I had visions of throwing elaborate dinner parties with exotic food and stimulating conversations. My background in journalism is partly to blame. Back then I just assumed everyone wanted to discuss Pat Conroy's most recent book, or the situation in the Middle East. All these years later, we're still in our starter-home but my dining room table is currently piled with clothes that need folding.

I count back to determine just how many years that is. Fifteen. Then I'm reminded that we bought the house when I was twenty-five, which means next month I'm going to be . . . *forty.*

"Maybe it's some creepy single guy who still lives with his mother," Ellie says.

Her suggestion gets my mind going in a different direction. Sound bites of television interviews play in my head.

He seemed like such a nice guy.

He was always quiet . . . kept to himself.

"Maybe it's a serial killer," I say. "He brings his victim here, rapes her, kills her, then dumps her someplace."

Sarah gives me a scowl. Or at least I think she does. She's just gotten a new facial treatment where they injected her own fat into the wrinkles between her eyes, so it's hard to tell. When she told me about the procedure, I wondered just how much fat they could suck out of my butt, and what it would cost.

Her head definitely wobbles with skepticism. "I haven't seen anything in the paper about any dead bodies."

"Maybe he's burying them."

"Come on, Rachel. What about missing women in the news?" Ellie asks.

"They could be hookers, or runaway teenagers," I offer. "We should save the condom for evidence. DNA."

"Ewww!" Ellie says again. "You're going to pick that up?"

"I'll get a glove, and put the condom in a Ziploc bag. The police can keep it on file. This could be the most crucial piece of evidence in a heinous crime."

Sarah glances at me over her sunglasses. "The only heinous crime here is your imagination."

Oscar pulls on his leash, prodding us to move along.

At the corner, Ellie pushes the crosswalk button and the traffic light at the entrance to Hamilton Farms changes. We hustle over to Braxton Lane.

Ellie has Oscar trained not to take a dump until he gets outside our subdivision. His favorite spot is the first house on Braxton, a rental that has seen better days. The pressboard siding is buckled and mold has invaded giving the beige paint a green cast. The front porch railing is a bit askew.

We've been speculating lately that the house is vacant. It's hard to tell because every single Venetian blind is drawn tight. Personally, I don't know how someone can live with no daylight coming in, but Sarah insists that lots of people keep their blinds shut so the sun doesn't fade their furniture.

Braxton Lane is one of those odd streets that started out as a country road decades ago. A few families built one-story ranches but still held on to their farming roots, adding small barns, and chicken coops, and turning the whole side yard into a giant garden.

Then urban sprawl oozed its way into Mansell County. The large farms were snapped up for subdivisions full of starter homes with two-car garages—that is if one of them is a sub-compact. And the connecting roads like Braxton Lane have become a hybrid of country and city with new homes right next to the old.

This first house on the street was designed to look like the homes in our subdivision: two stories, a token gable on the roof, but builder's grade flooring, fixtures and appliances.

The original owners took some pride in their new home— added some landscaping, kept the lawn mowed—but they didn't stay long and ever since the house has been a rental.

If you ask me, it's the perfect site for a porn house. I ran the idea by Brian a couple weeks ago but he didn't really get it.

"You know," I said. "Where they fix up a bedroom in red velvet or black silk and shoot low-budget porn movies."

At the time he was trimming his toenails over the wastebasket which I understand is extremely important so I wasn't getting his full attention.

"The video might have two minutes of a couple chatting in a living room," I continued, "and maybe some preliminary oral stimulation on a sofa, but the bulk of the action takes place on a bed."

He dug a piece of crud out from under a nail and flicked it, missing the basket. That was the end of our conversation.

I decide to present my hypothesis to Ellie and Sarah.

"A porn house!?" Sarah screeches. "Where do you come up with these ideas?"

"Think about it," I argue. "You never see anyone in the yard. They don't leave garbage cans at the curb. I don't think anyone *lives* in the house. They just come over late at night, or after work, and make porn movies."

"And no one notices anything unusual," Ellie chimes in.

"What's there to see?" I say. "The blinds are all closed. It's not like some drug house where there's traffic at all hours."

"You must have lived in some stellar neighborhoods before you moved out here," Ellie says.

To back up my suspicions, I tell them about a custodian I knew who started dating a guy that was into kinky sex.

"He took her to an apartment where there was all this crappy furniture, but his bedroom was tricked out like a bordello with satin sheets and mirrors on the wall. He bought her sexy lingerie, and while they were going at it, he encouraged her to moan and scream."

"So the guy liked sex," Sarah says.

"It was more than that," I say. "I figured the guy had hidden cameras to tape the sex."

"That's kinda sick," Ellie says.

I nod. "She didn't seem to mind. She got lots of expensive underwear out of the deal. And great sex, or so she claimed."

Oscar hunches in the front yard of the porn house and poops.

Sarah clicks her tongue as she surveys the yard. "Look at all this crap. You should pick it up."

"Why?" Ellie says. "Nobody complains. And I don't have Regina from the Homeowners' Association chasing me with a plastic bag." She turns to me. "She'll probably come after you when she sees you walking Oscar."

Ellie and her partner, Joanie, are going up to New York for Thanksgiving week. Shows, dinners, the Macy's parade. I'm Oscar's designated babysitter and in return Ellie waters our plants when Brian and I are gone.

"Regina ought to investigate this porn house instead of bothering pet owners," I say.

"Well for one thing," Sarah says, "this house is not part of the subdivision. And I doubt if you could convince her that there's something going on here either. She's too busy measuring people's American flags, and scrutinizing flower beds for edibles."

We all chuckle. It took a specially-called association meeting to vote in favor of those purple ornamental cabbages that you see all the time. Regina was sure residents were secretly harvesting the stupid things for dinner. She's still fighting the plain green kale.

At Ellie's house, we all stand at the end of the driveway.

"So, listen," I say. There's no easy way to broach the subject. "Has Brian said anything to either of you about planning a surprise birthday party for me?"

They both give me non-committal head shakes that are tough to interpret. Are they trying to hide something or is there nothing in the works?

"Because I definitely don't want a party." The mockery of black balloons and adult diapers doesn't sound like fun at all.

"Are you sure?" Sarah asks.

"Positive."

"Because you can't wait until the last minute and change your mind."

"I'm not going to change my mind."

Ellie and Sarah glance at each other but I still can't read the look.

"This is a big event," Ellie says. "Turning forty."

I think they've been discussing it, probably trying to talk Brian into doing something.

"Come back when you're about to hit that landmark," I say, "and let me know how you feel."

Sarah sighs and shrugs her shoulders. "So what are you going to do?"

"We'll probably go out to dinner. Maybe go to a movie," I say. "We've got a trip to Florida coming up after Thanksgiving. Maybe we'll celebrate down there."

Oscar yips and tugs at his leash. He's exhausted his supply of lift-the-leg sprinkles and he's smelled the other dog's droppings. He's ready to go home and eat.

Once I get back from my walk, I root through the fridge for lunch. I'm starving even though it's only been three hours since I ate a bagel with peanut butter.

I swear the instant the temperature dropped in November, my fat cells jumped into overdrive. It's a constant 'feed me' all day long and it isn't even Thanksgiving yet, the official kick-off of the eating season. First it's pigging out on dressing, sweet potato casserole, and pecan pie, then office holiday parties, neighborhood soirees, family gatherings and drunken late nights. There's no hope of keeping my weight in check until after the Super Bowl.

I can't decide between canned soup or a cheese omelet so I head up to the man pit to let Brian decide.

We both work for an outdoor/wildlife magazine called *The Good Life*, Brian as a photographer and me adding the local color of where to stay and what to eat while waiting for elusive wildlife to appear. Or not. We also cover the lesser-known scenic destinations, outdoor festivals, you name it. Our column is called 'Off the Beaten Path'.

We work out of our home because the magazine is too cheap to supply us with office space or equipment. Each of us has our own work area in the two extra bedrooms.

Now when I call Brian's room a man pit, I'm not talking about a cute little corner bar and tons of stereo equipment, or a massive TV with La-Z-Boy recliners. His home office actually is a pit. The closet has four shelves for storage yet his camera equipment is strewn all over the bedroom floor. And instead of using the file cabinet I bought him for Christmas last year, he has piles of papers that surround his desk chair like a Wiccan circle of protection.

The only way to retain my sanity is to keep his door closed and spend as little time in there as possible.

Lately, he seems to be morphing into The Thing from the Pit. Most days he sits at his computer in a tee shirt and boxers. When fall arrived, he added a ratty bathrobe I swear he's had since college. He rarely shaves unless he's going out but I can't complain about that since I'm on my own hiatus from grooming my legs.

"What do you feel like for lunch?" I ask. "Chicken corn chowder or cheese omelet?"

He stares at his computer monitor with rows of pictures from our recent trip to the UK. Our assignment was the murmuration of starlings. That's where thousands of birds fly in huge swirling clouds, constantly changing patterns and direction. While Brian stood on a pier in the blustery winds of Aberystwyth, I drifted from pub to shop in search of unique gifts and the best chips in the area. The pubs were not as cleverly-named as the ones in Martha Grime's novels but the food was tasty and filling.

After a couple days, we left the West coast for Cambridgeshire in the East and Brian hunkered in bogs while I sampled lambs liver with bacon and onions. Believe me, I had to walk from one end of the village to the other to work off all I ate.

It's all part of giving our readers the whole package.

"Is there any bacon?" Brian asks.

"In the freezer."

"Can I have a bacon and cheese omelet?"

I click my tongue and wait until he drags his eyes from his computer monitor so I can give him the tortured wife stare. He gives me his version of the endearing smile. It used to work—those soulful puppy-dog eyes and crooked smile. Of course, that was when he wanted some nookie. Now when he uses 'the look' it's for food or to get me to scratch his back so it usually just pisses me off.

He realizes it isn't getting the job done and changes tacks. "Cynthia called."

"Oh, brother. She wants to hear all about Kelly and Martin." My eyebrow lifts into the 'arch of disapproval'. "If she wants to get in on the drama she's going to have to walk with us."

"So what is the latest, Gladys?" he asks.

Brian gave me the moniker Gladys Kravitz years ago because he thinks I'm a nosy busybody just like a character from an old TV show called <u>Bewitched</u> that was popular in the 60s. Gladys Kravitz was the snoop across the street from Samantha Stephens who happened to be a witch.

"Hey, it's the journalist in me, wanting to know the details, the facts."

He taps his chest. "Don't forget who you're talking to here. I don't buy that crap."

"Right," I snort. "You want to hear the dirt just like everyone else."

His mouth opens like he's going to protest but then he leans back in his chair. "So what's up?"

So here's the scoop: Martin is a shithead. He cheated on Kelly with some woman from work. He confessed to Kelly and we thought that was the end of it, but she just found out he's been going back for seconds. And this time Kelly found out by accident instead of him manning up. She took her hurt pride straight to an attorney.

Unfortunately, when she and Martin sat down with counsel to discuss the division of property, they discovered neither of them has the assets or make enough money to go it alone. The real estate market sucks and selling their house at a loss is not an option. Martin asked if he could live in the basement for the time being and Kelly has agreed.

Although according to Sarah, Kelly has laid out some rules that she posted on the refrigerator. Rule Number One: *Don't ever bring that whore into this house.*

"Come on," Brian groans. "You don't really think Martin would bring his girlfriend home."

I give him the sideways eye squint *and* the smirky mouth. "Who ever dreamed he'd cheat on Kelly after she forgave him the first time?"

"Good point." He sits up in his chair. "So about the bacon and cheese omelet . . ."

I sigh. Why didn't I just fix myself a bowl of soup? Now I have to thaw and cook bacon. It does sound pretty good though, so I back out of the pit and head downstairs.

As I get the bacon out of the freezer, I wonder if Brian has ever thought about cheating on me. I'm not sure when he'd even meet someone willing but he does go to the gym on a somewhat regular basis. Maybe some big-breasted hottie in tight yoga pants—*who isn't turning forty*— finds him attractive.

I imagine some babe ogling Brian's butt while I herd strips of bacon around the skillet. Does he give the girls at the front desk that same sexy smile when he's trying to get a free towel for the shower?

What's even more unlikely is that some woman could persuade Brian to stray. Ever since he turned 40 last March, I swear he's entered male menopause. He's never been one to initiate sex but he used to get whiney if he didn't get it on a somewhat regular basis. And whenever I made the slightest innuendo—like an eyebrow wag or a flirty smile—he had his hand on his belt, ready to go.

Now he doesn't even catch on when I make a suggestive remark. A couple nights ago we were watching one of those crime shows; a man was walking a woman to her front door. She smiled up at him, and in a sexy voice, she said 'How about a little snack before you go home?' In the next scene, they were wrangling in her bed just before the program cut to commercial.

I turned to Brian and wagged my eyebrows. "How about a little snack?"

And do you know what he said? "Nah. But I'll take a beer."

.

CHAPTER TWO

It seems like the only time Brian and I get physical is when he's tweezing the hairs on my neck or I'm rubbing Icy Hot on his frozen shoulder. If I'm in the mood for some nookie—like when I'm reading a steamy novel—I pretty much have to pounce on him.

Although to be honest, my loins don't burn like they used to, either. We're middle-aged and boring, I guess. I'm trying not to obsess about turning forty but I can't help it; there's just no excitement in our lives. And we're together so much, both working at home and traveling, that there isn't even much to talk about anymore.

His once full head of brown hair has thinned and gone gray at the temples. Even with all the walking I do, the sand is piling up at the bottom of my hourglass figure.

While I'm at the sink draining bacon grease into an empty can, I notice movement out the kitchen window. It's Lisa Bradford cutting across the common area of everyone's backyard. She slips up onto the deck of their house and in through the sliding door. She should be in school. I think she's a senior. If she's sick and coming home, why wouldn't she use the front door? Obviously she is sneaking in and doesn't want anyone to see her.

I stand at the window with frying pan in one hand, paper towel in the other, waiting. I figure some boy is going to dash across the yard at any moment. Then it occurs to me he might use the front door, pretending to make a delivery.

Brian plods into the kitchen and comes up behind me. He looks past my shoulder and out the window. "I'm planning on raking the rest of those leaves this afternoon."

Interesting, eh? How guys are always wary of what women are thinking.

I give a little shrug. "I just saw Lisa Bradford sneak into her house."

"Who's Lisa Bradford?"

My shoulders slump and I turn to look up at him. "Really? The Bradfords have lived across from us for seven years and you don't know who Lisa is?"

He knits his eyebrows and wrinkles up his nose. "Is that the wife?"

What a faker. The expression alone is a dead giveaway. I can't begin to count the number of times I've walked into the family room and caught Brian gazing out the sliding glass doors instead of parked in front of the TV, mesmerized. He's hoping to get a glimpse of the lovely Lisa with the tight butt and youthful breasts.

Catching her in a bathing suit, sunning in the back yard can get a man an envious pat on the back at a neighborhood gathering. I know several guys who come over here to watch sports on our crappy 36" TV just because of the proximity to the Bradfords' house.

I back into Brian as I move away from the window and feel an erection in his sweat pants. Dear god, he hasn't even seen her and he's got a boner? What has he been imagining?

After throwing away the greasy paper towel, I pick up my cup of lukewarm tea. And nearly blow a sip out through my nose.

Skipping across the common area like a wood nymph is a girl with long blonde hair and colorful leggings tucked into a pair of Uggs. Before she even gets to the Bradfords' deck, Lisa has the sliding door open, a huge smile on her face. There's a brief kiss before they both disappear inside.

That ought to get Brian's stiffy at full attention. I'd take advantage of the situation but I refuse to profit from an erection produced by an under-aged teen.

* * *

Years ago, our relationship stumbled into existence while we were working on the campus newspaper. Brian hung out with the other photographers, usually with two cameras slung around his neck, and a backpack of lens and accessories sagging off his shoulder.

My friends were other writers who loved to smoke pot, drink beer, and wax philosophical over politics, the environment, the new world order, you name it.

Now and then, Brian and I worked on an assignments together, him taking pictures, me interviewing a student who had accomplished something phenomenal, like raising a couple hundred dollars to feed a starving nation, or a professor whose unorthodox teaching included not using a textbook. But we didn't really connect until I started nosing around one of our fraternities.

There was nothing new about drugs on campus, but if you stopped the average student and asked them where they got their drugs, the answer was usually 'the Delts.' This was no big surprise. Every school has that fringe affiliate full of wasters and drunks. But why did so many students know about the availability while the administration seemed blind to the fact?

Okay so this created a bit of a conundrum. On the one hand, I was scheming to expose my local supplier—kill the golden goose—and probably piss off half the student body. I tried to talk myself out of it, but the sleuth in me couldn't let it go. Little did I know that I was Gladys in the making even back then.

I didn't expect to catch Eric Donaldson, the president of the fraternity, buying a cache of drugs in some seedy motel downtown, but I figured he was part of the Delts drug-selling business so I started following him.

This wasn't some big-time stake out. I had a life; I had classes to attend. What I didn't have was a car to stalk Donaldson in my spare time. Not that having a car would have done me any good. Within fifteen minutes of parking, a campus cop would surely have given me a ticket. I imagined the write up in the student paper's Police Beat column: *Student's vehicle was cluttered with empty Starbuck's cups, Twinkie wrappers, and a mayonnaise jar full of urine.*

I did get a copy of Donaldson's class schedule and instead of cutting through Leeds Hall to get to my Gender and Media Studies class, I'd take a longer route across Winston Park to see if he showed up for his Business Ethics class. Big surprise—he rarely did.

Between classes, I'd usually catch him hanging out at the student center where he was always chatting up other students. I'm amazed he didn't wear one of those sandwich boards with the drug-of-the-day listed.

My first big break came one morning when I saw frat boy Donaldson standing at the side of Loews Hall in the shadows, arguing with Dean Stanley, overlord of fraternities and sororities. They both looked pissed.

Where did a student get off snarling at a dean like that out in public? And if a dean wanted to chew out a student, why not in his office?

This was back in the 90s, so I couldn't just do a quick Google search on my phone to see if the two were related. But I could go through the archives at the newspaper, and I could also ask if anyone on the staff knew of a connection.

The office was empty except for one of our typesetters, a freshman wannabe sports writer, and Brian. He was sitting on a desk fidgeting with a lens. I decided he was better than nothing and posed my premise: The Delt house seemed to have immunity. Was there a connection with Dean Stanley?

Brian jumped at the chance to do some real investigative sleuthing instead of roaming the campus taking artsy-fartsy group shots of students being students. And that was a boon for me. How was I supposed to keep track of two people?

We compared class schedules so one of us could be at Pemberton Hall during lunch to see if Dean Stanley left the building. And whenever we had free time, one of us tailed Donaldson.

Each evening, Brian and I met at the food court for updates. I guess that's when it started. We never had anything to report but we insisted on getting together. Our feelings for each other were so subtle that I don't think either of us gave it a second thought.

There was no love-at-first-sight moment, although the first time I watched Brian dip a French fry in barbeque sauce, I felt a vague shift in the universe. I'd never known anyone else who ate their fries the same as me. I guess he felt the same connection because from that point on, we were inseparable buddies. I know it sounds pretty sappy, like in the Lady and the Tramp movie when they eat the same piece of spaghetti. But that's how it happened.

Then one afternoon, Brian was tailing Dean Stanley; I was following Donaldson. Frat boy was lugging a beat-up leather briefcase I'd never seen before. Was he trying to impress a girl, or a professor? When he walked into the law library I was sure he was putting on a show for somebody. I mean, the guy was barely passing his business courses. I had his future pegged as either a night manager at a fast-food restaurant, or a cocaine kingpin who would die a bloody death in a hail of bullets.

I thought I might lose him when he got on the elevator. I scurried up to the closed doors and listened for the bell to ding on the second floor. It didn't. So once the elevator came back down, I rode it up to the third and top floor.

As I ran on tiptoes past an aisle of reference books, I saw Brian crouched behind a row of red-bound legal briefs. I slipped in next to him and he jumped like a dead frog that had just taken a jolt of electricity. After glaring at me, he pressed a finger to his lips, like I was going to strike up a conversation.

Two aisles over, we saw Donaldson hand Dean Stanley the briefcase. They didn't say a word during the pass but as frat boy turned away, Stanley hissed at him, 'Don't you ever stop me on campus again.'

I nearly ruptured my diaphragm stifling a yelp of glee. Brian dragged me to the end of the row and we each pressed against a bookcase panel until the dean and frat boy left. We followed Stanley, and the briefcase, back to the administration building but that was pretty much the end of the line.

All the way to the student center we hooted and stomped at what we had stumbled across: a payoff of some kind. Over fries—our favorite 'share' food—we hashed through what we had seen. I insisted it couldn't be just a pay-off. Even if it was a couple thousand dollars, there's no way frat boy needed a briefcase to pass it along. If the case was full, it had to hold a lot of money, possibly all the fraternity's earnings from drug sales for the month. Could it be a week?

Brian suggested the dean was laundering the money. Fraternities and sororities were always holding fund-raisers, but what did they do with the money? Sure enough, we discovered that all of the Greek houses had accounts with the same bank—except the Delts who had a second account at a small-time bank down by the airport.

After a few weeks of skulking around, Brian finally got pictures of both Donaldson and Stanley with the same briefcase and we broke the story. We didn't have any hard evidence, just a lot of speculation; but we didn't care. I mean, it was just the campus newspaper.

The day the article appeared on the front page, half the staff joined Brian and me at Mack's Tavern for brewskis to celebrate. We talked about follow-up stories, and new angles. By four o'clock, we were drunk.

As Brian and I staggered across campus, we stumbled into each other more than once. Brian accused me of getting fresh with him, and I said something about 'if I wanted to get fresh it wouldn't be in Winston Park.'

He threw his head back and sang an old Cure song: 'It's always tease, tease, tease.' He even affected a great British accent. And when he got to: 'You'll have me when I'm on my knees', he actually dropped to the ground.

I laughed so hard I toppled down next to him, and the next thing I knew, we were rolling in the grass our tongues in each other's mouth.

Someone from the paper broke up our love fest with the news that Dean Stanley was holding a press conference; speculation was that he was going to tender his resignation. The knowledge that Brian and I had brought about this cataclysmic event was not only sobering, but arousing as well.

With no discussion whatsoever, we hustled to his apartment. Before the door banged shut we were ripping each other's clothes off. That was the first of what I classified as my 'top five best sex ever' romps. It has never dropped from its number one position.

Unfortunately, that was our last big story. Once we graduated, the only job Brian could find was with a Georgia tourism magazine. I hired on as a cub reporter for the Atlanta Journal Constitution where I covered city sewage problems and department of transportation street improvement schedules. Even then, I got busted once for embellishing a story about the recurring sinkhole on Tenth Street. All I said was that someone in city hall was lining their pockets at the taxpayers' expense. My editor wanted concrete evidence of graft or at the very least a reliable anonymous source to back my claim.

Now, besides my job at *The Good Life*, I also write short stories for a couple magazines where I can exaggerate all I want and get paid for it. One of the publications is all about romance and my pen name is Lisa LaFlame. Sometimes the stories are sweet with a syrupy HEA. (That's 'happily-ever-after' for the unromantic.) Other times I write torrid erotica. Needless to say, I haven't told many people about my side job. I can't have my mother reading about women penetrating men with dildos, now can I?

Another magazine I write for features mysteries and thrillers and I write under Rex Rogers. The stories contain brutal murders which would surely keep my mother up at night, so she doesn't know about that one either.

One thing is certain. I'm about to turn forty and I'm a long way from where I thought I'd be at this age. The idea of covering the carnage of a war-torn country never appealed to me, but I thought for sure I would have exposed at least one crooked politician or corporate head by now. My visions of cleaning up a polluted river or getting a whole town growing their own produce are long gone.

Instead, I'm toying with a story about the condom at the curb. I can't decide if this will be a Casanova on a tight budget for the romance magazine, or a serial killer targeting high school girls in uniforms for the thriller publication. I'm leaning towards a dog uncovering the dismembered hand of the latest victim and dragging it home.

CHAPTER THREE

Ellie and her partner Joanie are flying up to New York early Monday morning for a week of Thanksgiving festivities, so I told Ellie she might as well drop off Oscar Sunday night. She walks him over around nine o'clock.

"He tinkled and pooped," she announces proudly.

"Good boy."

"I brought his binky." She hands me a ratty beige blanket that's in tatters, and a bag of doggy treats. "I hope I haven't forgotten anything."

"Ellie, you live on the next block. If I need anything, I'll go get it."

"Right."

I can see she's reluctant to leave but it gets really weird when crouches in front of Oscar for a round of open-mouth kisses that include way too much dog tongue. Then she stands, a bit teary-eyed. "I'll see you Saturday."

Her voice wavers; and she isn't looking at me, she's looking at Oscar.

I'll be the first to admit I'm cynical when it comes to relationships between people and their pets. I saw a woman just last week at the mall with a little dog in a pink purse. It was wearing a hat that matched the woman's. I wanted to rip that hat off and shove it up someone's ass but couldn't decide whether it should be the dog for tolerating that nonsense, or the woman for spending money on something like that.

I guess I'm missing some kind of maternal gene, or else my sister Gwen got all that lovey-dovey stuff while I got the vivid imagination. And it's not just pets. I'm not real fond of kids either.

When I turned thirty-two, I went off the pill. After years of being badgered by my mother and Gwen, I figured I'd let nature take its course; and crossed my fingers that once I got pregnant those long-hidden maternal instincts would kick in. Eight years later, Brian and I still don't have kids. And now that forty is about to bite me in the butt, I guess I'll give up thinking about it.

I'm not sure what disappoints me more: the fact that I couldn't conceive or that I spent all that money on birth control pills. Brian never pushed to be a father so I never insisted he get tested to see if he was shooting blanks.

Besides, experts insist that children need strong role models who impose safe limits. When Gwen's son Jackson turned eight, I bought him a bow and arrow set and a pair of elf ears to look like Legalose from Lord of the Rings. I never thought the kid would aim it at his sister for the last piece of pizza. And the first time Brian decided to cook on a grill, he doused the charcoal with enough lighter fluid to set off an explosion that curled the paint on the back of our house. Do we sound like responsible adults?

I'm not even a good disciplinarian with Oscar. If he wants another treat, I say why not? Ellie's partner Joanie is wise to me. She shook the bag of doggie treats at me the last time I took care of him.

"Two treats after his walk," she said. "That's it." But between the rattling of the crunchy bits and Oscar jumping into the air, barking for a treat, I wasn't sure if she meant two itty bitty pieces or two handfuls.

The first time I dog-sat, Ellie insisted all I had to do was go by her house a couple times a day to walk and feed him. Yeah, right. In a single day he managed to knock over the wastebaskets in every room, consuming anything that smelled even remotely edible, then barfed used Kleenex and peanut shells all over her hardwood floors. He even crapped out hair-embedded wax. And the moment I opened the front door, he attacked my bare legs like he hadn't had human contact in weeks. I still have a scar on my right shin.

Now he stays at our house where I can keep a close eye on the little psycho, and the wastebaskets.

"Don't worry," I tell Ellie, putting a reassuring hand on her shoulder. "He'll be fine. Have a fun trip."

Once Ellie is gone, Brian gets into a rousing game of roll-the-tennis-ball while he watches the first season of *Oz* on Amazon. This is where he holds the ball with his foot while Oscar frantically nips and digs at his shoe. Then just when Oscar seems to lose interest, Brian kicks the ball into the kitchen, Oscar scrambles after it—his toenails scraping down to the polish on my dirty vinyl floor—and brings it back. He drops the ball, Brian covers it with his foot, and the battle begins anew. This goes on until Oscar collapses from exhaustion.

Imagine my surprise when I am awakened at the crack of dawn Monday to shrill barking. I can only guess that the North Koreans have landed and are in my front yard with bayonets drawn.

Brian groans and drags his pillow over his head. I pry one eye open to check the time and temperature on our clock. 7 am. And a frigid 34 degrees. Indian summer is over.

Evidently Oscar hasn't sensed the dramatic climate change until he steps out into the arctic cold. Then he performs a full body shiver and sniffs the immediate area for a convenient spot to drop his load. I'm not having it. We power-walk through the subdivision, my head tucked down against the wind. There are no new condoms tossed to the curb. We work up a little heat as we dash across Barnsley Mill against the light.

As I wait for Oscar's haunches to thaw so he can squat, I study the porn house and its steep driveway that starts at street level and angles down to a basement garage. How does anyone get up that driveway if there's ice? Not that we get that many ice storms in Atlanta, but it happens.

While Oscar performs his finishing ritual of digging up clumps of grass with his hind legs, a woman walking her own dog strolls toward me.

"You're too late," she says.

Her comment throws me for a loop. Is she referring to Oscar?

"They rented the place about two months ago."

"Ah," I say, relieved that she isn't going to demand I pick up the poop. "Do you ever see the renters?"

"Nope. Pretty much keep to themselves."

She's a wiry, stooped woman probably in her sixties, with a gaunt face that suggests a lifetime of cigarettes and booze.

"A car in the driveway?" I ask.

"I seen them pull into the garage once. Sometimes they's lights on late at night. Upstairs mostly."

Yeah, when they're wrangling around on a bed gyrating and groaning for the cameras.

Her accent is definitely Alabama country. There's none of that breathless genteel cadence, just raw southern twang.

"This here's Milo," she says.

He's a black and tan mutt about the same size as Oscar but without the pedigree.

"This is Oscar," I play along. "But he's not mine. I'm just pet-sitting."

"I'm Milo's mama," she says. "Fran."

I reach out to shake hands as I tell her my name is Rachel but the gesture throws her for a loop. I don't think country women shake hands yet.

She tells me she and her husband Jimmy are retired. I envision him with a bright green John Deere hat, a beer gut, and a full beard that's harboring a few crumbs from yesterday's chicken biscuits. I'm sure Fran has coffee and cigarettes for breakfast.

They live in the corner house that faces Hamilton Farms. It's an older two-story with faded aluminum siding and a carport that looks like it was added later. The house was no doubt in better shape when Jimmy and Fran bought it forty years ago. It doesn't look like they've done much to maintain it since. They have the standard 'country folk' giant garden in their back yard; dandelions and clover serve as their front lawn.

Our dogs sniff each other's butts and decide to be friends.

"So do you ever notice anything unusual at the rental house?" I ask, trying to be vague.

"You mean like drug dealin' or Satan worshippin'?"

I'm not willing to share my theory with this woman yet, so I just shrug my shoulders. "I never see any garbage cans."

"Yeah. Jimmy figures they haul it themselves to save money."

"That's probably it," I say.

Oscar mounts Milo in an attempt to take a walk on the wild side so I pull on his leash. Keeping a tight rein, I tell Fran it was nice meeting her, and head for home.

I can't wait to tell Brian the latest.

"Huh. Lights on at night," he says while he stirs creamer into his coffee. "Like when they're getting ready for bed?"

Why did I think he was going to suddenly be intrigued? If I'm going to get him on board I'll have to find something more concrete.

As I pour myself a cup, I consider what it would take to get some evidence, and of course, how much effort I'm willing to put into getting it.

"The reason I never see anything going on at the porn house is because the action takes place at night," I tell Brian. "If I want to catch someone in the act I have to be there at the right time."

He shakes his head and walks away, one end of his robe belt dragging along the floor.

Once the sun goes down, the temperature drops to thirty. Brian is parked in front of the TV binge-watching old *Sunny in Philadelphia* episodes so he certainly won't want to walk with me. He got really pissed when Amazon suddenly started charging after episode six of *Oz*. Once his rant about unscrupulous marketing tactics died down, he switched shows. I think he was hoping I'd give him the go-ahead to pay for views. I don't know why. He knows we're poor.

I pull on my warm boots and stocking hat and wrap a muffler around my face.

Oscar is less than accommodating. He pees one long stream the moment he steps off the porch instead of visiting every shrub for a tiny squirt. Then he bolts back toward the house.

"No way, Pal. We're on a mission."

I drag him the three blocks to the entrance of the subdivision, and he's so reluctant I actually have to pick him up to cross the street.

I'm still holding him in my arms when I spot a fancy SUV parked at the bottom of the porn house driveway. The driver took the time to turn the car around before getting out; either that or he backed down. Planning on a fast getaway?

There are no lights on upstairs, or in the front rooms. Is there an orgy in progress on the kitchen table? If only I could come up with a reason to be in the back yard, I could see if all the blinds are drawn.

As I ponder the situation, a light goes out somewhere in the back and moments later the garage door rolls up. A couple scurries to the car. He's wearing all black, and she has on a short tight skirt and one of those fake fur shrugs. I can't see very well, but I bet she's wearing fishnet stockings, too. Her heels are real spiky, and when she grabs the car door handle, all of these bracelets jangle. 'Hooker' comes to mind.

He probably picked her up downtown, paid for a couple hours, and brought her here where he could secretly film their salacious romp.

I sprint home to tell Brian about this new development. Oscar is right on my heels.

"I was right," I say between gasps for air. "It *is* a porn house." Oscar jumps into the air and yips his own confirmation.

"How do you suddenly know this?" Brian asks without taking his eyes off the TV.

"I just saw a man and woman drive away in a fancy SUV."

"And your deduction comes from the fact they left their home after ten o'clock. Or was it the fact that they can afford an expensive car."

"You should have seen the way she was dressed."

"Just because you prefer sweat pants and bulky sweaters, doesn't mean all women do."

That takes me back a bit. Somewhere in the depths of my mind the word 'frumpy' taunts me. Tears sting my eyes. Have I turned into a bag lady? Now that I'm turning forty, will I start wearing those horrible 'house coats' with snaps? A 'bed jacket' for reading at night? Dear god, will I suddenly spend time pouring over yarn at Michaels?

I try to think back to the last time I wore a short skirt, or even a pair of tight pants. It might have been during the Clinton administration.

I always thought I had a good excuse; trekking through the wilderness calls for hiking boots, not fuck-me pumps. And wandering around towns eating local fare and checking out lodging requires loose-fitting pants and layers to be shed.

Could Brian's lack of amorous attention actually be my fault? When we first visited out-of-the-way places, we enjoyed getting frisky in hotel rooms. But as we got better at our jobs, we grew more distant. Brian is a sunrise to sunset kind of person. He wants to be in place at first light to capture early morning activity. And he often doesn't come back until after dark.

I tour towns rain or shine, hot or cold. And once I get back to our hotel, I want to get the details down on my laptop while they're fresh in my mind. I usually do that while dining alone.

Not only have we lost our edge as hard-hitting investigative reporters, we've lost the juice that made our jobs exciting. Now we're nothing more than middle-aged tourists who are paid to get fat.

It occurs to me that this whole porn house business might be a way for us to work together on something more thrilling than an annual bathtub race in Wisconsin.

"I've got to get a look inside that house," I say.

"What you've got to do is leave it alone—Gladys."

"You should have seen the tight skirt she was wearing. And short? Whew. I bet when she sits down you can see everything."

"And you think if I peek in their window, she'll sit down and let me have a look?"

He has a point.

But I have a good rebuttal. "When he's filming, I bet she really moans and claws."

"And I'll be on a ladder peeping in the second floor window, right?"

Okay, maybe I'm not going to rekindle our marriage with this scoop. But as I trudge out of the family room, I glance back. Brian is staring out the sliding glass door into the night. Is he thinking about peeping?

CHAPTER FOUR

You know those commercials where this huge extended family gets together for Thanksgiving? Someone unexpected arrives to everyone's delight, grandma and grandpa still gaze lovingly at each other after all these years, and a little kid commits a minor faux pas that they all think is adorable.

Well, Thanksgiving at my sister Gwen's house isn't at all like that. The only out-of-towners are my parents who insist on hauling their 33-foot RV all the way from Ocala to Atlanta so my dad can sleep in his own bed. We all know the real reason is that he can't handle Gwen's kids for more than a few hours, and he refuses to share a bathroom. That last bit is more than enough reason. If you've ever walked past an open bathroom door after my dad has been in there, you understand.

Gwen's oldest son, Sam is also an out-of-towner, but he won't be here because his band has a 'gig' Friday night in Topeka. At least that's what he told Gwen and Jake. I'm sure the real reason is because Sam's hair hangs to his shoulders. Jake's idea of a haircut is buzzing a clipper with a half-inch guard all over his head. Sam's ears are pierced in several places, and he's got tattoos running from his shoulders to his wrists. The only thing that could drive a deeper wedge between Jake and Sam is if Sam came out and told them he was gay.

I used to worry about my dad falling asleep at the wheel of his enormous quad cab truck while pulling their RV and wiping out four families at once, but now that my mom has the latest i-Phone, she keeps me posted on their travel progress with up-to-the-minute texts. Like:

Shouldn't have made your father oatmeal for breakfast. Riding with my window open. And then an emoticon of a dark cloud.

Or:

Stopping at Cracker Barrel for pralines.

Of course, I have to answer each text or she'll think I've been kidnapped by Muslims, so Tuesday I don't get anything done.

My mom insists on arriving early so she and her girls can spend the whole day Wednesday preparing to prepare Thanksgiving dinner on Thursday.

She tries to get Gwen's two younger kids Allison and Jackson (of the bow and arrow fame) involved in making table decorations, which never goes well. Allison is sixteen; need I say more? Jackson is now twelve. Last year the handprint turkeys he made had been stabbed with candy corn and left bleeding to death at each place setting.

I participate in the girls' food shopping extravaganza Wednesday along with four thousand other shoppers who waited until the day before Thanksgiving. Mom wants to be a part of the holiday shopping process which includes buying the last mangled bag of celery, settling for canned cranberry sauce because there are no more fresh berries, and waiting in line for 30 minutes to check out.

I go along hoping for fodder for a murder mystery; Gwen has to go or my mother will totally change the menu.

There's nothing more excruciating than standing in line with my mom. She tells total strangers what we're fixing then she analyzes their groceries and tries to guess what they're doing for Thanksgiving. 'Oh, a duck. How interesting.'

She also tries to strike up conversations with children who have been warned *not* to talk to strangers so they hover behind their mother in fear.

Or, god forbid, Mom gets into embarrassing conversations with Gwen and me. 'Did that rash on your inner thigh ever clear up?'

Thursday morning is pie baking. I choose my usual pecan pie and Gwen opts for apple even though she usually makes pumpkin.

Mom wants to try a new recipe using a fresh pumpkin, so there's lots of scraping and roasting. Later when I go to the bathroom I find an errant seed in my underwear. Go figure.

While pies bake, I peel potatoes. Mom decides to help since she and Gwen have already discussed all the cute kids they've seen on the Ellen Show.

"What are your plans for your birthday?" she asks.

"We're going out to dinner, and maybe a movie."

"That sounds boring for such a milestone," she says. "Isn't there some sort of party planned?" She glances at Gwen and gets some kind of snarly look.

Then with her eyes bugged out, Gwen says, "No Mom. You know how Rachel hates stuff like that."

Crap! My mom almost spilled the beans on a surprise birthday party and now Gwen's trying to cover it up. I've been hounding Gwen and Brian, and even Sarah and Ellie, NOT to plan a birthday party for me. I see nothing to celebrate about turning forty.

I'm going to have a talk to Brian as soon as he gets here.

He won't even come over until the football game starts at one. He and Jake are polar opposites. Brian has been known to paraphrase Nietzsche now and then; especially the one about whatever doesn't kill you makes you stronger. Jake thinks Nietzsche was a linebacker for the Green Bay Packers.

I'm sure they both have fantasies about women but in different ways. It wouldn't surprise me to hear that Jake forced himself on a few women in his younger days. Brian, on the other hand, wouldn't get aggressive if I patted my tushy and taunted him with 'Come on Big Daddy.'

My dad and Brian get along fine, as long as Brian is content to listen to my dad talk about fishing, his ailments, or dumping the contents of the black water tank in his RV.

"Jeez!" Brian fumed one night when we were driving home from a visit with my parents. "You dad walked me through the whole process of dumping the shit out of his camper and then making sure his grey water tank was full to flush out whatever was left in there." Then Brian actually clamped a hand on my shoulder. "Don't ever leave me alone with him again."

The only things all three of the men have in common are sports and eating. If Brian shows up for the kick-off, he and Jake and my dad can talk stats and eat buffalo chicken dip all afternoon while the women slave in the kitchen.

Naturally, my mom wants to use Gwen's good china even though it has to be hand-washed after dinner.

"Let's use the crystal, too," she says.

"No mom," Gwen says, but my mother is already pulling glasses out of the hutch.

"Oh, my look at all the dust," Mom says. Then she gasps and flies over to the sink. "There's a dead bug in this one."

She rolls her eyes at Gwen for being a lousy housekeeper. I roll my eyes at Gwen for not checking the glassware before Mom arrived.

Brian shows up right on time. I push him backwards into the small hallway off the kitchen.

"I thought you said you weren't planning a birthday party for me," I whisper.

"I'm not."

"My mom seems to think you are."

Brian gives me the vapid blink. "Why would she think that?"

Damn, he's good. Either that, or he's not planning it. Sarah or Ellie are, even though they said they weren't. I say a quick prayer that Gwen is not planning the party. If she is, my folks will be back for that.

I turn Brian loose and he scurries into the family room, answering the call of the Buffalo dip.

At four o'clock we all sit down to Thanksgiving dinner. I swear the conversation is always the same.

"Everything is delicious," my dad says.

"Uh," Jake grunts as he shovels in another mouthful.

Living with a writer has taught Brian one thing. Don't generalize. "The dressing is fantastic. Do I taste sage?"

My mom complains that the breast meat is dry. (Because Gwen left it in too long.)

"The whipped potatoes could have used some butter," Gwen shoots back. She harped at my mom all the time she was mashing them to add butter, but my mom insisted using chicken broth was healthier.

"Nice carving job, Dad," I say as I pick through the platter of decimated bird, looking for the dark meat.

By four-thirty the men are back in front of the TV.

I paw through Gwen's massive collection of plastic ware for lids while Mom picks every last morsel of meat from the turkey carcass. Now that the feast has been shopped for, prepared, eaten, and analyzed, we have nothing to talk about.

This is the most dangerous time of the parental visit; Gwen and I have had a couple glasses of wine, all the stress from the dinner is over, and our lips are no longer sealed.

Mom's first post-dinner question is a doozy.

"What size bra is Allison wearing now?"

That's the precursor to sticking her nose in Allison's business. Once we talk about her developing breasts, can questions about boys and dating be far behind? I figure I'll gain some points with Gwen if I change the subject.

"I think we have a porn house in our neighborhood."

I realize my Freudian slip—jumping from dating, to sex, to putting out to every boy on the football team—but Mom and Gwen haven't followed my train-of-thought.

Jake wanders in for a beer. "What's a porn house?"

He's a moose, with the broad shoulders that were perfect for mowing down other guys in football but I think he may have taken one too many hits himself in high school.

"You know," I explain. "Where they make porn films. I'm pretty sure that's illegal." He may be a cop but sometimes he needs a little nudge to make a connection.

He snorts and shakes his head like I'm stupid. "Why do you think it's a porn house?"

"You never see the hose dragged out. Or the flag up on the mailbox."

"And you stake out the house every day, so you'd know."

Brian wanders into the kitchen and drains the last of the wine from a bottle of Pinot Grigio. I suspect he's also there to intervene if I draw a knife out of the rack on the counter.

But I keep my cool. "There aren't any pets, or kid's toys in the yard. I don't think anyone lives there. They just use the house for filming."

"You don't have pets or kids," Jake counters.

Brian's back stiffens but he doesn't say anything. Behind Jake, I see Gwen shaking her head at me. The universal signal for 'Don't rile him up.' My mom has this really weird expression that kind of jumps from fascination to horror, like those holographic pictures of clowns that smile in one direction and frown when turned a different way.

All I can think of is how two girls born to the same mother and father have turned out so differently. Before I even finished college, Gwen was married to this neanderthal and pregnant with Sam.

When Gwen and I were young, she was the one who played with dolls, pretending to be the mama. I was reading the Choose Your Own Adventure books and the Chronicles of Narnia.

I remember my grandmother showing us through her old dusty attic once. I was captivated by an armoire, sure that if I climbed in I could come out the other side in some strange land. Gwen got all gushy over an old baby buggy.

In high school, Gwen paraded an endless procession of wrestlers and football players through our home. I brought home snails and interesting rocks. While she drooled over Tom Selleck, I tried to solve the case before Magnum.

All these years later, I'm still a mystery to both my mom and Gwen, and I'm still locking horns with Jake.

My mother has decided on horror, and gives me the high-sign to knock it off.

I'm not supposed to start something with Conan but it's okay for him to ridicule me? And the fact that a police officer—a detective no less—who has sworn to uphold the law refuses to even consider that I might be right. It just infuriates me.

"What if they're making snuff films?"

"In Batesville?" he says. Then he props a ham-y fist on his hip. "Do you even know what a snuff film is?"

I get right back in his face. "I just thought the police would want to know about something like this."

"You know what, Rachel? Cops can't just dream up wild stories and spread them around. We need evidence." He tilts his head back and guzzles half his beer like that kind of behavior is impressive. Then he waddles out of the kitchen.

I'm ready to charge after him when Brian catches my arm. "Can we go home now?"

His left eyebrow cocks up in a challenge so I throw my own back at him. "I'll go home as soon as you promise to help me get some proof about what's going on in that house."

CHAPTER FIVE

Brian has his coat on and is heading for the door when I grab his hand. We came in separate cars so I know he's hoping to make a fast getaway. I try to make it look like a lover's clasp of affection but after he tugs a couple times to get free it's pretty obvious he wants to escape the long goodbyes in the foyer.

I'm not even sure why everyone has gathered at the door. We're all getting together tomorrow for our festive Black Friday 'brawl at the mall'. This is where we draw names over breakfast at Gwen's—usually cheese grits, egg and sausage casserole, and mom's stick-to-your-ass cinnamon rolls—and then lumber to the mall to find the perfect gift.

Don't misunderstand. There is no secrecy in the name drawing. Last year, as soon as I got my dad's name, I groaned and showed it to everyone else at the table, who also groaned. That's because shopping with my dad will take a couple years off your life.

Confused?

Okay, here's how it works. Less than 1% of the American population actually has a good idea for a Christmas gift so we end up asking our friends and family members what they want for Christmas. But the gifter can still get into a lot of trouble even if giftee says 'I want a red cardigan sweater' because there are so many different styles of cardigans and colors of red. And of course before the Internet, the giftee had to flip through every ad in the Sunday paper hoping to find something remotely similar to what she wanted.

Our solution is to take the gift recipient shopping and let said recipient select the exact sweater color and size—and price. We set a price range so that nobody feels cheated on Christmas morning, and more importantly, to keep my mom from shopping at Goodwill.

Once the names are drawn and disparaging comments made, we divide into morning shopping and afternoon shopping with a break for lunch at the mall food court that is so crowded we've been known to sit on the floor with our burgers and lo mein.

Sound like fun?

While we're all standing in Gwen's foyer saying our goodbyes, my mom decides to tell us about her neighbor Brenda in Ocala who has started hanging around with new resident Burt. Mom has suspected the two are up to no good (that's code for shacking up). Then two weeks ago Brenda put her camper on the market. Shocking, eh?

No, not that Brenda intends to move in with Burt; that my mom had two days to relate this sordid tale but has waited until I'm trying to go home to tell us.

And of course she has to give us all the reasons why Burt is a no-account, a braggart, definitely a gigolo and quite possibly a criminal who preys on lonely women. Each time she lists one of his faults, she ends it with 'Isn't that right, Cal?' and my dad nods.

As I nod, I wonder if Brian will take the initiative and walk Oscar when he gets home; I'm sure he'll get there before me. And Oscar is not a part of my scheme for tonight, which is scoping out the porn house. I'm sure Brian is regretting that he agreed to my demands. His head bobbing is probably silent agreement that he's made a big mistake. I imagine as Gwen nods she's thinking about whether to empty her dishwasher tonight or in the morning. And Jake's pea brain is no doubt pinged around in that empty skull as he nods.

Oscar attacks as soon as I open the front door. Small wonder since he's been cooped up since noon. I can't even get his leash latched before he bolts out of the door and lifts his leg on the first bush he sees. How did Brian manage to even get past him?

It couldn't have taken more than a minute for the dog to get his business done, but by the time I get to our bathroom, Brian is brushing his teeth with one hand while attempting to step into his pajama pants with the other.

"What are you doing?" I ask.

He jerks his head up and gazes at me in the bathroom mirror, toothpaste drooling out of the corner of his mouth. His pajama pants fall to the floor around his feet.

"Ah wah genna weddy fa beh."

I cross my arms and give him my best cold stare. "I thought we were going to check out the porn house."

He leans over and spits, then takes an inordinately long time to rinse the residue off his chin. And then there's the blotting with the towel and the smoothing of the remains of his hair.

"I didn't realize you meant tonight," he says. "We've got a big day tomorrow."

"What part of 'as soon as we get home' confused you?"

I consider bringing up the fact that it is barely nine o'clock but starting an argument will do nothing to further my agenda.

Instead I smile sweetly. "Dress warmly."

He pulls a pair of sweats over his pajamas and skulks out. I step into a pair of my own sweats and find a matching black sweatshirt. For a millisecond I consider getting a piece of charcoal from the grill to blacken my face but I'm sure Brian will never let me hear the end of that. He'd probably even tell Jake.

I have to rummage around in the garage for a minute so by the time I get to the front door, Brian stands leaning like he's been waiting for hours. And he's wearing his bright yellow plastic parka. You know, like the kind policemen wear when they're directing traffic so they don't get run over.

"Really?"

"It's the warmest coat I have," he says.

"You do understand the objective here is NOT to be seen." I wave a hand down my front to display the black I'm wearing.

I dig through the coat closet for an old black hoodie for him and a puffy insulated vest for me.

My black knit headband keeps my ears warm but it's no match for the gusting wind that blows my hair into my face. I pick up the pace on Hamilton Farms Avenue to loosen up the muscles that automatically clenched the moment we stepped out of our front door. I figure a speed walk will work off a couple bites of pecan pie, too.

As we wait for traffic to clear at Barnsley Mill, Brian fusses. "I don't know what you think you're going to see in the dark."

"If I can't see anything then it'll be a short trip, won't it?"

I decide no good will come from telling him I have a flashlight. There's an off-chance someone will see the light and come to investigate. Or call the police.

Other than Brian's mood, my plan is perfect. I have Oscar's leash dangling from my hand, and I call his name as we cross the highway to Braxton Lane.

"Oscar! Here boy."

Even though there are no lights on inside, I march up to the front door of the porn house and knock. '*Have you seen my dog?*'

When no one answers, my plan moves on to phase 2. I'm going to pretend I hear barking in the back yard and Brian and I will scurry down the driveway to investigate. Brian's assignment is to stand guard at the back corner of the porn house, right by the garage.

"If anyone drives in, come and get me. We'll boogie around to the opposite side of the house while they're busy parking."

"You've got to be kidding," he says.

"How else can I see in the back windows? Hopefully there will be an open blind or at least a crack in some curtains."

"And when you see they have furniture that's a lot nicer than ours, what next? Am I going to have to get a second job?"

There's no point in carrying this conversation any further. He's not going to be happy no matter what I say. Best to keep things moving.

The backyard is small with a thin stand of trees separating it from a subdivision on down the slope. I don't see any lights shining from the backs of those houses. Either folks are already in bed or have slipped into a tryptophan coma in front of their TV.

I notice a faint light shining out of the only window on the first floor of the porn house, probably the stove light that everyone leaves on in their kitchen. But the window is too high for me to just walk over and peek in so I search for other options.

A small deck juts off the back. It's not more than three or four feet off the ground, and is barely big enough for a couple chairs and a grill. I slip up the two steps to have a look through sliding glass doors but they're covered with heavy plastic-insulated drapes. I fish my small flashlight out of my pocket, check over my shoulder once more for any signs of life, and then flash the beam between the little bitty crack in the curtains. I can't see a thing. I try the door but it's locked of course. I spot a broken broomstick wedged into the slider at the bottom.

Time is ticking. I figure Brian is good for about three minutes before he comes back to see what's happening.

I guess it's the kitchen window or nothing. I stand under the window and reach my hands up to the sill but even on tiptoes, I'm not tall enough to see in or strong enough to pull myself into a chin up.

Now I could get Brian and ask him to lace his fingers and boost me up, but of course he'll snort at the idea and declare the mission over.

Instead, I make a quick search of the back yard. No garbage cans, no picnic table. I squat so I can shine my light under the deck. Bingo! An old aluminum chair is wedged way back under the steps.

I know it's too cold for spiders or snakes, and I don't think rodents would set up a home in this drafty spot but I still can't force myself to crawl under there. I dash over to the tree-line searching for a dead branch on the ground.

With the perfect probe in hand, I drop to my knees at the deck and immediately feel wetness seep into my sweats. After the initial dismay, I reach the branch under the deck and snag the chair, but I pull too hard and the end of the branch breaks off. I hunker under a bit farther and try again, gently easing the chair along the dirt.

Once I have it out I'm disheartened to see that the webbing in the seat of the chair has disintegrated. Undeterred, I carry the chair over to the window, unfold the aluminum frame and put some weight on the arms. They feel fairly sturdy.

The ground steadily slops downward towards the garage, so I wedge the back of the chair against the siding of the house for some stability. Then I gingerly ease a foot up onto the aluminum seat frame while using my hands as a counterweight on the arms of the chair. Once both feet straddle the gaping hole where the seat used to be, I grip the windowsill, lifting as much of my weight as I can, and step onto the arms. The aluminum pings from the stress.

Why did I decided to investigate after eating the biggest meal of the year? As the chair sways, I think back to the dollop of mashed potatoes I licked off the spoon and the crusty bits of dressing I nibbled as I helped put leftovers away. I'm embarrassed to admit this, but while my mom and Gwen were arguing over whether to save the last two teaspoons of cranberry sauce, I snatched a big bite of pecan pie someone had had the good sense to leave on their plate.

I suck in a big breath, inflating my lungs into balloons that will magically float my bulk off the chair. Then bracing my forearms on the windowsill, I peek inside.

Just as I suspected, there are no small appliances on the counter, no canisters, no spice rack on the wall or dish soap bottle at the sink. This kitchen is not used. Something catches my eye on the far counter but the stove light is not bright enough to make out what it is. I slowly lift one arm off the sill and reach into my pocket like I'm fishing out a bottle of nitro glycerin.

Then I put the little flashlight in my mouth just like I saw Uma Thurman do in Kill Bill, and anchor my arms to the sill again. I aim the light at the counter beyond the refrigerator. Jewelry?

What's that all about? Do the women who perform get to pick out the accessories they're wearing in a scene? Does the director get them all dolled up? The woman I saw get into the car was wearing lots of bracelets. But why isn't the jewelry up in the bedroom where the filming takes place?

I try to raise the window but it's locked. And the added pressure of that lift makes the lawn chair groan. Time to abandon ship. I'm not going to see anything else anyway.

Rather than go through the whole acrobatic climb back down, I decide to keep all my weight on my arms, kick the chair away and drop the few feet to the ground. Just as I count to three, a brilliant light beams into the yard like a spaceship coming in for a landing.

A car has pulled into the driveway.

With the car beams as backlighting, I see Brian sprinting toward me. My guess is he saw me standing on the chair and all he could think of was 'dive' because he leaps, knocks me off the chair and onto the grass with an oomph.

The next thing I know, he has lunged on top of me and clamps a hand over my mouth. "Someone's here," he whispers in my ear.

My first reaction is to bite a finger. Of course I know someone is here. Why do men always think they have to tell women the obvious? But then I worry that whoever it is, has heard my aluminum chair clatter to the ground. Do porn creeps carry guns?

My heart thumps like Japanese women are beating on it with ceremonial drum sticks. I assume Brian's is fluttering, too. I know he's excited because his mouth is so close to my ear I can hear him panting. And a funny thing happens. As we lay clenched in each other's arms listening to a car drive into the garage and the automatic door rattle closed, I get this uncharacteristic tingle in my female netherworld. It's pretty obvious that Brian is in the throes of a similar stimulation because his hard love muscle is pressing against my thigh.

His lips graze the skin on my neck as he whispers, "Let's get out of here."

The flicker of my desire bursts into a raging flame. I haven't felt this aroused since New Year's Eve two years ago when Jack Thompson and Sue Bailey twerked to a Bruno Mars song. I'm not sure my excitement is due to my latest discovery or the fact that our adventure has aroused Brian.

We scramble to our feet like teenagers in lust; our objective is to get home and out of our clothes as quickly as possible. I do have my wits about me enough to grab the destroyed lawn chair and toss it into the woods as we sprint for the highway.

Once we're on Hamilton Farms Avenue, we slow the pace to a more comfortable trot. Between gasps for air, I tell Brian about the bare kitchen and the jewelry on the counter.

"Dang!"

Yep, that's all he says. So let me finish the thought. 'Dang. You were right. No one lives in that house. They're just using it to make porn movies.' And then I'm sure whatever swellage he's experiencing doubles at the idea of somehow getting a ladder, silently propping it against the house, and climbing up to watch live porn for free.

I'm so proud I was right that I want to throw my arms around him and squeeze.

"I'll race you to the front door," he says and I accept the challenge. It's only half a block away.

You'd think all our running would have tired us out, but my guess is we haven't had this much blood circulating to all regions in a long time. It's exhilarating.

As I stand wheezing on our front porch, I watch Brian fumble in his jacket for the keys. And a sinking feeling dampens my spirits. Did the keys drop out while we were wrangling on the ground? He also has this panicked look on his face as he digs through his jacket a second time. That's when I notice the additional bulge in his pants. I reach into the left side pocket, skimming my knuckles against his ball for just a moment before pulling out the keys. He grins and grabs my face with both hands.

Now I've never been a big fan of French kissing. I know, the romance books make a big deal about lovers' tongues searching passionately in each other's mouths. But I can't help wondering what they're searching for? The meaning of life? An old popcorn hull?

Regardless of my past feelings, when Brian slips his tongue into my mouth, that hard, probing appendage causes further moistening in my panties.

I moan, pressing my body against his. He backs me into the door for support and grinds his hips into mine. His fingers snake up into the sides of my hair. My hands grip his buns to keep our bodies close as we pump.

I'm just beginning to wonder what the neighbors are thinking when he breaks the kiss long enough to suggest we get inside. I unlock the door with fumbling hands. Behind me, Brian caresses my ass for encouragement. Then before I can push the door open, he grabs a fistful of my hair into a ponytail and pulls my head back so he can kiss my neck. I swear it's just like one of those BDSM billionaires who love to take control. I'm so turned on I even consider letting him spank me.

When he yelps and pulls his hand away from my hair, I'm convinced he's read my thoughts and even if he is a bit shocked, he's willing to start wailing on me right there.

"What is that?" he yells. Then he holds his palm to his nose and sniffs. "It's dog shit!"

He howls and casts his hand as far away from his body as possible. If he could, I'm sure he'd detach it and toss it in the bushes.

"What??" I say.

Now here's the real mind battle. Someone tells you you've got dog shit in your hair and the first thing your hand wants to do is check it out. I manage to keep my fingers away and instead I kind of shake my head. For the first time, I notice a little extra baggage back there.

Brian jumps off the porch and squats on the sidewalk, wiping his hand in the grass, and repeating at least ten times how gross it is. Then he disappears into the house.

I have a vision of him standing at the kitchen sink rinsing his hand and then wiping the rest of the poop off on a towel.

"Use the laundry room sink," I yell. Then I stand there cursing every dog within a five-mile radius.

I get an evil stare from Brian in the laundry room. He dries his hands, then lifts the offending appendage, takes a little whiff and bares his teeth at me.

"Why is it my fault? You're the one who tackled me in the yard and ground my head into the crap."

I guess he's harboring a grudge for having to stand guard on our caper. But if it hadn't been for the poo snafu, we'd be wrangling in bed right now. Isn't that worth something?

Evidently not because he pushes past me without a word.

I hold my head in the sink and run water through my hair until there is no more brown residue swirling down the drain. Why would anyone traverse that steep driveway to let their dog poop in the backyard anyway? Then it occurs to me that Ellie and other residents of Hamilton Farms aren't the only ones using the vacant lot as a dumping ground. The people in the subdivision below the porn house are using the backyard.

I grab the bar of soap at the sink to scrub my head without having to get my fingers involved too much. Once I feel like I've gotten it out, I wrap a towel from the rag box around my head and scurry to the shower.

I wash my hair two more times and completely scrub my body of any remaining stink. Standing in front of the mirror, I drag the towel off my head. Great. All that scrubbing has washed away half the chestnut brown I just colored my hair with to cover the grey. That's what I get for buying the cheap stuff.

By the time I get to the bed, Brian is sound asleep. The hot embers of our desire have gone cold.

I'm not tired so I shuffled to my office. First I log on to our bank account. No money is missing yet, but then my birthday isn't officially until the 17th of December. Has Brian been squirreling away cash so I won't notice? I just hope he doesn't spend too much money on this surprise party. And if he's not planning a party, what is he going to get me? He knows better than to waste money on flowers. And he's learned over the years not to buy me jewelry because then I'll want to get dressed up and go out, which he hates. If it's a household appliance, I'm filing for divorce.

CHAPTER SIX

Our Black Friday shopping extravaganza is the pits. I draw Jake's name at breakfast, so when he says he doesn't need anything I have to corner Gwen.

"He could use a new sweater," she says, further explaining that he refuses to wear a dress shirt or sport coat when he's not playing detective with the police department. "He needs something nice for when we go out for dinner or a movie."

Unfortunately, she didn't discuss this with him, so the minute I start digging through piles of sweaters at Macy's he gets all indignant. "I have plenty of sweaters."

"Yeah, I've seen them." A couple go way back to the days of the Bill Cosby sweater with all the fancy designs and colors, and they're so old they fit pretty snug against his ever widening beer gut.

When nothing sparks his interest at Macy's, we move along to Dillard's.

"You remember the house I was telling you about yesterday?" I say quietly. Once I got tired of trying to figure out what was happening for my birthday, I researched amateur pornographers. "I've read that a lot of men secretly tape women and then sell the videos online. It's become quite a cottage industry."

"Wow!" he says real loud as we fight our way through the crowd. "How much time do you spend looking at porn on the internet?"

A woman attempting to squeeze between us to get three feet further in the miasma of shoppers hears his comment and gives me a horrified stare. Then she barrels onward nearly crushing a young child.

What an ass! I swear I'm going to prove something is going on in that house if it's the last thing I do. And when I do, I'm going to rub Jake's face in it.

He refuses to look at any of the sweaters at Dillard's either. I'm tempted to wrap an empty box and leave it under his Christmas tree.

"You do understand what's happening here," I say. "This torture doesn't end until you make a selection."

"Fine," he says and randomly grabs a sweater off a table. It's over $200 dollars! The sign right there says they're all on sale for $49.99. How is it possible that someone laid this one particular sweater on the table instead of putting it back where it belongs? And Jake just happens to pick it up? Unbelievable.

My only hope is that he has selected a man's small, but no, it's an extra large. I head for the checkout line that snakes between the wallets and ties all the way back to the dress shirts. I turn to say something to Jake about a price limit in this gift exchange but he's gone.

What a break for me. I abandon the sweater on a table of men's scarves and slink out of the store. Then after my dad buys me one of those mini fryers that you can make your own beignets in, I hustle up the escalator to the men's department and buy Jake a sweater off the clearance rack. It looks pretty close to the one he picked out earlier.

Brian drew my mother's name so he's in a total snit as we drive home.

"She wants to wear leggings," he says, clicking his tongue. "A woman her age. And she insisted on trying on each pair and showing me." He shudders and his voice gets dangerously high. "I don't want to see your mother in yoga pants."

Frankly, I don't either.

I do my best to console him by offering to fix a pizza from the Take and Bake. He's still sulking even after I let him pick his favorite—the meat lover's with extra cheese—so I don't bother to tell him about my shopping experience with Jake.

Every once in a while, he takes his left hand off the steering wheel, cups it over his nose and sniffs; a not-so-subtle reminder of last night.

It takes all of my will power not to show him the abrasions from getting knocked off the lawn chair and scraping my forearms from elbow to wrist on the windowsill.

We eat the whole pizza while binge-watching old episodes of *X Files*. Well, not the whole pizza. I let Oscar gnaw on a piece of burned crust. He loves it.

In the morning, I tiptoe into my office, trying not to wake Oscar so I can check my emails before he needs to go out. Whereas Brian's office is a pit, mine is fairly neat although I have an inordinate amount of tiny post-it notes stuck to the sides of my monitor. It's the only way I can remember to call my dentist or take chicken breasts out of the freezer.

I pull out the drawer that holds my keyboard and wake up my computer. Oscar hears the drawer click and dashes upstairs. He hops and twists like a possessed dog in a Stephen King novel. I manage to get one email open. It's from the Gaylord Palms Resort and Convention Center in Orlando.

Brian and I have a trip coming up in two weeks. We're checking out a few December holiday celebrations in a non-traditional setting: Florida. The Gaylord Palms is a glass-enclosed village with every excessive amenity you could ever want: a grand hotel with rooms that look out over a lush, tropical oasis encased in a glass dome, expensive shops that sell everything from designer clothes to $100 souvenirs, restaurants that charge exorbitantly for even a plain hamburger, and all kinds of walking space through towering banana trees and frangipani. The cascading waterfalls are a great way to take your mind off how much you just spent on breakfast. There's another resort just like it in Nashville called Opryland.

If you catch a shuttle from the airport and get dropped at the front door, you only have to be outside for like 45 seconds. Evidently conventioneers love the idea of spending tons of money to travel to another city and getting hermetically sealed inside these behemoths because they don't like muggy weather and they don't like getting rained on—or in the case of the hotel in Washington DC, they don't like getting mugged.

I chose the Gaylord Palms because it's on the high-end scale of things to do for the holidays. The management pulls out all the stops to decorate the hotel in Christmas finery so if somebody has that kind of money, its surely going to be a holiday to remember. Thank god the hotel has comped us a room because our daily per diem from the magazine wouldn't even cover the bellman's tip.

Last year we went to Chicago's Daley Plaza where they have this German-themed marketplace. The year before, it was the Biltmore in North Carolina.

Ray, the publisher, wants us to try and boost readership at the magazine by being more inclusive, so Brian and I are driving all the way down to Miami after Orlando to experience the South Florida Chanukah Festival. Then we're going to swing over to the west coast and catch Christmas at Busch Gardens instead of the usual Disney parks.

Oscar is almost as excited as me about the comped room. Okay, so he's excited to get outside and relieve himself, but we both do a little celebratory dance before dashing downstairs.

I snap on his leash and off we go to pick up Sarah.

She comes to her front door with her upper lip snarled into a very unbecoming twist. This probably isn't a good time to gloat about staying at the Gaylord Palms.

"What's up?" I ask.

"That frickin' Ron."

Sarah's ex owes three months in back child support. He came crying to her in August that he thought he was going to lose his job and she let him slide. Then in September, she and I took a little ride past his condo to see how he was doing. It was a sunny Saturday afternoon, and there was Ron washing a brand new Honda Accord in his driveway.

I don't know why I gave that jerk the benefit of the doubt but I suggested maybe it was his girlfriend's car. Then the home-wrecker came bouncing out of the front door, pressed her silicone breasts against Ron as she kissed him goodbye, and hopped into a Miata.

Sarah was out of her car before the girlfriend's exhaust had dissipated. She got right in Ron's face and told him if she didn't have a check in five days she was taking him to court. Sure enough, a check arrived five days later—for half the amount owed.

She zips up her jacket and adjusts the headband that looks fantastic against her long flowing tresses.

"I've been calling and texting for three days but he won't return my messages."

"Sounds like he doesn't have the money."

"Well, how am I supposed to shop for Christmas?" she asks.

"I'm ready for another spy mission whenever you are," I tell her, rolling my shoulders back to open my chest. And yes, to accentuate the girls that aren't nearly as voluptuous as Sarah's. "In fact, Brian and I did a little spying on the porn house Thursday night."

"You did not!"

"We did. Only it was just one window. The rest are covered."

When she casts a doubtful glance my way, I tell her about the poop fiasco.

She laughs. "It serves you right for poking around back there."

"I wish I could get a better look inside."

We stop in front of the mystery house and glance up at the second floor.

"And the blinds are all drawn on the back, too?" she asks.

"Drawn and closed tight."

Sarah clicks her tongue. "Too bad. If the blinds weren't down, Brian could climb up a ladder with a caulking gun and pretend to fix a window."

Is it any wonder we're best friends?

* * *

Ellie got back a week ago so now I don't have Oscar to walk six times a day. And the weather has turned too cold at night to lurk in a backyard for hours. There is a rickety barn just up the hill from the porn house, but I can't imagine setting up a stakeout in there either. Several boards have fallen off the sides so it would be just as cold inside as out.

The solution to my dilemma is standing in the check-out lane at Publix supermarket. I'm finishing up my weekly Sunday shopping when I recognize Fran, owner of Milo and resident nearest the porn house, loading the conveyor belt with dog treats and toys.

I drive my buggy in behind her, and after reintroducing myself, I ask if she's trying to teach Milo new tricks. I nod at the incentives she's buying.

"Nah. Jimmy and me's takin' a cruise. We can't take Milo and he hates the kennel. I'm hoping if they give him somethin' special each day, he won't get too lonely."

"Oh, that's so sweet," I say. And just like that, the idea pops into my head. Of course, I can't spring my diabolical scheme on her all at once. I have to reconnect with Fran first.

"So is this your first cruise?"

"Yeah. Jimmy's nephew was gonna take his wife but she run off with one of his mechanics. She was keepin' Ricky's books at the shop."

"Oh, my. That's awful."

"The worst part is the boy that run off was one of Ricky's best. That guy could pull a transmission, fix the leak and have it back in by lunch."

"Wow," I say, raising my eyebrows to emphasis how impressive that is.

"Ricky said he'd let us have the tickets real cheap."

"That's great!" More head bobbing and grinning. "Where are you going?"

"Jamaica, I think. All I know for sure is that it's five days. We just found out Friday and we got to be in Miami tomorrow."

"Wow, that is short notice. But you'll have a great time."

"Jimmy ain't too thrilled about flyin' to Miami. Our flight's pretty early though so we won't hit no traffic drivin' to the airport. And Ricky says you can eat practically all day long."

"That's true. They even have a midnight buffet." I lean in to confide. "Don't take anything too tight. It won't fit by the end of the week."

She throws her head back to laugh and I see a mouthful of fillings and gaps. "Never thought of that. But I told Ricky I wasn't going to spend a lot a money on fancy clothes."

"I wouldn't either," I say, shaking my head. We're buds now. Friends for life.

I act like I've suddenly gotten a brilliant idea. "Hey, why don't I take care of Milo? I babysit Oscar. You saw how often I walk him. And Milo can stay in his own home."

Fran crunches up her nose. "He ain't good at being left alone either."

I have visions of Skol chewing tobacco barfed on her carpet, or a camo vest torn to shreds. But those are minor glitches. The main thing is that I'll be able to hang out at Fran's and keep an eye on the porn house.

"All I do in the evening is watch TV," I say. "I could sit in your living room as easy as mine and keep him busy. And if I take him on long walks, he should be good and tired at night."

I sound so desperate the cashier looks like she might report me to the police. Does she think I'm going to sell Milo to a Chinese restaurant?

I back off and tell Fran to think about it.

My short story about the serial killer who leaves a condom on the side of the road is coming along. I've made him a cop who hopes to frighten his community into being more vigilant, kind of like the firefighter who sets fires. The heroine is the only one who suspects him.

My cell rings and I check the time. It's almost eight o'clock. I don't recognize the caller name but I answer anyway. It's Fran.

She comes right to the point. "Are you still willin' to take care of Milo?"

"Sure."

"Well, me and Jimmy talked about it. We cain't really afford to pay for a kennel."

"I sure understand that. Their prices are outrageous." I have no idea how much it costs to board a dog but I'm sure the prices are steep.

Fran sounds relieved. But being a good southern woman, she can't accept my offer without a returned favor. She promises to bring me something back from Jamaica.

I understand the logic. She doesn't want to pay me, but she feels she'll owe me something. It was the same with Ellie. When she picked up Oscar yesterday, she gave us a fancy bottle of rum from the Barrio and a loaf of fresh-baked asiago cheese bread from Little Italy.

Having been to Jamaica myself, I'm sure Fran's gift will be either a hand-carved coconut, or a gaudy string of shells in a necklace. I don't care. My plan is coming together.

"Sounds like we got ourselves a deal," she says, like she just offered to sell me a car for $500. "I'll feed Milo and take him for a walk in the morning. We'll drop a key off in your mailbox on our way to the airport."

What a fantastic turn of events. I've got the next five days to catch these pornographers and when I do, I'm going to shove my evidence right in Jake's face. I might even take my evidence to the police station so everyone will see that he dropped the ball on this case.

For now, I need to practice taking videos with my phone in low light. If I'm going to get proof, the police will have to be able to get a license plate number or be able to zoom in on faces to recognize these dirtbags.

I stand in our garage and film cars driving by in the dark. The first few are pretty shaky and blurry so I work on panning. When our neighbors comes home at nine o'clock, I'm still futzing around so I video them pulling into their driveway. Then I replay the video to see if I can read their license plate. If I enlarge the picture enough, I can just make out the numbers and letters.

Tomorrow begins a new day of crime fighting.

CHAPTER SEVEN

I should have known something was up when Fran said she'd drop the key off instead of me going over last night to get it. The only defense for my stupidity is that my 'suspicion' radar was thrown off by my enthusiasm to uncover the porn people's business.

She also insisted that she'd feed Milo and take him for a walk before they left so I don't go over to let him out again until around ten. When I open the back door, I see wall-to-wall garbage on the floor: fast-food wrappers, Styrofoam meat trays, potato peels. There's even a pizza box open flat, its greasy middle substantially chewed or missing.

Milo comes running up to greet me with a smile on his face and a song in his heart.

"Look at this mess! Bad dog, Milo!"

YouTube has loads of funny videos of dogs getting into the garbage. There are a couple with the can lid and swinging door stuck on the dog's neck. Another video shows three dogs. When the owner asks who got into the trash, two of the dogs turn and out the third dog. The one thing all the videos have in common is guilt. The offending dog cowers in contrition, its eyes sorrowful and forlorn.

That's not the case with Milo. Even when I add more anger to my 'bad dog' voice, he acts oblivious, like he's never heard the phrase before. In fact, he must think it's a new game because he jumps up on my legs.

I grab his paws to push him back down. "No! Bad dog!!"

My hands are suspiciously wet. I look down to see why. There's a mound of barf on the floor, or what's left of it. When I opened the door, the sweep shaved off the top of the pile and smeared it in a lovely arc on the kitchen floor.

I groan as I stare at my hands, and clench my teeth. I move on to swearing, and Milo seems to understand that language because he backs up a couple steps. There are no paper towels readily available on the counter so I end up using a bunch of napkins from Bojangles to clean up the mess.

After tossing the napkins into the overturned garbage can, I kick the bigger pieces in with my foot and right the can. The floor is a mess, but I can't wait another second. I've got to wash my hands. Holding them out in front, I scurry over to the sink. And another string of expletives pour forth. Who leaves a sink full of dirty dishes when they're going to be gone for five days?

I scrub my hands with dish soap and dry them on my jeans because there's no hand towel. I don't have time to deal with the rest of this mess. Right now, I need to get Milo outside where he can dispense with the rest of his early morning snack. I snap the leash on his collar but he balks at the door. What the heck? He should be dying to get out by now.

I have to pull him along behind me to the end of the driveway. My objective is to check out the porn house and that's what I intend to do. Milo tugs at his leash to go back inside. It isn't that cold. What is his problem?

That's when I notice there's no leg-lifting and peeing on the scraggly bushes at the curb. Swell. I suspect I'm going to find more surprises inside.

There's no car in the porn house driveway, no way of knowing if anyone is home, so I let Milo drag me back to the house. The moment I unhook his leash, he runs to his food bowl. It's filthy. I swear it looks like it has never been washed. And his water bowl has tiny bits of swollen dog food floating on the top.

Disgusted, I pick up the bowls with the very tips of my fingers and drop then in the sink with the dirty frying pan and glasses with dried milk in the bottom. I find clean bowls in a cupboard so now all I need is something to put in them. I open every cabinet in the kitchen: under the sink with cleaning products, over the refrigerator where no one can reach, even drawers. I peek in canisters that usually hold flour and sugar. No dog food.

The house isn't big enough for a pantry or mudroom. The washer and dryer are in a half bath off the kitchen but there is no rolled up bag or recycled popcorn tin filled with food. I even check the carport for some kind of snap-top plastic container. Nada.

I do find a broom and dustpan hanging outside the back door so I sweep the floor while I ponder where else I might look for dog food. Milo whines at me but I ignore him. As I bend over to use the dustpan, I see some suspicious green paper. On closer inspection, I see that it's the corner of a ten-dollar bill. There are also a few shreds of notebook paper. The only readable pieces have the words 'Jimmy', 'asshole', and 'dog foo'.

"You turkey! You ate your food money."

I consider chasing the mangy mongrel around the kitchen with the broom, but I contain myself. It's not his fault. And at least a thimble of trust in Fran has been renewed. She did in fact leave money.

As I'm dumping a mound of garbage, I catch sight of an empty dog food bag. It's hard to tell because it's twisted into a tight rope like someone was so mad they wished they'd been wringing a neck. I unroll the bag to get the brand name.

Milo whines and I consider tearing open the bag and letting him lick the crumbs but I'm sure he'll eat the paper, too. Where are all the treats Fran bought at the grocery? Not on top of the refrigerator or tucked into the oven for safekeeping.

My last ditch effort is the refrigerator. It's a treasure trove of beer, diet sodas and at least seven jars of pickles but no half eaten can of dog food. And no partial carton of eggs.

I manage to scrounge up a meal of slightly slimy bologna and American cheese slices, and make a note to be back soon. I'm pretty sure the meal will blow out quickly.

As Milo wolfs down his gourmet feast, I search the rest of the house for obvious urine puddles. The living room seems to be his favorite squatting spot. It smells like an outhouse and the matted tan carpet has scattered pee stains from one end to the other. Right in the middle of the room is a nasty brown puddle, too. I'm going to need a lot more napkins.

Obviously, Fran does not feed Milo Eukanuba. I buy the smallest, cheapest bag I can find along with a spray bottle of Fabreze. I've seen the commercials. This will be a *real* test of its effectiveness.

The moment I get back from the store, Milo lets out a mournful wail and scratches at the back door. I snap his leash on and we dash down the driveway, across the street, and into the backyard of the porn house where he immediately hunches and drops a load. As I suspected, the bologna and cheese didn't digested well. Poor Milo even scoots his butt along the grass when he finishes.

While I'm in the back yard, I check to see if the drapes on the sliding door have been left open. No such luck. The blinds are still down in the upstairs windows so there's no need for a ladder. And I'm not going to prop myself up on the mangled lawn chair again to peep into the kitchen. I really doubt if any porn action takes place during the day.

I drop Milo off with a handful of dog food in his dish and a promise that I'll be back after dark. My strategy is to sit on a stool at Fran's kitchen window and watch the porn house through binoculars.

Head smack number one: There is no bar stool in Fran's kitchen, and no two-step utility stool in the laundry room or garage. My alternative is to sit on the counter and turn sideways, or sit on the front lip of the sink to look forward. Either way, my perch requires my feet in a sink that is full of dirty dishes. I wash all the plates and pans and leave them draining on a towel that I fished out of a piles of clothes on top of the washer.

Then after deciding that I prefer the forward stalking position, I pull the least dirty cushion off the sofa for extra butt support on the two-inch strip of counter, climb up, plant my feet in the sink, push the tattered curtains to the sides, and raise my binoculars to check my view.

Head smack number two: I find myself staring into the front of Jimmy's work van. I know, I've walked right by it at least twice, but it's one of those subconscious things I guess. Like continuing to turn the light switch on even though you know the power is out. Every other time I've seen the van, it was parked in the yard beside the driveway. But now that he's going to be gone for nearly a week, I guess he figures his tools will be much safer if the van is parked in the friggin' carport.

The doors are locked so I assume the keys aren't tucked behind the visor. I trudge upstairs to check the bedroom. Their bed is unmade; I'll just gloss over the fact that my bed at home is unmade as well. But I'm willing to bet my sheets have been changed in the last month.

The dresser is heaped with receipts for fast food and gas, lots of pennies and nickels—they must have scraped together the dimes and quarters to pay for the cruise—and old lottery tickets that have already been scratched. Why would anyone save a losing ticket?

There are no keys on the dresser or the nightstand. As I rifle through the pockets of a pair of grease-stained overalls I find on the closet floor, I spot the grocery bag of doggie treats Fran was buying when I saw her at Publix. The woman has some serious memory issues.

With no way of moving the van, I have to amend my plan. I wander into the other two bedrooms upstairs but the windows are facing the wrong way. At the end of the hallway is the only other view to the porn house, a small window high above the bathtub. I'm not even going to discuss the moldy shower curtain or the wad of hair in the drain.

This is dull stuff. I'm standing in the tub with binoculars around my neck but there's absolutely nothing to see. Braxton Lane is seldom used, so I can't even watch cars go by. I detect a bit of activity in the house behind the porn house. Focusing my binoculars, I watch some guy put a dirty dish in the sink, and I stay focused for a while waiting for the wife to come in and rag on him about not putting the dish in the machine, but there's nothing. He turns out the light and the show is over.

I refocus on the porn house and its shabby siding. I count the rows, wondering how much it would cost to get it all replaced. How many porn flicks would they have to sell? How much do they even charge for a single download?

It would depend on how inventive the sex is, and how big the woman's breasts are, I suppose. Do they get a lot of repeat customers? Does the guy ever get rough? Does she get kinky?

I imagine a woman binding a man's hands to a headboard with a silk scarf. She climbs on top, straddling his hips and runs her tongue across his nipples. When they rise to little pebbles, she nips at them and he groans.

I wonder what Brian would do if I nipped his?

I wonder what Brian would do if I nipped his nipples while he was lying in a bed at the Gaylord Palms in Florida?

I wonder what Brian would do if I hid a camera and nipped his nipples. . . Whoa! Wait. No cameras please. I don't need a shot of my naked butt to know it's large.

The plan is doable, I just need to find some silk scarves. Or handcuffs. Maybe Sarah has some.

She gets all excited when I call her.

"Your very own sexcapade! How exciting."

"So I was wondering . . . didn't you tell me once you had handcuffs?"

"You naughty girl," she giggles. "You've definitely got to get something sexy to wear."

"Forget it. I've seen our bank balance. And I don't think they sell sexy lingerie at the Goodwill."

"Gross."

"I could record some music on my phone," I suggest.

"Oh, yeah!"

Naturally we both agree on 'Nasty Girl' by Vanity 6.

"I could practice a few moves to go along with it."

"Maybe the hotel will have a four-poster bed and you can do a little strip tease like Jamie Lee Curtis did in <u>True Lies,</u>" Sarah says.

"We leave Monday. I'd need two years to lose weight, get in shape, and learn how to dance like that."

We argue over who's sexier, Marvin Gaye, Barry White, or Isaac Hayes and finally settle on 'Let's Get it On.'

"You've got to have 'Putting out Fire' by David Bowie," she adds.

By the time I hang up, I've got at least ten songs. This is going to be tricky since Brian will probably only be good for about seven minutes from start to finish.

After I hang up, I check the time. It's only been thirty minutes?

I raise my binoculars again to see that nothing is happening. This is the reality that you never see on cop shows. On TV, the partners have a meaningful conversation in the front seat, then the bad guy shows up and the cops make an arrest right before the commercial.

I decide I need my own commercial break so I head downstairs for one of the beers from Jimmy's stash. Milo evidently hasn't been getting the kind of attention he thinks he deserves even though I left the TV on and a new chew toy for his amusement. He has dragged a sock into the kitchen and gnawed it to shreds. I'm guessing it's one of Jimmy's work socks and the aroma must have driven Milo into an orgasmic frenzy.

I open a beer and take a long drag. Then I wander into the living room where the chew toy lies in pristine condition on the floor.

After another worthless attempt at shaming Milo, I snap on his leash and march him up and down Braxton Lane. As we pass the rickety barn next to the porn house, I glance across the street to the only crop field still in our area. It won't be long before it becomes another subdivision.

I wonder how these country folks felt about us moving in to their quiet little corner of the county. And I realize I'm going to be disappointed when this last stretch gets bulldozed for houses. That's the classic paradox: it's okay that I moved up here for the peace and quiet but I don't want anyone else coming along after me.

When we get back I guess Milo is tuckered out from all the sock chewing because he hops up on the sofa to crash. I tuck his little chew toy under a paw just in case he gets restless later. Then I spend another hour staring out the bathroom window before I give up and go home. Tomorrow night I'll be prepared.

CHAPTER EIGHT

I load one of our barstools with a swivel seat and padded back into Brian's Jeep. And with a bribe of pork skins and beer, I convince him to join my after dark stake out at the porn house.

I sit on the barstool in the tub with a screw-top bottle of Merlot. Brian perches on the closed toilet playing Solitaire on his iPad. He gets quite a rhythm going after a while: slug of beer, a fistful of pork skins, then he tosses a dog treat down the stairs, Milo tears after it, swallows it whole, and comes bounding back for more.

This lasts for about an hour. Once the pork skins are gone, Brian wants to leave.

"At least let me walk Milo one more time," I say. "After all those doggie treats, he probably needs it."

"Stay out of the minefields."

He's referring to the poop garden at the porn house.

I trudge along Braxton Lane, contemplating how boring stakeouts are. Maybe that's why Jake is a jerk; he spent his first years on the police force doing the menial stuff that no one else wanted to do.

Then I think back to the first time Gwen brought him home to meet the parents. I was a junior in high school. My science class had watched the launch of the Hubble Telescope so I decided to dazzle everyone at the dinner table with my worldly knowledge.

My dad was just as enthusiastic about the scientific implications. (I think I was the son he never had.) Jake's only comment was that the satellite would probably get hit by a meteor and come crashing back down on Earth. He was a douche long before he was a cop.

I snap out of my memory by headlights coming at me. The porn guy? My heart goes pitty-pat and I hold my breath as it drives by. But it doesn't turn into the driveway.

Once Milo has dribbled on at least ten shrubs, we head back to Fran's. I stomp up the stairs to relieve Brian of duty. "I thought for sure I saw the porn car."

"But . . ."

"It didn't stop."

He gives me a fake frowny-face. "Don't worry. You've got three more nights."

His lack of sincerity is obvious even without the barely concealed smirk. Once he's gone, I make myself comfortable on my barstool and pour myself another Tervis tumbler of wine. Even Milo abandons me, either to go to sleep on the sofa, or to chew up one of Fran's bras.

At least Brian was thoughtful enough to leave me the iPad, so I check my emails, catch up on Facebook, play a little poker.

I'm just about to give up when an old beat-up van swerves into the porn house driveway. As I grapple for my binoculars, I drop my tumbler. It takes a crazy bounce on the tub floor splattering red wine everywhere. I don't have time to worry about that though. I train my binoculars on the action.

The garage door opens, but the van is so big that the driver has to jockey back and forth a couple times before he can make the right turn into the small garage.

Now why would someone go to all that trouble instead of just leaving the van in the driveway? Is there a woman in the van dressed in a revealing costume? Or two women?

I watch the light in the garage fade as the door runs back down.

Maybe the woman is bound and gagged? Or what if the van is filled with young girls? Dear lord, these aren't porn makers, they're sex slave traders.

I'm so excited I can barely focus to punch up Brian's number.

"There's a van!" I shout into my phone. "It just pulled into the garage."

Brian sounds groggy. "What time is it?"

"I don't know, but I just saw a beat-up van. And they closed the garage door so no one could see them unloading under-aged girls."

"It's one o'clock." I hear him flop back on his pillow. "You need to come home."

"No, you need to come over here, and bring the Jeep. When they leave, I'm going to follow them."

"You're going to stay there all night?"

"I'm sure they won't be here all night," I say. "I figure maybe an hour; if the guy is paying some woman he must be on a time schedule. If it's someone like Cheryl, the custodian, she has to work tomorrow."

"Okay, whatever," Brian says. "If you want a car, come and get it."

What is he thinking?

"I can't leave my post. The porn people might get away."

There's a long silence where I'm sure he's thinking about hanging up and dealing with the consequences in the morning. But we've been together too long for him to think that will turn out well. In the end, he agrees to bring my Cooper.

"Now if they leave before I get there," he says, "you're not going to throw yourself in front of their vehicle are you?"

What a funny guy.

The excitement has my bladder spasming. I definitely should pee before the action starts. But I'm so afraid the van will leave that I turn off the bathroom light and stand to relieve myself. I figured if the porn house garage door opens I'll see the light in the darkness. Unfortunately, there's a bit of sprinkling which adds to the wine spillage on my grey sweats.

A few minutes later, Brian pulls into the driveway. I'm going way too fast when I hit the stairs, and if I hadn't been clutched the railing I'm sure I'd have tumbled all the way down. It occurs to me that I might have had too much wine.

I bolt into the kitchen just as Brian comes in the back door. He's wearing his pajama pants and a hoodie. Like a traffic cop, he holds out his hand. "Geez, Rachel. Slow down!"

I straighten the binoculars that are slightly askew from my dash down the stairs. He gives me one of those tilted-head, squinty-eyed inspections.

"I think you've had enough excitement for one day," he says. Then his eyes roll down to survey my wine-splattered sweat pants. "Why don't you just come home with me?"

"No! This is the perfect opportunity to see where these people go."

Brian draws his head back. "You're drunk! Did you finish that whole bottle?"

"No!" I answer with even more conviction. I'm pretty sure I didn't. But then I remember draining the bottle on that last pour. But then I also remember dropping my tumbler and spilling at least half a glass, so technically I didn't drink it all.

"Either you're coming home with me or you're walking. I'm not giving you the car keys." With that Brian turns and walks back out to my car.

I'm right behind him, jabbering about how it's my car, and I'm perfectly able to drive. I'm lurching wildly at him when the porn house garage door rolls up.

"Shit! They're leaving."

I make one last grab for the keys as the van pulls up the driveway. Great. Whoever is driving sees a man in his pajamas fighting with a woman who has pee and wine stains on her pants.

71

The van turns left and stops at the red light on Barnsley Mill Road.

"They're getting away!" I hiss between clenched teeth.

Call it divine intervention. Call it an alignment of planets. For some reason Brian stops arguing with me and hops into the driver's seat. I run around to the passenger side. He backs out of the driveway and we take off with a squeal of tires.

"That's not the same van I saw the night you were peeping in the back windows," Brian says, leaning forward to scrutinize the vehicle. "This one is a blue Ford. The one I saw was a white Chevy."

"Maybe they have vans coming from Texas and Florida. You know, with illegal immigrant girls. Or maybe they come in on boats, like in Savannah and New Orleans, and then they get transported up here."

"What's with the sudden switch to human trafficking?"

Uh-oh. This is a new theory for him. I need to shut up or my drunk talk will convince him to turn around. I sit back as he putts along at a conservative distance. But then we get close to a major intersection. It has one of those handy pedestrian crosswalk signals that count down so the driver knows when to speed up.

I watch the numbers: 7 . . . 6 . . . 5. If Brian doesn't pick up the pace, we're going to lose them.

I turn to the side and drape my arm on the back of his seat. "We need to make this light," I whispered. Then I run my other hand up his leg and let it slide along his inner thigh. He steps so hard on the gas I think he might run right into the back of the van.

We make it through the light with two seconds to spare. But my tease between the knees has Brian even more convinced we should turn around and go home.

"Can we review exactly why we're following this van?" he asks. "I'm trying to get the big picture here, you know, what you hope to accomplish?"

"I need to get a picture of the plate."

"Maybe a little bit bigger picture," he says, pinching his fingers for effect.

"Well, we may see where he drops off his porn star. Or we can see where he parks the van so we can tell the police where he lives."

"Where he lives?" Brian says. "Jeez, Rachel, that could be Stone Mountain. Or Douglasville."

"I'm sure it's not Douglasville. We're going the wrong direction."

Brian curls his lip into a snarl. "So get a picture of the plate."

I prop my phone on the dashboard and snap a couple shots. Then I worry that he'll think that's enough and want to go home.

"The thing is," I say, "we haven't been investigating this long enough to even know what we're looking for. We just have to keep our eyes open and see what happens."

"You know, you probably wouldn't be pursuing this if Jake hadn't ridiculed your idea."

"That's not true." Although I guess it is, partly. I decide to be honest with Brian, and myself. "The biggest reason is that every morning when I wake up, I'm one day closer to turning forty. If I can prove I'm right about this, maybe I won't feel like such a loser."

He clicks his tongue and I expect him to come back with something snarky. Instead, he looks over at me and gives me a smile. "You're not a loser, babe."

Once we get onto Alpharetta Highway, it's easier to blend in with traffic. Unfortunately, there are more traffic lights, and Mr. Safe Driving Record taps his brakes when the light turns yellow at Old Milton Parkway. The van turns left.

"Go!" I screamed. "Go! Go! Go!"

I can see the debate raging in Brian's head. He doesn't want to run the light, even though it's after one in the morning and nobody is around. (I take a look behind to check.) But he also doesn't want to listen to me bitch all the way home when we lose the van.

"This intersection has cameras," he yells as he hits the gas and speeds through the light. Since I'm turned around, I get a nice view of the camera flash as it records our license plate.

I'm expecting the van to get on the expressway and head for downtown Atlanta, so you can imagine my surprise when the driver pulls into the entrance to the mall.

This is definitely a problem. We can't follow them into a deserted parking lot. How obvious is that?

"What's he doing?" Brian asks.

"I don't know, but maybe we should watch from here." I nod at the Hampton Inn off to our right. Brian turns in, douses his lights, and drives to the far end of the parking lot where we can see the mall beyond.

I train my binoculars on the van as it careens into the Sear's parking lot. The driver stops, gets out, and walks away.

"Something's fishy," Brian mumbles.

"No kidding. Where's the hooker?"

I focus on the driver's face, trying to decide if he looks like the guy I saw dressed in black and driving the fancy car, but this guy is wearing cargo pants and a hoodie so it's hard to tell. And where's the woman? How do you make a porn movie without a hot babe? Are there really young girls locked in the back, waiting for a replacement driver to take them to Chicago?

Suddenly an SUV speeds across the parking lot at an angle, heading straight for the guy. I'm sure it's the same car I saw in the porn house driveway.

"That's the car! I told you it was fancy."

"It's an Escalade," he says, like any moron should know that.

Why do men retain all these worthless facts? Because when they're supposed to be listening to their wives, they are memorizing car models. It's an SUV and it's expensive. That's all anyone needs to know.

The *Escalade* gets closer to the guy in the hoodie. Are these rival gangs? Will we witness a shootout or a hit and run?

"He's abandoning the van," Brian says. "It must be stolen. But why?"

"They wrecked the van while they were coming across the border with the girls."

"Young girls? What are you talking about?"

"I'm thinking these people are sex slave traffickers."

"When did you come up with this idea?"

"While I was staking out the house."

He shakes his head. "It's probably drugs."

At the last second, the SUV squeals to a stop right next to the guy and he hops into the passenger seat. What the hell is going on?

Brian doesn't even wait for my encouragement. The instant the Escalade drives back past us, he follows them to the highway 400 interchange and we head south. This is perfect because there's enough traffic that we can hang back.

Ten minutes later, we're on I-285, Atlanta's beltway around the city, or as I prefer to call it, the Atlanta Raceway. It's even in a circle to give drivers more encouragement to switch lanes constantly, cut each other off, and push their speed to eighty whenever possible.

It's also teaming with tractor-trailer rigs at all hours of the day and night. Brian ducks between two of them to hide out for a while. Hopefully, the pornographers don't see us one lane over. Once they take an exit ramp, we'll slip back over one lane and follow.

We cruise along to an oldies station. Guns-N-Roses comes on with 'Knocking on Heaven's Door', one of Brian's favs. He does a terrible impression of Axl Rose but I've never pointed that out, and Brian has never critiqued my rendition of Imogen Heap's 'Rollin' and Tumblin'."

I even join in when he sings 'Hey . . . hey . . . hey, hey, hey' in that deep gravely voice. He's having a good time, I'm having a good time—of course I'm blitzed on wine but what the hell. We're hot on the trail of people who are doing something they shouldn't be.

Once the song ends, the commercials start. This is always a crucial time when men's minds have time to wander. I don't want Brian to get antsy about how long we've been following the perps.

"The McGrew's got new garbage cans delivered yesterday," I tell him. "I guess they got tired of paying those high Waste Management prices. They're going with North Metro."

Whereas Brian goes to the gym to stay in shape, I walk every day, even without Sarah and Ellie. I tell myself I don't want to pay more for the family membership at the gym but it's really because I can't compete with 20-something babes who strut around on pencil legs and show off their six-pack abs.

The advantage to walking every day is that I see a lot of what goes on in our neighborhood. I don't think that makes me a busybody. I consider myself more of a concerned citizen.

All I get from my garbage can tidbit is a harrumph so I move on to juicier info.

"I think Al Nelson got a new riding lawnmower. I saw him using it this morning."

This gets a grumble out of Brian. "Poser."

"Right? I mean, how many feet does he have to mow?"

This is usually a good ploy because men love to estimate things: lengths, heights, weights, distances.

Brian thinks a minute. "He probably doesn't have more than 1500 square feet. We've got 1350 and I can mow it in fifteen minutes."

I click my tongue at the absurdity.

"Was it just a mower or a small tractor?" he asks.

What's the difference?

"I'm not sure," I hedge.

"Maybe he got one of those John Deere mini tractors with the interchangeable attachments. I wonder if he got the bucket scoop?"

Gosh, me too.

Before we can get into just how much earth Al could move per hour with that bucket attachment, the Escalade turns off at Lawrenceville Highway. This isn't really a problem even at one in the morning because there's a quasi-stream of cars getting off with us. But when the SUV takes a right onto Montreal Drive I get a bit anxious. We are the only two cars on the road.

My worst fear is realized when the SUV brakes and pulls to the side of the road.

"Shit! They've seen us," Brian says. "We gotta get out of here."

"Are you kidding? They'll follow us back to our house. Then they'll break in some night and slit our throats while we sleep."

"What do you want me to do?" he yells.

I frantically look around. "Pull into the Red Lobster."

Brian swerves into the restaurant's parking lot. "Now what?"

"We need some excuse for being here," I say. "So they won't think we were following them."

"They're closed!"

He's getting a bit hysterical. Okay, so am I. The SUV is turning around. Shit!

"Let's pretend we're having sex," I say.

"In a Cooper!?"

"Lean your seat back."

The Escalade barrels straight for us. I lean over Brian and pretend I'm giving him a blowjob. For an instant, he's so stunned by my action that he tries to push me away. But then Mother Nature kicks in and his stiffy pokes out between the folds of his pajamas. I figure, what the heck, it's there, why not add some realism to the scene. I latch on.

The Escalade's headlights shine into our car and suddenly all I can think of is: *Don't let them ram into us.* I read <u>The World According to Garp</u>. I remember what happened in the front seat during a blowjob.

As the car pulls up next to ours, I bob my head with enthusiasm. They're so high up in their fancy SUV that I'm sure they can see everything. Brian gets into the act as well, his hands on the back of my head, encouraging me with hisses and groans.

Then I swear I heard a faint cheer and tires burning rubber. I stop and take my mouth off his organ. "Are they gone?"

But Brian holds my head down so I can't see. "No, they're still out there. Keep going!"

CHAPTER NINE

I don't fall for Brian's nonsense. Once I'm sure the coast is clear, I sit up.

"Aw, come on," he pleads. "You're just going to leave me hanging like this?"

I glance down. He's at full attention. "I don't see anything hanging." I turn and look out the window. "Where did they go?"

He nods out the windshield. "Into that apartment complex," he grumbles while his hands are busy tucking himself back into his pajamas.

"Let's go see if we can find their building at least."

It's a great plan until we get closer and see the electronic gate. We aren't getting inside unless someone else comes along. The odds of that happening at this time of the morning are nil. And we also can't just sit out here with the car running. The complex must have security. I know, it's some Barney Fife in a golf cart but I guarantee he's got a cell phone to call the police. Plus, what if the porn people see us sitting out here.

I toy with the idea of parking the car in one of the empty spaces in front of the rental office and walking in on foot, but the directory map on a nearby post is a mind-boggling maze of drives and buildings. With our luck, we'll get lost in there, and then the security guard will come puttering around wondering who we are.

We've accomplished a lot. Instead of pushing it, I tell Brian, "Let's quit while we're ahead."

When we get to our exit, I ask Brian to swing by the mall for just a second so I can get pictures of the abandoned van.

"You already got pictures of the license plate."

"I know, but maybe I'll get one more quick shot of the van from the side."

He believes I'm going to snap a couple pictures from the window as he slowly cruises by. (Guys are so trusting.)

"Stop. I want to get out."

His head turns so fast I hear his neck pop. "You're kidding."

He whines something else but I'm already out of the car. I cup my hands to peek in the driver's window. It looks like a construction worker's van with a rack of hanging tools. The floor is surprisingly clean. I'm relieved that there are no girls clinging to each other in the dark.

As I wander around the van, I check out the front end that is totally banged up. I take a bunch of pictures with my phone, marveling at how the guy even got it to run. Naturally, I try the door handles but it's locked up tight.

I jabber about the front bumper that looked like it was about to fall off as Brian drives us home.

"Did you notice how the front quarter panel on the passenger side was white?" he says. "And it was part of the damage which means this is at least the second time he's wrecked it."

"I totally missed that," I admit. "Did I get a picture of it?"

I scroll through my phone and there it is. The white replacement panel. My clenched stomach relaxes and I turn the phone to Brian.

"Got it."

As he cruises through the deserted streets of Alpharetta, I take another look at all my pictures. "We've got some great evidence. I'm just not sure of what."

While I ponder the situation, Brian reaches over and lays a reassuring hand on my shoulder.

"Sooner or later we'll have enough to take to the police," I insist.

"That's right," he says, massaging my shoulder for encouragement.

"And I intend to tell whoever is in charge that I suspected something way back at Thanksgiving but Jake Haggarty wasn't interested."

His thumb strays down to my breast. I'm not even aware of the shift in contact until he rubs across my nipple and I get this tingling jolt of arousal. Is he intentionally trying to turn me on? When I glance over, he appears to be off in a daze, eyes straight ahead, one hand relaxed on the wheel.

Time for the tried and true litmus test. I reach over, slip my hand between his legs and skim up. He's hard as a rock again.

By the time we get home, we're both rubbing and squeezing. I think I might have groaned back at the turn to Barnsley Mill Road. We clamor out of the car and make a mad dash to the door.

Who knew adrenaline had this kind of side effects?

In the morning I let Brian sleep while I hustle over to Fran's house to take Milo for a walk and feed him. When I get back, Brian is awake but still in bed watching the news.

I crawl across the mattress and give him a kiss. "Thanks for a great time last night."

"You were pretty sensational yourself," he says. My V-neck sweater gaps a bit so he hooks a finger into the fabric to enhance his view. "Red Lobster is my new favorite restaurant."

I smile and tickle him. "You don't say."

He pulls me on top of him and then rolls over, dragging the covers with him and pins me to the bed. I'm embarrassed to admit I squeal like a girl when he kisses my neck, his scruffy beard waking up all kinds of nerve endings. One is a direct line to my toes which curl with anticipation.

'Thieves used a utility van to commit a daring robbery at a pawn shop in Duluth last night,' the announcer on TV says.

Brian's kisses stop. He turns his head to look at the screen.

"Holy crap!" he says as he rolls off me.

I sit up to watch a replay of a van smashing into the front of a store.

"That's the van!" we both say at the same time.

We watch glass and metal fly in slow motion, see the front bumper collapse with the impact, and the white quarter panel come to rest against a floor display of stereo speakers in a pawn shop. Then two thieves quickly go to work, the shorter one raking jewelry from a broken glass case while a larger guy loads an arm full of rifles into the side of the van.

"Do you think the shorter one is the woman?" I ask.

"You mean the one in the fishnet stockings who was going to sit down and show me her stuff?"

I snatch my phone off the nightstand and dial Jake's cell. It goes to voice mail after several rings. The jerk. He probably saw it was me calling and decided to ignore it.

I fume as I type a text: *We know where the van is that was used in last night's robbery.*

His reply comes back so fast that I know he was ignoring me: *So do I. It's in County Impound being dusted for prints. I'm busy. Leave me alone.*

"What an ass," I say as I turn my phone so Brian can read the reply. He stares at it for a long time.

"He's right, you know," he finally says.

"About what."

"We need to leave this alone."

"He said 'leave *me* alone'."

His lips purse into a tight line and he gives me the 'glare.' He doesn't use it often but when he does, I know he's not buying into whatever I'm selling.

He rolls off the bed and pads into the bathroom. This is just my luck. I finally get him interested in checking out the suspicious house, and now he's going to walk away from it.

I make one more effort to keep the caper alive.

"Okay, I agree," I say as I follow Brian. "Seeing that guy load rifles into the van has me a little hesitant, too. But guns are hot ticket items. I'm sure he's just selling them. He probably doesn't even know how to load one." Probably.

Brian doesn't look back at me, he just climbs into the shower. And he doesn't invite me to join him.

My aspirations of busting open a crime pop like a balloon. No, not a pop. It's more like that high-pitched squelch from air slowly escaping.

* * *

Thankfully, Fran will be back tonight. I don't think I can stand opening her door one more time to the smell dog pee and cigarette smoke. It's become even more unbearable since there's no reason to stake out the porn house anymore.

The temperature hasn't been above forty-five this whole week but I still had to walk Milo a hundred times a day. And for what? This is what I get for sticking my big nose in other people's business.

Brian has been moping around, too. I've been tempted to bring up our investigation again, see if he's softened at all but I don't really have anything concrete to offer. He's right. They're probably dangerous.

Tomorrow is my birthday. And so far I haven't caught anyone revealing that against my wishes, a surprise party has been planned. You know how you run into someone at the grocery store and as they're leaving they say 'See you Saturday.' Oops!

Brian and I plan to go to our favorite pizza place and then instead of dropping twenty-five bucks on a movie, we'll just come home, find something on Netflix and drink our own beer.

Then we're driving to Florida first thing Monday for the magazine article. I've downloaded some sexy music on my phone just in case the opportunity arises.

Hopefully all the traveling will get my mind off the whole porn/robbery business. Four days of warm sunshine and good food should brighten both our spirits.

Milo tugs at his leash to get a whiff of some other dog's poo in front of the mystery house but I'm not in the mood.

"Do your business and let's go," I growl.

A car drives along Braxton Lane and slows. I turn to see Angie Ferguson, the neighborhood realtor. I can always count on a postcard in our mailbox once a month reminding me not to forget Angie if we decide to sell our home. I try not to take it personally. She's not hoping to be rid of us, she just wants our money.

She gives me her thousand-watt smile. "I didn't know you had a dog."

"I don't. I'm just watching him for a friend."

"What's his name?"

"Milo."

Her cheeks twitch as she tries to hold the professional smile while she thinks of something to add to the conversation. She could care less about Milo but I'm sure the realtor's handbook has a rule about staying engaged with neighbors.

I help her out by turning towards the porn/mystery house. "I don't suppose you can find out who's renting this house?"

"Sure." She takes a quick glance in her rearview and puts her car in park. "Do you know someone interested in renting it?" she asks while she taps on her phone.

I don't want to give her any encouragement. If I say I know someone, she'll hound me for the details of whoever is looking for a house.

"Not really," I say. "But it's kind of an eyesore. It doesn't give a very good first impression to people looking to buy a home in Hamilton Farms."

Angie nods slowly as she taps and clicks. Ten seconds later, she has an answer.

"The title is held by Atlanta Community Bank. But I don't see a notation that it has been rented. According to this, it's vacant."

"Are you sure?" Wrong response.

Her smile morphs into a pucker momentarily, but then she gives me a weak chuckle. "Of course I'm sure. It's my job." Then she turns her phone to show me a notation: *Not available to show*.

"What does that mean?" I ask.

"Hard to tell. Could be a problem. Maybe it's under contract but the listing agent hasn't taken it off the market yet. The bank could be debating on whether to rent or sell."

I can't get away from Angie fast enough. And time's up for Milo. I drag him back up the driveway, shove him into the house, and sprint home. I must tell Brian this news.

He's standing at the open refrigerator. No, he isn't trying to decide what to fix for dinner. He's trying to see what I'm fixing.

"You won't believe this," I say as I come in huffing and puffing. "According to Angie Ferguson, that house is NOT rented."

"How can that be? We've seen people coming and going."

"What if they're squatters?"

"How do they know about the house?" Brian closes the refrigerator door and moves on to a cupboard. "How do they get in?"

"I don't know. Maybe one of them works at the bank. Or they figured out how to override the garage door."

"No way. What if a realtor came by to show the house?"

"Angie says it's not available to show," I say. "Like maybe there's been damage."

He considers that for a minute while he reaches into a box of crackers. After taking one bite, he closes the cardboard top and puts the box away. Those crackers have been up there for months so I know they're stale. They're stale because somebody never remembers to fold down the plastic bag inside to lock in the freshness. I don't have the will power to throw them away, but I haven't made macaroni and cheese lately where I could use them for the crumb topping.

"Like the owners flooded the upstairs bathroom," he says, "so the floor and ceiling have to be replaced?"

I nod with enthusiasm. "Yeah. Or remember that house in Dunwoody?"

A few months ago the news had a story about a house that had been completely gutted. The homeowner was so pissed when the bank foreclosed that they not only took the appliances, but also the built-in cabinets, the granite countertops, the marble tile in the foyer, the garden tub in the master bathroom; they even took a brass knocker off the front door.

Brian snags a bag of tortilla chips and goes back to the fridge for salsa. This is a key moment. If I rush him, he'll get spooked like a deer and his brain will go loping away. I have to give him time to think about the mystery house and what could be going on.

While the refrigerator door is open, I take a peek inside, wondering what I *am* going to fix for dinner. Looks like it's going to be something with eggs.

"But why do they keep going to that house?" I ask as I pull out the eggs, a half a bag of shredded cheese, pepperoni slices, and leftover peas.

CHAPTER TEN

What a fun way to spend my birthday: cleaning house. Yes, unlike Fran, I clean my house before I go away. I'm not going to spend four days in Florida and come back to a mess. Or god forbid, our house would catch on fire, a fireman would break down our door, and immediately deduct that the cause of the fire was my slovenly housekeeping skills.

While I'm picking up and putting things away, Brian is busy spreading even more junk around the floor of his man-pit. Will he need the 70x300mm lens? The macro? The regular tripod or the carbon fiber? Which backpack? Will he be carrying both Nikon bodies?

Once all of these critical decisions are made, he fills a bucket with soapy water and takes it outside to wash the car.

I'm debating whether to take everything off surfaces and really dust or just drive the Swiffer around knick-knacks.

Brian comes back in for the vacuum. "Randy wants me to come down and work out at his gym."

"Today?"

"Yeah." Brian shakes his head and gives a little shrug. "I made the mistake of inviting him up to Crabapple after they added the pool and the new weight room. So now he wants me to check out his gym."

"Where is it?"

"In Midtown. On Tenth."

"Yuk. Where are you going to park?"

"I think I'll take the train down."

I've let out a lot of line here but so far I haven't gotten a nibble. Time to be direct. "When will you be back?"

"Don't worry. I'll be home in plenty of time to get a shower and take you to Antico for pizza."

It's fine with me. I'm spending the afternoon trying on winter capris to see which ones fit. Yes, I have summer capris and winter capris. Don't all women? I mean, in the summer I'm at least five pounds lighter and the pants are more colorful. And I have to factor in that I'm traveling after the Thanksgiving gorge. I settle for two different pairs of black pants—one with a subtle grey pin-stripe—and several blousy tops.

Once Brian's gone, I haul the laundry basket downstairs and sort it all out into piles. I'm shoving the whites into the washer when I see his favorite gym towel on top of the dryer. How could he forget that? After I washed it last time, I laid it right on top of his gym bag.

While I wait for the wash to finish, I pack my laptop into its carrying case, make sure I have a fresh notebook and several good pens. It's weird writing a magazine article that won't appear until next November's issue. The final layouts have to be done in August since it will go to press in September and get bulk-mailed in October.

Thus, Brian and I will pretend we're a year ahead. I can't make references to dates or prices since they can change. And Brian can't take pictures that include newspaper headlines, or some guy's tee shirt heralding the latest World Series victor.

The washer beeps that it's done. I move the whites to the dryer and see Brian's towel again. That's so strange. Why wouldn't he take his towel?

Because he didn't really go to the gym.

I didn't watch him pack his gym bag so I don't know what he took. But it is gone. Where could he be?

Voices in my head shout in unison: *Surprise!*

No way. Even though I told everyone NOT to plan a party for my birthday, that's what they've done. And since the party obviously is not here, it must be at Sarah's or Ellie's. Please don't let it be at Gwen's. That would mean my parents are already back and intend to camp in Gwen's driveway until Christmas. Surely my sister is not that stupid.

At four o'clock, Brian texts me that he and Randy are going to swim some laps. Is it okay if he gets home at five-thirty?

I won't need to take a shower. Just change my clothes, he texts.

Sure, I text back.

I should be mad that he's been gone all afternoon on my birthday and all I've done is work, but I remind myself that he may have had to run a vacuum or carry out garbage at Sarah's house to help get ready for the party. He may be running errands, picking up vegetable trays or a fancy cake.

The cleaning is done, I don't have to fix dinner. I fix a cup of Chai tea, get a handful of gingersnaps (also stale) and flounce onto our bed. With feet propped up, I click through TV channels to see what's on TCM. Of course, once I'm comfortable, I notice how gnarly my toenails look. I should polish them just in case I wear open-toed shoes to my party tonight.

I can't get into Joan Crawford so I carry my tea into the bathroom to take a shower and wash my hair. I was going to wait until tomorrow since we're leaving early Monday morning, but I can't go to a party with this mop.

With a towel wrapped around my head, I lay out potential tops to go with a pair of black slacks. Once I blow-dry and curl my hair, I'll make my final decision. If my 'do looks bad, I'll wear the plunging v-neck sweater to draw attention away from the disaster.

It's close to five o'clock when Brian calls. He sounds freaked out.

"Randy broke his wrist!"

"What?"

"He broke his wrist!" His voice rises. "I heard it snap!"

"I thought you were swimming."

"We were going to but then some hairy ape came in talking smack to Randy. They decided to do some stupid weight-lifting challenge and the next thing I know—snap!"

"So did he go to the hospital?"

"No, we're waiting for the ambulance."

"Okaaaay."

What else can I say? 'Tell Randy it's my birthday and you have to come home?'

"It shouldn't be too much longer," Brian says.

"That's fine. I'll see you when you get here."

I go back to watching Joan Crawford but I can't concentrate. It sure didn't sound like Brian was at a gym. I mean, I've been inside his a few times. The music is blaring, metal weights are clanging, feet are stomping on treadmills. But I couldn't hear any background noise at all.

He's still busy decorating for my party. Or there's been a glitch on picking up the balloons. I have to hand it to him, he did a superb job of sounding upset. Ellie or Sarah must have coached him. I wonder if they wrote out exactly what he should say.

It's six o'clock. My hair is done, my toenails are polished, my makeup has been expertly applied, I'm dressed. Brian should come walking in the door any second. At least I hope so. My hair will only look good for so long and I want to walk into the party on a high note. I've practiced my 'surprised' expression a few times. I'm all set.

My phone rings. It's Brian.

"Hey," he says.

"Hey," I say back. Then I wait.

Evidently he's forgotten his lines, or Sarah is signaling some last minute change and he's confused.

He blows out a sigh. "I'm at Emory Midtown."

"You're at the hospital?"

90

"Yeah. Randy begged me to drive his car down here so it didn't get towed. He's still waiting to see a doctor. Can you believe that?"

What I can believe is that there's definitely a snag in the party plans and Brian's supposed to keep me from getting pissed. I wonder if they've hired a stripper.

"I'm really sorry," he says. And he definitely sounds like he is. "I'll get away as soon as I can."

"Don't worry about it," I say, all light-hearted and forgiving.

"Really?" This time his sigh is filled with relief. "So, why don't you go over to Sarah's or Ellie's to wait for me. You can have a glass of wine. Talk about shitty husbands."

And there it is. The ruse to get me to the party. I have to admit this has been well thought out. I assumed he just come home, we'd get in the car and instead of going to the pizza place, he'd drive to someone's house.

"That sounds like a great idea," I say.

Interesting that he has given me a choice of who to call, but of course Sarah doesn't answer her phone. I call Ellie.

When I ask her what she's doing, she says she's just waiting for Joanie to get home. I tell her about being stood up and she immediately invites me over. As I walk toward her house, I wonder where they have parked all the cars.

She answers the door in the rattiest pair of jeans she owns. Geez. She could have dressed up a little.

"Wow," she says. "You look great."

I play along. "Brian's taking me out for pizza if he ever gets home."

I don't want to sound too bitchy in case everyone is huddled in the family room, listening. But as I follow her into the kitchen, I don't see anyone lurking. There are no cut brownies or deli trays on the kitchen counter. I even glance out the deck door. Nothing is cooking on a grill.

"I'm making meatloaf," she says. "If he doesn't show up, you're welcome to eat with us."

And here's the crazy part. It does smell like something's baking.

Joanie gets home and I start on my second glass of wine. They're both just chit-chatting about their days, minutiae about working. Then at one point, Joanie kind of gives Ellie a puzzled look, so Ellie slaps her thighs and stands.

"Okay. Who wants meatloaf?"

The truth finally hits me. There is no surprise party. Brian really went to the hospital with Randy. I am an idiot.

"You two go ahead," I say with a big smile. "I'm going to walk back home. I'm sure Brian will be there soon."

I stomp up the stairs to our bedroom, raking my sweater off and throwing it on the bed. The necklace and earrings are tossed into my jewelry box. And once I have my pants peeled off, I go into the bathroom to get my nice comfortable sweats off a hook on back of the door.

I stare at myself in the mirror, at the eye makeup and lipstick. "You idiot."

Disgusted, I pull out my brush and drag it through my hair with a vengeance. How could I be so stupid? Thank god Ellie and Joanie don't know what a fool I've been.

I throw the brush back in the drawer but when I slam it shut, my finger is in the way. I howl in pain and tears come gushing out. As I run cold water on my throbbing finger, I cry and curse.

"You stupid, stupid, stupid idiot."

Brian pokes his head around the corner. "Rachel?"

I turn my face away so he can't see the snot running down to my lip. Or my red puffy eyes.

He comes further into the bathroom. "What happened?"

"Nothing." Oh, my god, I sound like a whiney baby.

I reach blindly behind me for a tissue.

"Are you hurt?"

All of my frustration bursts out like a lanced boil. "I thought you were planning a surprise party for me so I did my toenails, and my hair looked perfect, and I went to Ellie's and made a fool of myself, and when I realized how stupid I was I smashed my finger in the drawer, and now I'm probably going to lose the nail, and if it doesn't grow back right I'll always remember the day I turned forty and couldn't even catch some stupid robbers."

I'm out of breath and my knees buckle. I slump to the floor and boo-hoo some more.

"Oh, honey." Brian comes over and sits on the floor next to me. He puts his arm around my shoulders and with his free hand, he offers the whole box of tissues.

I snatch two.

"I thought you said you didn't want a party," he says.

"I know." I sound so pitiful. No wonder men give us funny looks. There's no predicting what we want. "But then you didn't take your towel."

"I know," he shakes his head. "I had it right in my hand but I guess I laid it down because when I got to the gym, I didn't have it."

Okay, that makes sense. He's always laying stuff down and forgetting where. But I'm still disappointed.

"I couldn't find a present in the back of the closet, either."

He chuckles. "That's because I know you snoop. I hid your present in my desk."

"You did?" I swipe at tears with my sleeve.

"Yeah. I was going to give it to you in Florida. Do you want it now?"

My voice is still quivery when I tell him no.

"Look," he says and pulls me closer. "I'm sorry we didn't catch Bonnie and Clyde. I was really getting into it, too."

I blow my nose. It's really more of a honk. Then I look up at him. "You were?"

"Hell, yeah. That's the most fun we've had in years."

I bust out crying again. "I know."

CHAPTER ELEVEN

The highlight of our Florida trip is the Gaylord Palms. No, not because of the extravagance that we didn't have to pay for. That first night when we got to our room, Brian gave me my birthday gift. When I opened the box he laid in my lap, I discovered a foofy pink sweater and a colorful glass pendant on a gold chain.

I tried really hard to look happy but the truth is I hate pink. I guess it's the feminist in me; I don't want to look like a bimbo. 'Try it on,' he says so I do. Then he insists it's perfect. I was trying to think of some way to gently suggest how I loathe pink when he says, 'Remember when we were tracking that frat boy at school, trying to make a drug connection? We met in the student center one afternoon and you were wearing a pink blouse. It was this exact shade of pink.'

I went all gooey inside.

"I saw it when your mom and I were shopping on Black Friday. She said it was nice but it wasn't really special enough for your 40th birthday. She insisted I get the necklace, said it would go with everything."

I don't think he even noticed at first how emotional I was getting. But the way he remembered something I had worn almost twenty years ago blew me away.

Needless to say, I never got a chance to play Marvin Gaye. Brian was delighted to rake that sweater back off me before we tumbled onto the bed.

And guess what? I look fantastic in that sweater. I had to giggle when Brian told me my mom insisted he buy a large. But he went for the medium. It shows off the girls perfectly.

The rest of the trip is pretty boring. We did get fodder for a good magazine article with lots of pictures. As an added bonus, I got a gruesome idea for a short story in the crime magazine.

While cavorting at the Gaylord Palms, a family of four—handsome son, darling little daughter, loving mother and father—takes a stroll through the verdant atrium of tropical plants, cascading water, and cabanas stocked with expensive beach towels. The young girl skips ahead only to discover a dead body floating in the crystal clear lagoon.

On the drive home, I tell Brian about my idea. "I haven't decided yet if it's a negligent husband or a naked woman."

He clicks his tongue. "You're one sick puppy."

So much for conversational banter. I'd love to doze off but it's my job as the navigator to keep him from falling asleep at the wheel. We've already exhausted the license plate game. That's where you take the letters on a plate and make a word. And we've played the radio game where you scan to the next station and try to be the first to guess the band.

I'm tired and it's too dark to play 'I See Something'. If he doesn't want to talk about my story, I'm out of ideas. I give up on and just keep my eyes glued to the road in case Brian nods off and careens into a ditch.

I'm working on my strategy—*grab the steering wheel, pull his leg off the gas, brace for impact*—when Brian says, "They've got to be using that house to stash the stolen goods."

What?

Out of the clear blue, he suddenly comes up with that? Has he been thinking about the robbers ever since I told him about the house not being rented? I've got to play it dumb here and see where this is going.

"You mean like all the jewelry I saw on the kitchen counter?"

"Yeah. And the big-screen TVs and computer stuff. You can't just rob a place and then carry the loot into your apartment. You've got to have some place to stash it until you can fence it."

"Wow. I never thought of that."

96

"If we could tip off the police that the stolen goods are in that house . . ." He's thinking out loud. Best not to disturb.

But he takes so long to complete the sentence that I'm afraid he's drifted off course. "You mean like, take pictures?"

"Yeah. Hard evidence, just like Jake said."

Isn't this a turn of events? All of a sudden Brian is planning our next move. So what changed his mind? My sniveling breakdown? Jake's belligerence? The fact that these people aren't just taping raunchy sex, they're ripping people off. Or could it have been the heart-pounding, adrenaline-infused sex we were having while we pursued justice?

"We'll have to get inside," I say.

"Of course. We've got to see what all they've got in there."

I turn slowly to make sure it really is Brian sitting in the driver's seat and not some alien with a pointy head and long, spindly fingers.

"There might be an alarm system," I suggest.

"No way. An alarm would bring the cops. They don't want that."

He wrings his hands around the steering wheel. "If no one really lives there, it's unlikely that even an upstairs window has been left unlocked."

I cross my legs, perch my elbow on the arm rest, and drum my fingers on my chin. "And we can't break a window. They'd notice that right away." I'm being facetious to see if he's just pulling my chain. But he sounds dead serious.

"Yeah, broken glass would definitely tip them off."

He grips the wheel and raises up his hips. Wait. I know that move. He's getting swellage in his pants. I almost snort. Is he having some kind of James Bond vision of rappelling onto the roof from a helicopter? Or seducing the lady thief—aka 'hooker' woman—and snatching the house keys from between her breasts?

"It's the garage door," he says. "That's how they go in and out. That's the key."

* * *

It's one in the morning and I'm exhausted. The suitcase is dumped in our foyer, the cooler abandoned in the kitchen. I'm even tempted to skip brushing my teeth but I give them a quick swipe.

I crawl into bed, cooing at my pillow like it's Johnny Depp and we've been apart way too long. Brian is right behind me but instead of flopping out like a dead fish, he reaches over for a half-hearted squeeze of my breast. He must be kidding. Now?

I feel obligated to give him some semblance of pleasure. After all, we're back on the case and he's had this hard-on for the past hour. I give him a little personal attention and thirty seconds after I cap the gusher with a washcloth, he's out like a light.

I wake up at ten o'clock because my mouth is so dry from snoring, my tonsils are stuck together. I gulp down a swig of water from the glass I keep on the nightstand, then flop back and glance over. Brian is already up?

The bathroom is empty. I don't smell coffee brewing. Confused and groggy, I shuffle down the hall to his office. He's sitting at his computer in his ratty robe. Four days on the road tasting sugar-laden treats, smelling apple cinnamon candles, listening to Christmas music, and seeing millions of twinkling lights has thrown me into sensory overload. I cannot compute that he is already wading through the hundreds of pictures he took. Usually I have to threaten him five days in advance that I'm absolutely, positively going to have the article ready to send tomorrow and *I need pictures*.

"What are you doing up so early?" I ask.

"I'm researching automatic garage door openers."

"Huh." His renewed interest is so unexpected, I can't come up with anything else to say.

Brian stares intently at his monitor. "You know how crooks have come up with a device that can read the signal from your car fob and open your locked door? I thought I could find something like that for garage door openers, too."

Not only does that sound impossible to find, but expensive. And I have a funny feeling that since this is his plan, he'll be the one who gets to go into the house; I'll be the one standing guard far from the action.

"The problem is figuring out if that particular garage door opener is one of the older models that uses a dip switch or if it's new enough to use rolling codes."

My brain locks up and I tune out his techno-blather. The bottom line is that he can't just go on Amazon and get a hacking device with free shipping.

"I'm going to take a shower," I say.

He swivels around in his chair. "Need some help?"

Isn't he full of vim and vigor this morning? I know what I've said about his slovenly habits and his abysmal dress code, but with that tousled hair and man-stubble on his face, the invitation jumpstarts my mojo. He must read something in my face because he practically leaps out of his chair and his smile clenches the deal. He really is quite attractive with his broad shoulders and sinewy legs. Have I mentioned he works out at a gym?

Now here's the thing about sex in the shower. It's not nearly as easy as it looks in the movies. Either the woman is under the water with the spray running down her face or he's under the water and her butt is freezing. And all the while, both parties are kissing while water sprays in their face and hopefully they're getting turned on.

First Brian tries to lift me up so I can get my legs around his hips, but that goes nowhere fast. I even try standing on the little corner bench so I'm higher to hop aboard. But once I get my legs around him, he staggers and we both crash against the glass side of the shower stall. I make a note to add weight loss to my New Year's resolutions.

Next, Brian sits on the little corner bench and pats his lap for me to climb on but when I try kneeling on my knees, my hips groan and my knees pop.

Finally, he turns me around and I manage to lower myself down and bounce on his lap like a cowgirl. Yee haw!

Once we've sated our animal lust, other primal urges surface, like hunger. After all that wrangling, I'm starved. I'm sure Brian is, too. And what he needs right now is brain fuel. Before our interlude, he was working on a way to get into the robbery house. I need to get him back on track so that his gelatinous green blob of an idea morphs into a distinct, well-formed plan.

"Why don't you get back to work," I say as I step up behind him and wrap my arms around his bare shoulders. "I'll go get us some coffee."

I broil slices of cheddar on top of two bagel halves in the toaster oven and carry them and our coffee up to the pit.

I know I could possibly cause a coronary infarction or something by being so nice but I'm willing to take the risk to keep Brian motivated.

His eyes bug out almost as far as they do in cartoons when he sees what I've brought.

"Wow. Thanks," he says. Then he snatches one of the bagel halves off the plate like they both might be for me.

I set a mug of coffee on his desk, then sit in his Packer's folding sports chair with a breakfast tray on my lap. Patience is key. I don't want to make any sudden movements or say anything that will distract him.

"I had another idea," he says, then takes a big bite of bagel. While he chews the wad, he continues. "I'm going to sneak into the garage while the door is open. Well, technically, when it is closing and they are leaving."

"Uh, correct me if I'm wrong, but don't most people sit and watch their garage door close before they leave? I know I do. At the very least, I glance out of the rearview mirror to make sure it closed all the way."

"Oh, trust me," he says taking another huge bite. "The plan is foolproof. That is as long as you provide a good enough diversion."

Oh, boy.

Naturally, Phase One of his master plan involves surveillance.

"You know how *The Good Life* has cameras that can be mounted in trees to observe wildlife?" he says.

"Yes." My voice is tinged with more than a little skepticism.

One of the magazine's cameras is currently sending back live feed from an eagle's nest in North Georgia. People can tune in to the magazine's Facebook page and watch the parent eagles bring food home to the young. It's pretty disgusting since most of the time it's fish which the baby eagles tear apart and gobble up. These cameras can also be set up to send back live feed to a cell phone.

"I figure we can get one of those cameras and watch the robbery house so we know when the garage door is open," he says. Then he sits back, proud of his accomplishment.

"You want to get a remote camera from the office," I say. "Aren't you forgetting about Madeline?"

The surveillance cameras—as with everything else from paperclips to underwater equipment—are guarded by Madeline, the magazine's very own Cerberus. In fact, it would probably be easier to get past the multi-headed dog that guards the gates of hell than to get into the locked closet at the office.

"Oh, yeah," he says. "I'll look for one online."

"On eBay."

"That's what I meant."

I'm halfway through my first draft of our Christmas article when Brian shows up at my door.

"The cameras on eBay are out of our price range, but I called Randy. He's got an older one he's not using."

Randy is not only a gym rat but also a freelance photographer who sometimes submits to *The Good Life*.

"Good thinking," I say. "How's his wrist?"

"The doctor says he's going to need surgery."

"Damn. Does he have insurance?"

"I don't know. I didn't ask."

Is there a husband anywhere in the universe who would?

"He says the camera's picture is grainy and the sensors need some calibrating, but that doesn't really matter. All we need is a signal when the garage door opens. Then if all goes according to plan, we'll be there when the robbers are leaving and the door starts to close again."

That's when Brian will leap into action. And supposedly, I will cause the diversion.

We discuss mounting the camera on the old barn next door to the robbery house and angle it so when the garage door goes up, the motion detector will beep on Brian's phone.

Sounds easy, right? But there are a few stumbling blocks in the project.

"First of all," I say, "we can't very well drag our ladder over and prop it up against somebody's barn."

We used to have one of those smaller two-step ladders but the last time Brian pruned back the red maple that hangs over our driveway, he left it out and I backed over it.

It's on our list of things to buy when we have the money but we haven't yet so every now and then when one of us is feeling cranky, we bring up whose fault it was: mine for not looking, or his for leaving it out. I'm too stoked about our scheme to bring it up now.

The next problem is that we'll have to carry out our clandestine mission at night so visibility will be low. We don't want passersby to see us mounting a camera but it might make drilling holes more difficult.

My solution to the ladder is a couple plastic milk crates like everyone stores junk in. When stacked, they should boost Brian up enough for our purposes. Once the coast is clear, he'll climb up, his electric screwdriver in hand, and while I shine the flashlight, he'll mount the camera. It shouldn't take more than a couple minutes.

We park up the road next to the open field and walk back to the barn. Wading through the waist-high weeds is a breeze until we get to a patch of prickly blackberry bushes. I have come prepared with yard gloves so I lead.

Brian yelps and I turn around to see him clutching his cheek. One of the vines I pushed out of the way must have whipped back and got him in the face. We should take the brambles as a sign to stop but we both come from a long line of hearty pioneer stock—or is it morons—so we forge ahead.

"This looks like a good spot," he says after two seconds of surveying the barn and its proximity to the house.

He stacks the milk crates and climbs up. But immediately, disaster strikes via one of those pesky physics laws—something about: if you're standing on wobbly crates and you exert pressure to drill a screw into a piece of wood, you're going to lose your balance and fall into briars.

On the second try, I plant my hands on Brian's butt to act as the counter-balance but he can't see the holes in the camera mount because I'm not holding the flashlight. He can't see the screws either. Thank goodness he has a pocketful because he drops several into the tall grass. I have to hand it to him, I never would have thought to bring extras. If there are four holes, I would think four screws would be plenty. But then I'm not a guy.

The third attempt is the winner. I brace his back with my head, wrap my arms around his thighs, and aim the flashlight in the general direction. Total time for our two-minute job? Twenty-five minutes.

* * *

There seems to be a major flaw in Phase One. Last night, every dog, cat, cardboard lid, squirrel, deer, plastic bag, possum, or raccoon that moved across the robbery house driveway set off the camera. Poor calibration, my ass. I'm just thankful most of the leaves have fallen or the beeping would be constant.

First thing this morning, Brian calls Randy about recalibrating the camera.

"Is it possible to make the sensor less sensitive?" he asks.

Since I'm listening to a one-sided conversation, I must interpret Brian's facial expressions. His mouth is in a grimace, afraid to hear the answer. Randy says something and Brian's lips relax a little.

"Do I have to take the camera down and fidget with dials or switches?" he asks next.

His cheek twitches at the thought of wading through briars again. At times he looks relieved as he listens, then disheartened. Once he gets off the phone, he gives me the scoop.

"The camera can be recalibrated in the software. According to Randy, I can narrow or expand the detector field so that it ignores part or most of what it is videoing. And he says that according to the manufacturer, I can make it less sensitive. It will need more movement or for a longer time in order to trigger."

I have no idea what all that means, but I say "That's great!"

104

"Yeah, well then he said that it's nearly impossible to get it calibrated correctly. If I go too far, it won't trigger at all."

He fiddles with the program on his phone for a while, but I suspect it's just for show.

No sooner does he leave for the gym than the stupid beeper goes off, and I'm right in the middle of making Christmas cookies.

Seven of us ladies in the neighborhood have an annual cookie exchange. I bake four dozen Snickerdoodles, Sarah usually makes four dozen Mexican wedding cakes, Ellie brings truffle candies that are to die for, and so on.

When all the goodies are spread out on someone's dining room table, we walk around taking two of each until they're all gone. Then we each have a lovely variety of cookies for the holidays, or in the case of Brian and me, for the next two days.

One time I made the mistake of popping a truffle in my mouth as we were dividing up the treats and I nearly got banned from the next year's exchange. I thought I was going to have to get my cookie box inspected before I could leave the house.

So I'm up to my knuckles in cookie dough, rolling perfect little balls, when the phone beeps. I try opening the app with my elbow, my nose, even my tongue. I finally have to suck all the dough off my fingers. (Hey, I'm not going to just rinse all that cookie goodness down the drain.)

Naturally, there's nothing showing on the screen by the time I get the phone turned on: no car in the driveway, no movement of the garage door. As I ponder the situation, Fran and Milo come out of the backyard and set off the detector again. I wonder if she suspects something's going on in that house, too. If she makes this bust before me, I'm going to be pissed.

When Brian gets back from the gym, he tells me he's going to start practicing the 'sensor dodge' with our garage door. This is an integral part of the entry proposal. (We're avoiding the term 'break in'.) He has to get over the infrared sensor at the bottom of the track that keeps little dogs and toddlers from being crushed by the door when it comes down. But it's a lot trickier than you might think. The door is rolling down while you're standing there trying to take a giant step over the invisible beam. Yeah, I know Matt Damon makes it look simple but it isn't. Brian does take a tip from the fearless star. If he somersaults over the sensor he'll be closer to the ground and won't get gonked in the head by the door. And once his hands drop inside the garage, his legs swing up and out of the way.

A knot on his head and a sore back remind Brian that he is not in fact Jason Bourne, but after slipping a bulky stocking hat on his head and donning a second sweatshirt he has added enough padding to make the tumble less painful.

I have no way of practicing my diversion but I do rehearse the plan in my head now and then.

* * *

Night time is the worst for enduring the random beeps. The whole situation reminds me of exhausted mothers who have to get up to feed a baby at two in the morning.

Yes, I know, I don't have to actually get out of bed and tend to an infant, but it's an ordeal just the same. I have to enter the passcode on Brian's phone and then open the monitoring app cleverly designed with a bright yellow background and red lettering that leaves after-images on my retinas, enter another passcode because heaven forbid someone might want to hack into my surveillance camera and watch hornets build a nest, and finally turn off the beeping. All the time I'm battling the phone with tired, squinty eyes, my heart is thumping and my mind is racing with strategic details. *Pee first, then jump into some sweats, drive over to Braxton Lane, drop off Brian—*

Needless to say, I'm not getting much sleep. Is this my payback for not trying harder to get pregnant?

Brian rolls out of bed grumbling about getting new blinds without gaps that allow the early morning sun to wake him prematurely. I ignore him and drift back to sleep. The beeping phone wakes me in the middle of a dream that I have won the lottery and I'm spending the whole day at the Container Store. I'm sure it's another damn squirrel but I check the phone anyway.

"Holy shit!" I yelp as I watch the Escalade pull into the garage. "It's them!"

I scramble out of bed, tripping over a tangle of sheets, and dash into the bathroom.

"It's them! It's them!" I repeat in an endless loop.

Brian stares out at me through the glass door of the shower. "Who?"

"Bonnie and Clyde!!"

Ever since Brian discovered the pornographers are really thieves, he's been calling them Bonnie and Clyde. I know, these two don't shoot people—as far as we know—and they don't rob banks. But then he calls me Gladys and I'm not a crotchety old bat with no chin who spends her days peeping out her front curtains.

Brian lovingly rinses non-existent soap off his boys, fondling and juggling as he ponders the situation. I, on the other hand, can barely containing my excitement. I yank a towel off the rack and hold it out impatiently.

"Why would they rob somebody at eight o'clock in the morning?" he says.

"I don't know. Just hurry up!"

Once he takes the towel, I rush back into the bedroom, step into a pair of sweats and lay out boxers and sweats for Brian. He comes out of the bathroom, massaging the boys with his towel this time.

"Come on!" I urge him, tossing the boxers at his chest.

"I really don't think our plan is going to work in broad daylight," he says as he slowly steps into his drawers.

I hold his sweats, stretching the elastic waistband in and out in agitation. "We're going to miss our window of opportunity."

"It's rush-hour," he says. "There's traffic. People are standing in their kitchen windows gulping down that last sip of coffee. Someone is bound to see me."

What he's saying makes sense, but I can't tamp down my urge to find out what's going on. I come up with the only retort I can think of. "You promised."

I know, it's lame.

He opens his mouth to point out how illogical I'm being when the phone beeps again.

"Shit!"

I swipe and click. The Escalade is already backing out of the garage. It zips up the driveway and is gone.

"I can't believe it," I say as I stare at the screen. "That was a really short visit. I wonder why?"

Brian chews at the corner of his bottom lip. "There's no way they pulled a heist. I'm thinking they just got an order for a diamond broach or a sixty-inch TV."

Of course. I feel like a knucklehead for not thinking of this myself. They don't just drop off stuff, they come back to retrieve it and sell it.

CHAPTER TWELVE

The neighborhood Christmas party is at the Bradford's so all the husbands come dressed with extra care in the hopes that the lovely teenaged Lisa will make an appearance, spot a balding, paunchy middle-aged man that shows promise of rocking her world because he's wearing a gaudy polyester print shirt with an extra button undone, and she'll seduce him into following her to the basement for some carnal activity.

Sarah and Ellie are camped at the vegetable tray where they won't be disturbed.

As I join them I hear Ellie say, "I'd love to destroy their fantasies by telling them she's a lesbian."

"You talking about Lisa?" I ask.

"Who else?"

"Leave the guys alone," Sarah says. "It's a hoot to see them suck in their guts every time they hear a female laugh and think it might be her."

"A lot of guys get turned on by the idea of two girls going at it," I say.

Ellie snorts. "And one of these fools is hoping they'll get invited to watch?"

I grab a little paper plate and fill it with baby carrots, celery sticks and broccoli nubs. Sarah gives me the stink eye when I add a big heap of spinach dip. I'm sorry I told her my proposed New Year's resolution is to lose ten pounds.

But then again, this is *why* I told her. So she'll make me stick to it. Her resolution is to badger Ron to get current with his child support. I can't wait to assist with that.

You know what Brian said when I told him about hounding Ron? "People who stir up the shit pot should have to lick the spoon."

He ought to be in a comedy club.

Anyway, New Year's is less than two weeks away. I might as well get started. I scoop up a nice blob of spinach dip with a baby carrot, bite off the end, and plow it into the dip again. Hey, I could have gone for the much higher calorie French onion dip or worse, the triple chocolate brownies with dollops of cream-cheese frosting swirled through the regular fudge icing.

We all shift 45 degrees to get a new view of the party.

Ellie clicks her tongue. "I don't see how they can afford a lawn service."

"She only works part-time," Sarah says.

"Who does?"

"Misty Cramer," they both say.

"Maybe they got a Groupon," I say, then twirl a broccoli head into the dip to get it nice and coated.

"I'll bet their credit cards are maxed out," Sarah says.

That's when I spot Brian further down the food table. I don't want to get into that whole credit card discussion since ours are maxed out too, so I wander over.

"What are you doing?" I ask when I step up next to him. He has a cracker in each hand loaded with Buffalo chicken dip.

He shoves one into his mouth and immediately reaches for another. "I love this stuff."

"I thought we were going to cut down on the junk food."

"It's not the new year yet," he says, spewing crumbs.

I try to glare at him but I can't keep my eyes off the huge bowl of cheese-topped, bubbly-hot chicken dip. I love Sarah like a sister, but I decide to take the low road with Brian. Besides, I need something more substantial than raw vegetables to absorb all the alcohol I'm swilling.

My biggest fear is that Brian's phone will beep and I'll have to go play super sleuth in my holiday best which is a pair of black jeans I found in the back of my closet. They're more than a little snug but I hid some of my extra baggage with the long sparkly grey sweater I bought at the Salvation Army.

This fear has a close second. What if we do have to leave? It's going to be hard to explain why we have to dash all of a sudden. I have visions of the wild party in the movie *The Chase*. Rumor has it the fugitive, Robert Redford, is hiding at the city landfill. The sheriff, Marlon Brando heads that way to make an arrest and all these drunks at a party decide to go watch. Oh, and to set the whole dump on fire in the hopes of smoking Redford out.

I made a pre-emptive strike when I came in the door, though. I told Nicole Bradford that Brian has been toughing out some kind of bug the last couple of days. I even leaned in close and whispered, 'Diarrhea' with a sympathetic nod and a shrug. So we're good to go at a moment's notice.

We actually get some false alarms: twice by Fran and Milo, and once by a raccoon but there's no Escalade; no opportunity to swing into action.

* * *

I wake up to Brian retching in the bathroom. What is it about going to a party that encourages people to drink way too much booze? It must be all the talking and eating and music that keeps getting louder as the evening progresses. I didn't pay much attention to how many drinks I had until I patted Stan Richardson on the ass and asked him if he used the Rough Rider condoms or the Ultra Thin.

I knew it was inappropriate but my brain was too pickled to know why. All I remember is Brian pushing me out of the Bradford's sliding glass door and me tumbling down the last two steps of their deck. Somehow we managed to stagger across the common area to our own sliding glass door and evidently got inside because we did not spend the night on the chaise lounges on our patio.

I also have a faint recollection of lying in bed, my head spinning, my stomach roiling, and screaming at Billy Idol to knock it off with the rebel yell.

The toilet flushes. But instead of Brian wobbling back to bed, I hear him collapse on the bathroom rug. I've got to pee but I'm not going in there. In fact, I'm not going anywhere too fast. I'll have to do this in stages.

First I roll to the side of the bed and gauge how much that movement shook things up. Not bad. I'm not nauseated so that's definitely a bonus. I ease my head up, then use my arms to raise my torso. My hands begin to shake so I quickly cock out my elbow to keep me propped up. No use losing ground.

That's when I hear this hideous rumble and realize it is coming from deep within my bowels. I must get up. And I can't just go stumbling over Brian in the master bathroom. I've got to career down the hallway to the bathroom between our offices.

Once seated, my head slumps between my knees. My arms resting on my legs are the only things keeping me from tumbling off the toilet. I give the wastebasket next to me a quick glance. (It's always good to have a contingency plan.) That's when I notice the big bruise on my thigh.

How did I get that? Later I'll have to get on Facebook. I'm sure someone has posted a picture of whatever I did. Nothing is sacred anymore with phone cameras everywhere.

By the time I get back to the bedroom, Brian has returned. He's propped himself up a bit with two pillows. His face is as white as a kabuki dancer. And even at half-mast I can see how bloodshot his eyes are. Poor guy. I hand him my glass of water from the nightstand and he takes a tentative sip. Then he groans and dashes back to the bathroom.

By midafternoon, Brian has the strength to turn on the TV. Between dozing off and hobbling to the bathrooms, we watch the

Falcons stomp the Saints. I'm actually feeling good enough to go downstairs and fix us each a cup of weak chicken broth. I bring them back with a sleeve of Saltines.

Brian has recovered enough to add the color commentary to the eight o'clock Vikings/Bears game. He hates both teams so he can inject twice as much rancor. 'Ray Mandera was a douche at Ohio State and he's still a douche.' 'That guy would make a better bouncer at a tittie bar than a blocker.'

I doze off during halftime and I'm sure I would have slept through the night if Brian's phone hadn't beeped.

My head jerks up off the pillow, a strand of drool slapping against my cheek. *Please be a deer* I pray as I pick up the phone. Brian groans and tries to grab his phone away but I get to the app just in time to see a different van pull into the garage.

"Shit!"

Brian drags his pillow over his head. "I'm not going."

"Yes you are. We've been waiting and planning for days."

We take the Jeep since the thieves will surely remember my Cooper and our front-seat sex. At the entrance to Hamilton Farms, Brian hops out.

"I'll call you when the garage door goes back up," he says, leaning into the car.

The color is back in his cheeks and he actually appears stoked.

"Don't forget about the sensor."

He shoots me a cold stare. "Yeah. Thanks for reminding me. I might have forgotten the last twenty times you warned me."

I can't stop worrying about that damn sensor. If he trips it, he'll get caught standing inside the empty garage, or he'll have to make a mad dash and hope the thief doesn't jump out of his car to pursue. I had my doubts that horny porn guys carry guns, but I'm not as sure about robbers.

I give him a meek smile as an apology before he sprints across the street and into the robbery house back yard. I guess the adrenaline in his system has cured him. A new kind of 'hair of the dog.'

There will be very little time once the thieves open the garage door to leave so I park at the entrance to Hamilton Farms and turn off my headlights. Brian and I have discussed my 'distraction' several times and decided the best approach is from Barnsley Mill Road.

If I pull this off it will be a miracle.

As I sit in Brian's Jeep, I imagine the two thieves unloading the van, carrying TVs or stereo speakers or armloads of designer blue jeans up the basement stairs to their storage facility. Or maybe they've come for a load of computers they already stole. How long does it take to find buyers for all that stuff? Or do they have a fence who moves the product for them? If he's driving a fancy Escalade, my guess is Clyde doesn't use a middle man who takes a cut.

As the minutes tick by, I start to worry. What if they spotted Brian running through the back yard? We've been avoiding the conversation about guns but now it's all I can think about. Is the woman holding Brian at gunpoint while they discuss shooting him here or driving him to a deserted location to knock him off and roll his body into a ditch?

My hands start to sweat as I wring them around the steering wheel. What's taking so long?

I actually scream out loud when my phone vibrates in my pocket. It's a text from Brian: *GO!*

I put the car in gear and roll up to the traffic light, which of course is red. After looking both ways I zoom across Barnsley Mill and onto Braxton Lane. Ahead, I can see the light of the open garage door of the robbery house. Show time.

I hit the gas, jump the curb, and plow the Jeep into the front yard. I guess I go a little too fast because my wheels spin in the grass, throwing sod and mud. As I skid across the yard, I glance down the driveway. The driver has jockeyed the van enough to get it pointing up the drive, its front-end definitely crumpled. The two occupants gape at me through the windshield so they aren't watching the garage door go down.

I careen to the left and clip the mailbox before my front tires hit the dry pavement of the driveway. My swerving stops; I zoom across the drive and back out to Braxton Lane. Thank goodness no one is coming the other way because I overcorrect and almost drive into the field across the road.

My heart is pounding, my hands shaking. I slow down and blow out an audible 'Woo! Hoo!' as I drive on up the road. Just like we discussed, I'll circle around, go back to the robbery house and join Brian for a thorough search of the premises. But when I look in the rearview mirror, the stolen van is following me.

What? Naturally I assumed they would turn left to get as far away from me as possible. I mean, who would follow a drunk driver? They're in a stolen van! What if I get pulled over by the police?

The van comes up behind me so fast that I panic and the Jeep zig-zags across Braxton Lane, which in hindsight is a good idea since I'm supposed to be some lunatic or drunk.

The short road dead-ends at Hickory Flat Highway. The van's headlights shine through the back of the Jeep. I repeat a mantra: 'don't get out . . . don't get out', hoping the driver doesn't come up to the side of the Jeep and shoot me. Then I glance back at the red light and switch to 'turn green . . . turn green.' The headlights are so bright I figure they can see me pretty good so I rub my face and head like I'm trying to sober up.

When the light turns green, I take a left away from town assuming they will turn right. But they don't!

It's almost two miles to the Publix shopping center and any hope of witnesses. What if they decide to run me off the road? Or shoot out my tires? I make a couple perfunctory weaves in the road, speeding up and then slowing down like I think a drunk might drive. As the lights of our little urban shopping center come into view, I get an idea.

I swerve into the Waffle House parking lot and rest my forehead on the steering wheel for a couple seconds before opening the door and nearly falling out of the driver's seat. I'm pretty sure Bonnie and Clyde won't recognize me. The last time we were this close, all they saw was the back of my head bobbing in the front seat.

The restaurant is half-filled with other late night diners in various stages of drunkenness or boredom. Honestly, who hangs out at Waffle House on a Sunday night? I stumble to a booth where I can see outside and scan the parking lot as I steady myself with the table. The van has parked. They're watching me!

I plunk down in the seat and let my head fall onto the table. (I'm telling you it's an Oscar-worthy performance.) When the waitress comes, I order coffee and raisin toast. She instantly produces a cup and fills it.

Brian must be getting worried. I need to text him but I don't want Bonnie and Clyde to see me using my phone. I slide to the window end of the booth, and turn sideways with my feet on the seat and my back to the window. I let my head loll, and then holding my phone between my shins, I send Brian a message: *Momentarily delayed. Don't leave!*

I look up to see Bonnie walk up to the front counter. She speaks to the waitress but she's looking at me. Holy crap! I'm going to have to up my game. The only thing I can think of is to sing.

What you want?
Baby I got it.
What you need?
You know I got it.

I slap my hands on the table to give myself a beat and bob my head to the tune. I know I sound awful because everyone in the room is staring at me in disbelief. The waitress's face is screwed up in a scowl. I'm sure the Waffle House likes their drunks quiet and orderly.

All I'm askin'

For a little respect when ya come home

Tap ta tap tap.

Hey baby

Tap ta tap tap.

I think the lurid wink I give the old guy sitting at the counter finally puts the waitress over the edge. She reaches under the counter for the phone. That gets Bonnie scooting out the front door.

I stop singing and wave a hand at the waitress. "Sorry. Sorry. I'll be quiet."

She hesitates a couple beats before she puts the phone down. I doubt if she wants the cops here any more than the rest of us do.

She comes over with my raisin toast. Her nose twitches as she sets it down along with my tab. I'm going to have to leave a decent tip.

I fish through my purse and come up with enough change to pay. Then after scanning the room to see if everyone has resumed chowing down on their smothered and covered hash browns, I turn and glance out the window. The van is gone.

I grab the raisin toast and bolt for the Jeep.

CHAPTER THIRTEEN

I park in Hamilton Farms. I don't need Bonnie and Clyde coming back by and seeing the Jeep in their driveway. There are no lights on inside. By the moonlight, I can see the ruts I left in their front yard. I remember clipping the mailbox but in my haste I forgot to check the Jeep for damage.

As I trot down the pavement, I see that the garage door is closed. Did Brian make it inside in time? If he didn't get in, why hasn't he texted me? I'm fishing in my pocket for my phone when he steps out from behind the back of the house. I scream.

"Jeez!" he hisses. "Why don't you wake up the whole neighborhood?"

"What are you doing lurking back here?"

"This is a B & E. Remember? Did you think I'd wait for you on the front porch?"

"I figured you'd be inside casing the joint."

He shakes his head. "Are you channeling Sam Spade?"

I ignore his barb. He's got the jitters; so do I. And I'm really glad I don't have to do this by myself.

"I'm not going to get caught alone inside," he says. "If we go to jail, we go together."

"Aw. Isn't that sweet?"

I kiss his cheek and then pat it gently. That reduces his snit a couple degrees. In fact, his eyes light up.

"Look what I found." He holds up a backpack. "It was on the garage floor. I figure they set it down while they were hauling loot inside and forgot to pick it up when they left."

"So have you been inside?"

"Yeah." The snit drops another degree. "It's pretty amazing."

He waves me around to the back of the house, then with great stealth he slides open the sliding glass doors and we slip in past the heavy drapes. It's pretty dark so I fumble for a light switch.

"What the hell are you doing?" Brian screeches, his eyes blinking from the bright light of a cheap chandelier.

"Fran said she sees lights on inside. Stop worrying."

The small dining room is totally empty, more proof that no one lives here. Brian sets the backpack on the floor and unzips it. My fingers twitch to be the first to examine the cache but in all fairness, it *is* his find.

He pulls out two ski masks, gloves, duct tape, and a small spiral notebook. He tosses the notebook on top of the gloves and I pounce on it like a cat on a mole while he rifles the zippered pockets.

He finds a folded city map in one of the pockets. While I scan the notebook, he unfolds the map and spreads it flat on the floor.

"What do you think?" he asks.

There are random numbers written with a Sharpie but I have no idea what they mean.

"Let's get a picture."

While he's busy with that, I take a closer look at the notebook, starting back on the first page. There's a street name: *Moreland Avenue*. Under the name is a list of numbers and prices, like LG5700-55—$600. Obviously this means an LG fifty-five inch TV priced at six hundred dollars. I flip to the next page. *Dahlonega St.-Cumming/Pawn* and a list of merchandise, mostly jewelry.

"Holy crap! They've kept a record of their break-ins." I turn the notebook so Brian can see. "And what they took."

He skims down the page. "They even lined up the prices in a column." His eyes roll up at me. "A thief with OCD?"

I have to smile, not just because he's funny but because he's excited about the find.

"This is fantastic!" I snap the notebook shut. "We've got a paper trail of their crimes." But no sooner are the words out of my mouth than I realize this book will be missed immediately. "Oh, boy. We need to take pictures of these pages and then you're going to put the whole pack right back where you found it."

"And we need to get out of here. They may have already missed it."

I hold the book steady as Brian snaps away with his phone. Then he starts jamming stuff into the pack.

"Hold on," I say. "The gloves go in before the ski masks."

His eyebrow twitches in disbelief that it makes a difference. But we've been together a long time. He's resigned to the fact that sooner or later he'll have to comply. And I'm usually right. In the long run, it's just easier to do what I say.

I rush through the rooms of the house while he takes the backpack down to the basement. The living room has TVs, stereo components both in and out of boxes, and a few speakers. The items are separated and categorized, and every piece has a post-it note with a description and value like they're going to be listed on Craigslist. OCD indeed.

The kitchen has more jewelry than it did when I peeked in the window. Some of the pieces still have a little white tag with a price. Holy smokes. One of the bracelets costs $1500 and there's only a couple diamonds on it. The jewelry is tastefully arranged in clusters around different post-it notes. One reads CRTVL. What does that mean?

Upstairs, the first bedroom is empty but when I open the closet it's full of designer jeans. They're even hung according to size. In the next bedroom, the closet holds fabulous designer jackets and full-length coats. The force is strong, but I resist the urge to try on a darling blue satin jacket with raglan sleeves. Stacked along the back wall are shoe boxes: Stylish sandals in one section, evening wear in another. They are arranged with smallest sizes at the bottom, and sub-divided by colors. I've got to say, if Bonnie wasn't a thief, we'd probably be best friends.

I see a pair of Christian Louboutin open-toed heels for $945. And they're in my size!

I fight back tears as I force myself to move on to the master bedroom. It's full of computer stuff: laptops, tablets, fancy monitors. The sight of all this electronic junk snaps me out of my funk. I even manage to convince myself that there would never be an occasion where I could wear three-inch heels or a sparkly satin jacket.

I'm taking close-up pictures of serial numbers and bar codes on boxes when Brian rushes in. "Let's go. We've been here way too long."

"What do you think about leaving a window unlocked? In case we want to get back in."

"Good idea. I may come back and get me a 60-inch for the Super Bowl."

I know he's kidding—sort of. But he doesn't object. At first I consider unlocking the kitchen window. Then I have a vision of me with my butt hanging out, my legs flailing, while some nosy neighbor calls the police. The front door is definitely out of the question. With a little trepidation, I hide the broomstick that has been blocking the sliding door. I figure with the heavy drapes, there's no reason why Bonnie or Clyde will see the bar missing or test the door to be sure it's locked.

On the walk back to Hamilton Farms I nearly crow with enthusiasm. "I can't wait to see Jake's face when he finds out we cracked the case for him."

"Yeah? I can't wait to see your face when Jake arrests you for breaking and entering."

"We had probable cause."

"Rachel," he says, reaching out to stop me with his arm. "You are not, nor have you ever been an officer of the law. I don't think probable cause pertains to you."

He's right of course. My euphoria quickly fades. We have all this evidence that we can't use.

"So how are we going to catch these guys?"

* * *

Our adventure last night might have ended in some rambunctious nookie if we hadn't realized it was all for naught. I was more than a little bummed that we can't report the robbers' loot to the police without incriminating ourselves. I had aspirations of not only solving this case but possibly getting my name in the paper. Now I realize that's probably not going to happen.

My state of mind is mellower this morning. The wheels are turning in my head again. I don't think we've reach the end of our investigation yet. I just don't know where it's headed next.

While we lie in bed waiting for news of a break-in, I notice that Brian is pitching a pretty large tent.

We missed the headlines at eight o'clock so we'll have to muddle through weather, traffic and sports before they come around again at eight thirty. I reach under the covers to better gauge the tent pole's length and girth. It's impressive.

His fingers get involved in stimulating my magic button and the next thing I know, I'm breathless and teary-eyed from a bodacious orgasm. I've never been much of a morning-sex girl but after the cowboy ride in the shower and now this erotic interlude, I may have to change my mind.

We're flat on our backs in recovery mode when the top news stories begin again. Sure enough, there was a smash and grab in Newnan, Georgia—a fashion boutique in a strip shopping center. The thieves got away with thousands of dollars in designer jeans, women's boots, and expensive jackets. What? I didn't see any boots.

122

My mind flashes to the bedroom closets. Did Bonnie and Clyde steal any black boots in an 8 ½? Could I possibly sneak back over there while Brian is working? I mean, I do need to check and see if they retrieved that backpack—

The urge to commit larceny passes as I watch the grainy video of the break-in on the news. The two thieves toss armloads of clothing into the side door of a late-model mini-van; the one that followed me to Waffle House. I'll bet it didn't take longer than three minutes to gather up everything I'd seen in the bedroom. I get a little tingle just thinking about the crime.

After I get out of the shower, I tell Brian, "I better go see if they've been back for their pack."

He's still in the bed like a sexually-sated slug. "They did."

"How do you know?"

"My phone went off."

Crap! I really wanted to get back inside that house and—

"Wait a minute. You saw them open the garage door and get the pack?"

"Well, no," he admits. "I was taking a dump the first time the phone beeped. But when it went off again, I saw the Escalade drive away."

Aha! Mere conjecture. Be still my heart. I *do* have an excuse for going over but I can't let Brian know. He'll think I don't trust him and he'll want to go along just to prove he was right.

"Okay, great," I say. "So what are you up to after breakfast?"

"The same thing I'm up to every day." He gives me a funny look, wondering why the sudden interest.

"Yeah. Good. I've got to run by Sarah's for a minute."

"What for?"

What's with the third degree? He never pays any attention to what I do. But I've got the conversation stopper. "Female business."

I scurry over to check on the backpack. It's gone. On my way out I pass right by the stairs to the second floor so I figure I might as well confirm that these are the same robbers. I discover a stack of boot boxes behind a long coat in a closet. And I'm proud to say I do not try a single pair on. There isn't an 8 ½ in the bunch.

I do slip on the Louboutin 4-inch heels. I get the vapors just having a pair of $945 shoes on my feet. I figure I've gone this far, why not check out the jacket. It fits like a dream.

In the master bath, I kick myself for not wearing some black slacks instead of these awful navy blue sweats but if I squat low enough all I see is the jacket in the mirror. I wish I could see the shoes but there is no long mirror behind the door.

As I unzip the jacket to put it back, I hear a rustle in the living room. Double crap! Bonnie and Clyde have come back. There's a flurry of thoughts bumping around in my head like circus clowns.

Bonnie grabbed the wrong size jeans so they had to turn around? They came to pick up something, like a computer or a necklace, but on their way back to town, they got a call for something else? They thought the backpack was lost so when they saw it in the garage, they were so ecstatic they forgot what they came for?

I press index fingers to my temples to silence the voices. The reason doesn't matter. The fact remains that they are here.

Sweat gushes under my arms. Those Japanese girls are back pounding on my heart. If I'm going to continue with the spy business, I'm going to have to get a prescription for Xanax.

I stand at the top of the stairs, my head cocked, listening for more noise. The longer I wait in this frozen state, the more I wonder if I even heard anything. Was it outside? At a neighbor's house? Wouldn't I have heard the garage door open? Have they heard me moving around up here? Does Clyde have a gun aimed at the stairway, just waiting for me to come back down?

So what are my options? I visualize silently raising a Venetian blind, opening a window, tying blue jean legs together, and rappelling down the side of the house. (I know. I'm losing it.)

My only real option is to hide until they leave. But should that be in the closet with the coats and boots, or the one with the blue jeans? On second thought, what about the bathrooms? I can hide behind a shower curtain.

I tiptoe down the hall, sure that they can hear each step I take on this cheap carpeting. And guess what? There is no curtain at the tub. Duh.

That's when I hear the sliding glass door open. What the hell? There's no way Bonnie or Clyde have a key to that door. They always come in through the garage.

I dash into a bedroom and pull the blind back in time to see Brian sprinting towards the stand of trees behind the house.

That little stinker.

This is one of those instances where you can't bust the other guy without incriminating yourself. But when I get back home, I find a tape measure on the kitchen counter. Was he checking the width of a TV to see if he could get it into his Jeep?

After I change my sweaty shirt and panties, I head to my office to download the pictures we took last night on Brian's phone. Then I get a map of the city and plot all the addresses from the notebook pages. An online search shows that there was some kind of robbery in each area; some were smash and grabs, others were break-ins of warehouses. At some locations, a stolen car was abandoned right there. Other times, a stolen van or truck was found in an empty parking lot, like the one we saw at the mall.

The robberies are so random that I can hardly believe it's the same two people. But then, that's probably what they intend. The police won't connect the dots. There isn't even any rhyme or reason to when they strike. Some robberies were during the week, others were on weekends.

Could I somehow trace a TV or laptop to Craigslist or eBay? That seems highly unlikely. There are thousands of listings. How many of them are legitimate and how many have been stolen?

Once I realize how futile my online search is, I consider tracing the jewelry to pawn shops. I'll wait a couple weeks, then take some of the pictures we took at the robbery house and see if I can find a matching watch or necklace that has been hocked. That idea lasts about thirty seconds. I call up a map of the metro Atlanta area that shows pawn shops. There are hundreds of them.

I put myself in Bonnie's shoes. (I assume she's the one who is keeping such good records.) If Clyde and I rob a jewelry store in Canton, we'll take the goods to Jonesboro to pawn them. And now I understand why the jewelry on the kitchen counter was arranged in clusters. The post-it that read CRTVL meant Cartersville. So *if* I had the time and the inclination, I'd search pawn shops in Stone Mountain or Conyers for that $1500 bracelet. Jeesh. This woman works a lot harder than I do.

Which reminds me that I'm supposed to be writing a piece about lesser-known festivals around the country. So far, I've found a cardboard superhero costume parade, a roadkill cookoff, a testicle festival, and a cow-chip throwing contest.

I start a new search online but it's no use; I can't stop wondering how much Bonnie and Clyde pull in per year. Maybe if I tell Brian about the festivals I've discovered, he'll keep me inspired.

He recoils as expected when I tell him there's actually a tarantula awareness festival.

"Gross! I hope Ray doesn't find out about that one."

"No kidding," I agree. "That'd be like him to pay all the expenses just to send us to California for a spider festival."

126

He smiles and leans back in his chair. "How's the robbery research coming?"

So much for keeping me on track.

I flop down in his canvas sports chair to tell him what I've discovered so far. "They're very clever. They never use their own car in a robbery. I guess because of all the cameras. Sometimes they abandon the vehicle in a parking lots. Once they drove a car into a tree, like kids had gone on a joyride or something."

Brian rubs his hands along his armrests as he thinks. "I guess we'll just have to outsmart them."

CHAPTER FOURTEEN

I'm wracking my brain, trying to figure out our next move as I wander out to the mailbox. Amongst the flyers and catalogs is an official looking envelope. Actually it's one of those perforated letters like paycheck stubs come in. As I fold and tear, I glance down the street.

There's a pick-up truck with ladders and equipment, parked in front of the Anderson's. The lettering on the tailgate is for a roofing company. I didn't know they were thinking about getting a new roof.

The guy on their porch rings the doorbell, then knocks. When no one answers, he peers into the narrow windows on the side of the door. Then he crosses their yard and rings the Collin's door bell. What is he up to?

I open the letter and see a picture of my license plate. It's a traffic violation for running the red light in Alpharetta. And they have three excellent shots of my Cooper just in case I don't believe it. *Merry Christmas!*

How am I going to pay for this? I already shop at Aldi's and Costco. The power bill is due in four days and I won't get paid for a story about a woman who gets away with killing her husband by pushing him off a cliff until January fifteenth.

I imagine me standing on a street corner in downtown Atlanta with a stockinged-leg cocked at a seductive angle. I even visualize me in the Louboutin 3-inch heels and the fancy blue satin jacket. That just increases my depression; who would pay for sex with me?

I'd do better making a sign that reads: HELP ME. I'M TOO OLD FOR HOOKER HEELS and beg for loose change.

The roofing guy is heading my way and gives me a friendly wave but I'm definitely not in a friendly mood.

"There's no soliciting in this neighborhood," I say, then I walk inside and slam the door. From our living room window, I watch him get into his truck. Is he worried that I'll called the cops? What if I do? He'll just drive to the next subdivision and start again.

I've watched plenty of cop shows. By the time the police arrive, it's too late. And they can't arrive too early either or they might thwart the criminals and then they'll just go someplace else. It's really a flawed system.

That's when it occurs to me: we need to figure out where Bonnie and Clyde will strike next and make sure the police are there.

Back at my desk, I scroll through the pictures until I come to the unfolded map. I zoom in on Cumming, Georgia and the number 17. What does that mean?

I flip back through my notes on previous break-ins and there it is. The pawn shop in Cumming was robbed on October 17th. Next, I check a robbery in Jonesboro. The map has a 3 and sure enough, a boutique was robbed on November 3rd.

But how does this help me decide which day is their next scheduled hit? I see a 14 over in Conyers. According to the news reports, there has not been a robbery on that date. December fourteenth has come and gone so does this mean they plan to rob some place in January? Are they looking far enough ahead to February? That's pretty gutsy. And on Valentine's Day no less.

That triggers an idea. I scroll to another part of the map and enlarge it. There's a 25 in Roswell but the map is buckled at a fold and I can't really pinpoint the location. I Google the same area and compare. It looks like they plan to rob some place on Mansell Road. And I'm almost positive it will be December 25th. What could be more perfect? The stores will all be closed; the streets deserted.

I can't think of anything along that stretch except car dealerships and restaurants but investigating possibilities along a street will be a whole lot easier, and cheaper, than driving all over town looking for pawn shops.

* * *

I'm right about Mansell Road. There aren't many shopping centers. The first one I pull into has a 24-hour vet, a liquor store, the usual nail salon, and a Mexican restaurant. No pawn shop, no electronics store.

The next shopping center has a clothing boutique but it's a consignment shop. No respectable thief is going to steal used clothes. That's when I spot the store at the end. The sign reads: *Charles Martin and Associates* in fancy script. I assume it's insurance or an attorney but I walk down anyway. In tiny lettering under the name is: Jewelers.

I glance into the display window. Bingo. High-end jewelry. The storefront is so unassuming that I almost missed it. How can Charles Martin do business when no one knows he's here? That's when I notice the chunky gold necklace. It's gorgeous and it must cost a fortune. An old saying comes to mind: *If you have to ask, you can't afford it.* Evidently the women who can afford this stuff know he's here.

I step out into the parking lot and take in the whole picture. The front door is glass, the façade is brick but I doubt if it would stop a speeding car. And just beyond the store is Warsaw Road that parallels the side of the building. Clyde can drive a stolen car into the store, rake up the goods then dash out to the waiting Escalade.

It's a perfect plan. No, not the robbery; the plan where Brian and I will be somewhere nearby to call the cops and catch the buggers red-handed.

I lay it all out for Brian, how we'll stake out the jewelry store and be ready to take pictures of the whole break-in. So what do you suppose he wants to do first? Go check out the jewelry store for himself. Why do men have such a distrust of their wives' suggestions?

For instance: I've been telling him for years to stop drinking diet sodas because the chemicals will kill him but did he listen to me? Nope. Then he's chatting with the *garbage* man one day while he's dumping our bin of recyclables. When he saw all the cans and bottles, he told Brian that diet drinks were bad for him. So right away Brian declares he isn't going to drink them anymore. What the—

Nevertheless, we drive to the jewelry store for his second opinion.

"You know there's definitely a problem with our stakeout vehicle," he says. "They've seen us wrangling in the front seat of your Cooper, and who could forget the night you plowed through their front yard in this Jeep."

I gnash my teeth. He's right. "What can we do? I'm not going to ask to borrow someone else's car."

I imagine Ellie or Sarah finding a traffic violation in their mailbox, or seeing a crumpled front bumper from a high-speed chase.

"I'm sure I can find a rent-a-wreck company that leases used cars," he says.

We both chuckle. One time Brian was attempting to get close to a pond in Maine known to be frequented by moose. We were cutting across a small clearing when our rental car sank up to the wheel-wells in muck. After lots of rocking and wheel-spinning, Brian managed to push us out but not before he was covered in the foul-smelling mud. (Well, I guess I chuckle more than he does.)

"I'll check out their rates," I say, hinting that I might nix the plan if the rental cost is too much. But who am I kidding? I'm determined to see this through even if I have to pay full price. I delude myself into thinking we can afford this by justifying that it'll only be for one night.

This is why we never get ahead. While we're out and about, Brian is going to swing by a coffee shop in Roswell to pick up a check for two of his photographs that sold. But instead of paying the cable bill, I'm ready to squander the money on a rental car. Of course, if we catch these guys I'll be able to write a piece and make some money. I've got to remember to save my receipts to write off the expenses.

The minute he gets out of the car, he comments that the jewelry store is in a perfect location. Not for business, mind you, but for a heist.

"Look how easy it would be to drive a car through the door." He turns and looks out on Mansell Road. "And they have several options for a getaway: Warsaw Road, Alpharetta Highway or Georgia 400."

Exactly what I told him earlier.

He holds the showroom door for me— the first time in probably ten year—and tries to take my hand as we stroll into the store. If he makes goo-goo eyes at me, I'm sure I'll blurt out a laugh.

The sales clerk looks like he's in his early fifties, and spends most of his commissions on sweets. But I suppose it is boring, working at Charles Martin and Associates and waiting for a rich customer to buy a single item that will pay his commission for the day.

His chubby cheeks force his eyes half-closed when he smiles. I think he has powdered sugar on his tie.

Brian tells the clerk he wants to buy me something special, but it has to be within our budget. So I'm going to pick out three or four baubles that I think we can afford (Ha!) and then he'll come back and buy one so I'll be surprised.

The sales clerk thinks it's a wonderful idea. "More couples should shop together. Women have very distinct and discriminating fashion sense."

He proceeds to interview me on my tastes, and my preference of necklace, earrings or bracelet.

"There sure are a lot of hearts," I say as I lean over the counter.

"We're stocking up for Valentine's Day," he says. "Women love hearts."

We do? I always thought they were dorky. But then I'd never have the money for a diamond-encrusted symbol of our undying love so what do I know.

I settle on earrings and give the clerk an exorbitant amount we're willing to spend. Brian nearly chokes on his tongue which is counter-productive to his mission. His assignment is to casually lay his phone on the glass counter and take a few pictures of the jewelry in the cases.

I hold various earrings to my ear and look in the hand-held mirror acting aloof like all of my jewelry is real gold. Now and then I turn to Brian. "What do you think, Sweetheart?"

"Whatever you like, Babe."

It is kind of fun pretending that I'm going to get some gorgeous earrings. I can't imagine an alternate universe where we'd have enough money for me to spend this much on a simple gold hoop.

The clerk makes a big deal about writing down my choices for Brian. When he asks for a name, Brian says, 'Eric Cartman' and gives the guy a phony telephone number.

We get back in his Jeep and as he pulls into traffic, I review our plan. We now have pictures of the goods before they're stolen. We'll stake out the store and wait for the police to respond. And if they don't get there in time, we'll follow the thieves, giving their exact location until the cops catch up. Case solved.

"The pictures were probably overkill," Brian says. "I'm sure the shop owner has an inventory."

"Yes, but he may not have pictures. This will give the police a good head start if all else fails."

There's no point in getting negative, like the police wondering what we were doing in the jewelry store taking pictures. Once the arrest is made, they'll appreciate our foresight.

We don't have a good excuse for why we're hanging out so close to a jewelry store at the time of a break-in, but I figure we'll just say we were driving by when we saw the car crash into the window. Then once we saw the robbery in progress, we reacted like any good citizens would; we followed them.

I push the discrepancies out of my head. When it's all over and Bonnie and Clyde are locked up, we can reveal how clever we were.

Brian turns into a car dealership across the street from the jewelry store and drives along the outermost row of cars to check on available parking.

"They picked a great time on Christmas night," he says. "No traffic. Probably half the usual crew at police stations."

"Hang on a minute," I say. "Their robberies aren't really at night. They're early in the morning. So does the 25 mean early in the morning of Christmas day? Or Early in the morning of the day after Christmas?"

"Crap!" Brian bangs his hand on the steering wheel.

"Yeah, which means we'll have to rent the car for two nights just to be sure."

"No, I mean this is no good," he says, flailing his hand towards the windshield. "They have all their new models parked in this outside row along Mansell. Even if they sell a car, they probably plug the hole with a new one immediately. We'll never find a space for surveillance."

"What about in the next lot with the used cars?"

Sure enough, there's a much better selection of empty parking spaces close to the road, plus the lot is filled with older models. It's a much better cover. Brian even parks in one of the spaces to get a feel for the location. No one will notice us here late at night surrounded by other cars. The jewelry store is in plain sight but we'll be hidden.

"It's going to be cold," I mention.

Brian slowly nods his head. "We need to look for something with a big back, like an SUV. And tinted windows so no one will see the light from our iPads."

"We can back the car in and get comfortable. Bring some blankets and pillows."

Brian turns and gives me a sly smile. "Maybe an air mattress for extra cushion."

I wonder if Bonnie and Clyde get as turned on after a caper as we do before.

CHAPTER FIFTEEN

The SUV we rent is an old Toyota Rav4 with a back door that swings open to the side. The rental office is closing early since it's Christmas Eve so we have to pick it up at noon. Once Brian folds down the back seats, our air mattress fits quite nicely. I load pillows, two blankets and my fleece Snuggly. I come across the big bag of snacks Brian has smuggled onto the floor of the back seat.

"What about our New Year's resolution to eat healthy?" I ask.

"It's still not New Years," he says, his head wobbling at the obviousness.

I reach into the bag. "Ding Dongs, M&M peanuts. Kettle chips? Those are the worst!"

"No one brings baby carrots on a stake-out."

Truth be told, I'm not too excited about gnawing through celery sticks for a month, either. I mean, what's the point if you can't dip them in Blue cheese dressing or slather them with peanut butter?

Once the car is packed, I stand at the back, surveying it all. The only thing missing is a campfire.

Brian has a small camera set up on a mini tripod. When the action starts, he'll take pictures. My binoculars hang from the clothes hook. The air mattress has been made up like a bed, our pillows propped up like a photo shoot in Architectural Digest. I've got a box of Kleenex nearby, a small cooler with water, a couple battery-powered clip-on lights so we don't run down the car battery. Cozy.

At eleven o'clock, Brian drives over to the used car lot, backs into a parking space, and we settle onto the air mattress. It's Christmas Eve and we're staking out a possible crime scene. In a way, it's kind of romantic.

I check the view with my binoculars. Actually, I have clear sight without them. I don't really think we'll miss the moment when

Bonnie or Clyde drives a stolen car into the front of Charles Martin and Associates, but what the heck. I brought them, why not use them? Brian even did his 'man-thing' and cleaned the windows. Now we wait.

And wait.

Brian kills time by playing solitaire on his iPad. By midnight, he's sound asleep. That's fine. In fact, it's better this way because we have to be at Gwen's for Christmas festivities at nine in the morning and it's never a good idea to be cranky around my parents—or Jake.

After Thanksgiving, my folks drove their RV to the Outer Banks, then made their way down the coast to Hilton Head, Charleston, and Savannah. They got back to Gwen's earlier today but Brian and I begged off the midnight service at church by saying we had other plans.

I'm reading on my new iPad which turns out to be a bad idea because it makes me tired. My brain is conditioned to read for about an hour and conk out. That's pretty much what happens.

I wake up with a start. What time is it? I turn on my phone while I wipe drool from the corner of my mouth with my shoulder. It's six-thirty! My head bangs on the car roof when I sit up too fast. Then I twist and duck to see out the side window and my back screams in protest.

There is no car smashed into the front of Charles Martin Jewelers, no flashing police lights, no sirens blaring. Damn! I should have known Bonnie wasn't anal enough to consider two a.m. as the next day. When she wrote 25 on the map, she meant Christmas Day. We'll have to come back tonight.

* * *

Christmas morning is a repeat performance of the Black Friday breakfast. We stuff our faces with Gwen's standard egg casserole and cinnamon rolls while we wait for Princess Allison to get up.

"Why don't you go wake her?" my mom asks Gwen.

Gwen gets this horrified look on her face like my mom has just asked her to climb a tree and pull down a hornet's nest with her bare hands.

"She's sixteen," I tell Mom. "No good will come of waking her before she's ready."

At first I think Gwen is happy that I have intervened but then she looks pissed like I think she's a coward. Being the parent of a teenager must be a bitch.

Allison finally graces us with an appearance at eleven. She plunks down on the sofa with a sour expression, fires up her phone, and begins texting. I'm sure she is saying vile things about all of us to some other teenager.

At least we can open our presents and get this show on the road.

"This isn't the sweater I picked out," Jake grumbles.

There's a collective gasp at my holiday faux pas but I'm ready for this calamity.

"The one you picked out was fifty percent wool," I say, "so it would have to be hand-washed."

Now it's the women only who gasp, thanks to the magic words: hand wash.

The only sports on Christmas day is basketball so Brian and I can skedaddle right after dinner at three. My folks are leaving early tomorrow morning. They've got to be back in Ocala for their annual mile-long yard sale on the twenty-seventh.

It's really pretty clever. All the folks in their retirement community get new stuff for Christmas. But something old has got to go because they've all downsized into these tiny houses and they've got to make room for the new blender/weedwacker/lopsided pottery vase made by a grandchild. Thus, the yard sale to cull out the clutter.

Once we get home, I change into the fleece pants and v-neck top that Brian got me. We compromised on the outfit. He got me nice roomy pants, but a tight top. We lounge on our bed with the newspaper strewn about, killing time until we leave for the stakeout later tonight.

Brian picks up the remote and surfs until he finds 'A Christmas Story' which we've seen at least ten times.

"Do you think you really could put an eye out with a BB gun?" he asks.

I shake my head. "His mom says *he'll* shoot his eye out, like he's going to turn the gun around and blast away."

"Maybe he shoots the gun, it hits a metal flag pole, ricochets back and gets him in the eye."

"How old is this kid? Ten? And you think he can shoot with that kind of accuracy?"

This goes on until I get bored and go back to reading the comics page. Brian gets hungry and goes to make a sandwich from leftover turkey Gwen gave us.

"New Year's is seven days away!" I call as he lumbers down the stairs.

Stake out: Night two.

Tonight, I'm staying awake. I dozed during the movie so I feel pretty good. And instead of reading, I'm jotting down notes for an article about our adventure. How ordinary citizens knew something was wrong and didn't give up until the perpetrators were caught. Hopefully I can sell the story to the Atlanta Journal or maybe even a national magazine. I'm thinking of calling it *See Something, Say Something*.

By one o'clock, Brian is sick of consuming chips without beer. He's put a good dent in the sweets as well. Even though I've been drinking water sparingly, I've got to pee. I open the rear passenger door and climb out with my salsa jar.

I know the clock is ticking on when he will get so restless he'll want to give up but I'm still surprised when I get settled back in the car.

"They're not going to hit this store," he says. "We've got the wrong place."

"But you said it was perfect."

"I don't care anymore." He shifts and groans. "My back's killing me from sitting like this."

"Lie down. Do some stretches."

His top lip curls into a snarl.

"It's just now one o'clock," I say. "Let's give it a little longer. The other break-ins usually happened later."

I can tell I'm losing him. What he needs is some motivation. I shrug out of my zip-up jacket.

"You just need to relax," I say in my best sultry voice. Then I push him down onto the mattress. "How about a last-minute Christmas present?"

His grimace turns quickly into a boyish grin. "What have you got in mind?"

I straddle his thighs, rocking side to side a couple times to get good and comfortable. Brian makes that little humming noise in the back of his throat. Then I slowly unbutton my flannel shirt to imaginary music as I continued to bump and grind my hips on Mr. Happy.

I know it probably isn't a good idea. If we get busy wrangling in the back seat the robbers could strike and we'll be caught with our pants down—literally. But if I don't do something, Brian will want to go home.

Besides, I figure we'll surely hear the initial crash. Then it will take the robbers at least three minutes to wipe out the jewelry store. Brian is notorious for his marathon completions. We have plenty of time.

He rolls over on top of me and spreads my shirt wide so he can slip his hands under my bra. With a practiced flip, he has the girls out and the bra up to my neck. The bulge in his jeans is growing by the second, so I unzip his pants and slide my hand into his tighty-whiteys.

We're right in the middle of overcoming Brian's subconscious obsession that he was not breastfed enough as a child when the hatch flies open. Cold air rushes in, and Brian turns to see what's happening.

He's dragged off me and pulled from the car. I watch him tumble to the grassy patch between the parking lot and the sidewalk. It all happens so fast, I don't have time to even register what's happening before two people grab me by the ankles and haul me out as well.

Don't ask me why but I grab one of the tripod's legs like it's going to save me. It comes along as I'm hauled out of the back. At the last second they drop my feet and I land in a squat, then drop to my butt and bang my head against the bumper. The camera and tripod clatter to the ground beside me.

I wobble to standing just as Brian rolls to his feet, hastily pulling his pants up. We stand facing two thieves wearing ski masks. One is decidedly smaller than the other. Bonnie and Clyde.

Bless his heart, Brian doubles up his fists and widens his stance like he's going to punch someone's lights out. That's when Clyde pulls a gun out from the back of his pants.

"Gimme the keys," he says.

"What?"

The guy waves his gun in Brian's face. "The keys."

My hands shoot into the air, which isn't easy considering my breasts are dangling. I try shrugging my shoulders to shimmy my bra back down but that's useless.

The guy doesn't seem too interested anyway. He's concentrating on Brian fishing the keys out of his pocket.

What is he going to do with our keys? Throw them into a cornfield so we can't follow them? We're in an urban area. There isn't even any tall grass.

And when Brian doesn't move fast enough, the guy punches him in the stomach. With an oomph, he drops to his knees; the keys chink onto the sidewalk.

I think Bonnie might be ogling me. Either that, or she finds my gyrations hilarious. The keys shift her attention however, and she swoops down to grab them. She tosses them to Clyde, then runs off into the jumble of used cars. Clyde pushes Brian back down to the ground face first. He reaches into Brian's back pockets, takes out his wallet and tucks it into his own pocket. Then he slides out Brian's phone, drops it onto the sidewalk, and stomps it with the heel of his boot. After he kicks it into the street, he dashes to the driver's side of our rental.

As we stand on the sidewalk watching, Clyde drives out of the parking lot, across the street, and into the front of the jewelry store.

CHAPTER SIXTEEN

I'm not even sure how long we stand there watching. I remember seeing Bonnie drive their Escalade out of the used car lot. It wasn't parked more than five or six cars away from us. She crosses over to Warsaw Street at the side of the shopping center and sits with the motor running as Clyde wipes out Charles Martin and Associates.

The headlights of our rental shine into the store, glinting off the shattered glass cases. I see the silhouette of Clyde as he moves along the row, raking loot into his pack. The store's alarm blares. Even from our vantage point, it's loud. It must be deafening inside the store. Has Clyde learned to carry ear plugs?

Seconds later, he crawls over the crumpled hood of our rental, slings the backpack over his shoulder, and sprints to their SUV. It hasn't been more than five minutes from the time they dragged Brian out of the car until they disappear into the night.

Once I'm sure they are gone, I pull my bra back down and button my shirt. I'm shivering—and stunned.

My mind races through all the things in our car: my purse, my phone, my sweater, our jackets, the blankets. I actually look down at my feet to reassure myself I still have on my boots.

Brian dashes into the street to pick up his phone and scurries back to the sidewalk, his head shaking as he presses buttons. It's a goner.

I'm not too concerned about calling the police since I can hear sirens in the distance. Our rescuers are on their way.

Brian grabs my arm. "We gotta get out of here."

"Why? We're eye witnesses."

My first thought is to dash across the road and get my purse and coat while we wait. But as the sirens get closer I realize that the police seeing me climb out of our smashed car is not a good idea.

"Pretend you're Jake for just a moment," Brian says as he grabs my hand and drags me between two used cars. "All our stuff is in a rental car. Obviously, we were staking out the place. You've been obsessed with these people and the robbery house."

"I wasn't obsessed."

Brian rolls his eyes at me. "You've talked to Jake about it how many times?"

The situation is looking bleaker by the second. Even if we claim our innocence—including the fact that we don't have the stolen jewelry in our possession—all evidence points to the contrary. The police will merely say we stuck around to avoid suspicion but passed off the jewelry to an accomplice.

I squeeze Brian's hand. "We're in deep shit."

I hop up to run but he remains crouched, staring at the empty parking space where our car was. His camera and tripod lie crumpled and broken on the pavement. It's like the classic scene where the chaos has died down enough that little Billy realizes his dog Buster is dead.

"I'm so sorry," I say as I lay a hand on his shoulder.

We don't have time for this, but I let him have one last moment with his beloved Nikon D300. He unscrews the tripod which got mangled when the car backed over it, then cradles the camera at his side before he backs away and we sprint off into the night.

I pick up the pace as we zig-zag our way through a cemetery behind the car dealership. Thank goodness Brian is still wearing his shoes, too, but he's down to his jeans and a tee shirt. He's also carrying the destroyed tripod and dead camera. I'm sure when he takes it in for repairs, the quote will be so high he'll be better off buying a new one. Which translated means a newer model at a much higher price.

At Alpharetta Highway, we wait until a lone car zooms by, then sprint across the street and into another parking lot, sticking close to the storefronts so we won't be seen by passing cars. But Brian has different worries.

"A lot of these places have security cameras," he yells as we round the corner to the back of the shopping center. "We can't be identified anywhere near the crime scene."

We skulk around dumpsters and through back brush until we get off the main drag. His wallet is gone so we have no money to pay for a cab even if we could find one at this time of the morning. We have no phone to call someone. And I can't imagine that anyone driving by will pick us up at this ungodly hour. More likely they'll call the police to report two suspicious people lurking in the shadows.

Our house is at least seven miles away, and we will be walking the whole distance.

"I can't believe it," Brian mumbles as we cut behind a church on Houze Road. "They were staking out the store the same time we were."

I shake my head. "Evidently, they were staking us out, too."

"Shit!" Brian's voice echoes. "I bet they couldn't believe their good luck. We provided them with the ramming car."

"And suspects."

"What are we going to tell the police?"

By now I'm too cold to think. My flannel shirt and leggings don't provide any protection from the bitter cold. Okay, the bank sign said it was 38 degrees, but the wind chill must be minus seven.

"I'm freezing!" I yell at the universe.

"Me, too," Brian says, his bare arms hugged to his chest.

Then he says he has an idea and runs over to one of those waste receptacles the city provides. After gingerly setting his camera down, he wrenches off the metal lid and pulls out the opaque white plastic can liner. It's nearly full of fast-food Styrofoam, dumped sodas and who knows what else.

He smiles. "You can wear this as a poncho."

Without waiting for my snarky reply, he dumps the garbage into the bin and shakes the bag—like those two little shakes will remove all the rotting food and germs and slime.

"You've got to be kidding," I say when he hands it to me.

"It's not that bad."

"Oh, yeah? Stick your face in there and smell."

He actually opens the bag and takes a whiff. "How about if I turn it inside out? The outside's clean."

"No thanks."

He isn't deterred. He pushes the bottom up into the bag until it's gunk-side out. Then even he is repulsed by the black smears of mold and clinging bits of rotting food.

"Okay, so it's not a great plan," he says. Then he drags the bag across some weeds to remove the excess. With a finger, he pokes a hole in the top and widens it. He slings the camera strap over a shoulder and across his chest before pulling the bag over his head.

And this is the man who was disgusted because he got a little doggy doo on his hand.

With his arms snug inside, the white bag makes him look like an alien wearing camo.

"You can't walk with your arms in there."

"Why not?" he asks. "It feels great once you get the inside warmed up." He wriggles his shoulders to demonstrate how comfortable he is. Whatever.

After nearly a mile, we come across a construction site. New homes are going up as fast as builders can cobble them together. One of the houses already has siding and windows.

I'm so cold my fingers are numb. My nose is running and I can feel where I've been wiping it on my sleeve. It's going to freeze soon.

"Let's see if we can get in," I say.

Naturally the house is locked up tight to prevent thieves from stealing copper wire and light fixtures. But the garage is open. Tucked in a corner is a painter's drop-cloth.

I shake it out and examine it for wet paint blobs. It looks fairly dry even though it's splattered with years of neutral tones in semi-gloss latex. And it's scratchy canvas, not soft fleece. But who am I to complain? I wrap it around me like a blanket.

Once the chill fades and I begin to warm up, my shoulders relax and my teeth stop chattering.

Brian is sitting under a beam of light coming through one of the garage windows, examining his camera. He looks through the viewfinder and turns towards the light.

"It doesn't look like the lens is cracked."

"Thank god," I sigh with relief. Even if the camera gets out of this without a scratch, I'll be hearing about it for years.

Satisfied that the camera doesn't need triage care, Brian loops it back over his chest and crawls back into his garbage bag. He stands and straightens the bag like it might be riding up at an unflattering angle in the back. Then he glances over at me wrapped up like a burrito.

"Better?" he asks.

"Oh, this is ideal. We make quite an attractive couple don't you think?"

He tosses his tripod into the construction dumpster before we head back out. My drop cloth trails along like the train of a wedding gown. I take the lead so the odor drifting from Brian stays behind.

After another mile, my brain thaws out.

"I guess we need to work on our story. Eventually the police will trace that car back to the rental agency and then to us."

When I don't hear a snarky comment about 'if I'd mind my own business we wouldn't need stories', I turn to see what's going on. Brian's mouth is in a kind of sickly contortion.

"What?" I ask.

"The rental contract is in the glove box."

"My purse is in the back. We're toast no matter what," I say. "We've got to come up with a plausible excuse for all of this fast."

"Have at it, Gladys."

"Okay, what about this: we were going to Tallulah Falls for a shoot but we couldn't afford to book a room so we decided we'd sleep in the car. But neither the Jeep or Cooper were big enough so we rented an SUV."

"Wait a minute. We can't afford a room but we can rent a car?"

"Yeah, okay." I erase the idea with my hand. "What if we were going to track some animal? Or we wanted to be close to a mating site?"

"And we couldn't take the Jeep because—"

"The back isn't big enough to sleep in."

Brian gives me a shrug. I know he'll work on the details of what we were tracking; all I need is the set-up. "We decided on a dry run to see if the air mattress fit in the rental, and to see if sleeping in the car would be too cold."

"Where?"

"How about Providence Park?"

His head waggles from side to side as he thinks it through. "That might work. It explains the blankets and snacks."

"Exactly." I march along Arnold Mill, the gears in my head running at full speed. "We're fast asleep in the car when someone yanks you out of the back. Blah, blah, blah, they drive away with our rental."

"And why would two otherwise intelligent human beings sleep in an unlocked car?"

I like to stick to the truth whenever possible. "I had to go to the bathroom and I forgot to lock it again."

Brian gives me another shrug. If he's buying it, surely the cops will too.

"I can live with the police thinking I'm stupid." I start walking faster. "But we need to get home and report the SUV stolen."

Once we have our story straight, my mind begins to conjure up new crises. "Bonnie and Clyde probably have my purse, my phone, both our credit cards, the house key on your key ring."

"Shit! They know where we live. They've probably wiped out all our stuff."

"At least I don't have any expensive jewelry. And there's no cookie jar with hundreds of dollars in it."

Brian groans. "What if they take my Braves Bobble-head collection? Or my Packers Shareholder Certificate?"

"Really? That's what you're worried about?"

He has a framed certificate that proves he is the proud shareholder of stock with the Green Bay Packers. Value? Zero dollars.

Heat caused by fear makes my scalp prickle. "Those bastards better not take my Keurig machine. I was the last one on our block to get one."

The moon has disappeared making it even darker by the time we finally get to Hamilton Farms. My feet are killing me, the muscles in my arms are locked up, and my fingers ache from clinging to this stupid drop cloth.

I want to cry when I see our house in the distance. But then I also notice a car sitting in front. The engine is running, and there is the unmistakable hump of police lights on the top.

Brian panics. "Oh, crap. They're waiting for us. We're going to be arrested. Shit, shit, shit. We're going to jail."

"Knock it off," I hiss. "This works out perfectly."

I shrug off the drop cloth and start running straight for the cop, my arms out front in supplication. When I get closer, I call out. "Help us! Please help us!"

By the time I get to the policeman's window I'm panting and sobbing. "Thank god you're here! Someone stole our car and left us on the side of the road." I take a moment to suck in a shaky breath. "We've been walking for hours."

The policeman shines a flashlight in my face, then on Brian and his garbage bag. He orders us to back up then slowly gets out of his patrol car. "Can I see some ID?"

"We don't have any. When they stole the car they got my purse, my phone, even our jackets."

"And my wallet," Brian adds.

I start shivering again to prove how cold we are but the policeman wants the full story right out here in the street.

"We're freezing," I say, my voice rising to the level of almost-pissed-off woman. "Can't we at least go into our house where we can get warm?"

He must be married and recognizes the warning signs of woman-on-the-edge because he finally agrees. And once he sees that Brian knows the code to our garage door, he takes his hand off his gun.

Brian shrugs out of the trash bag and tosses it into our garbage can. The policeman, Officer Davidson, follows me inside. As soon as we walk into the living room, I grab the afghan off the back of the sofa, wrap up tight, and sit down.

Officer Davidson gives me a funny look then glances at poor freezing Brian standing in the doorway. Oops. I motion for Brian to come sit next to me, and wrap a loving arm—and a corner of the blanket—over his shoulder.

It's only later that I realize what a smart move that was. If Brian had gone hunting for his own blanket, Officer Davidson might have started questioning me alone. It's much better that we're together to keep our story straight.

Officer Davidson flops into the chair across from us with a sigh. That was quite a trek from his car to our living room. He pulls out a little notebook from his front breast pocket along with a pen. "What time did this incident occur?"

Most of our tale is the truth which makes the telling a whole lot easier. And I do most of the talking. I mean, I'm the one with a degree in storytelling. Brian offers his smashed phone as evidence.

"Did anyone else see the thieves?" the officer asks.

I shake my head. "I don't remember any cars driving by."

"How did you come home?"

"We walked!"

"No," he says. "I mean what route did you take? Maybe someone was up late getting a glass of water, things like that."

"Oh. Yeah. Well, it was mostly Providence Road and Arnold Mill." I turn to Brian for confirmation. Men always like it when women check with their husbands to be sure they're right. I figure this cop is no exception.

The problem is that once I veer away from the truth, Officer Davidson looks a touch suspicious. And I always thought I was a good liar.

I clap my hands to my face and bend over. "It was awful!" I cry. "I thought they were going to kill us. I've never been so scared in my life."

Brian pats my shoulder as I tremble. I even manage to get a sob out.

"I just want to take a shower and get warmed up," I say. "Can't we finish this later?"

Officer Davidson gives each of us what is probably a practiced glare and says he wants us to file a complete report by noon today. We swear we'll be there as we escort him to the front door.

The instant that door clicks shut, I scurry to the kitchen to pour myself a big glass of wine. But when I turn on the light, I freeze. There on the kitchen table are Brian's credit cards—cut into little pieces.

"Oh, my God. They were here!"

Brian comes in after me. "What the hell is that all about?"

I stare at the mess for a moment before it comes to me. "I suspect they tried to use one of our cards for something big and got rejected. I think this is a message for us to stop charging."

Brian looks into the den. "They didn't steal the TV. What? It wasn't good enough?"

Even my old laptop is still on the table. They didn't bother with it either. And glory be, they didn't taken my coffee machine.

I wake up the screen on the laptop and see the article about unusual festivals. "At least they didn't see all the pictures from the robbery house, or the map."

"How do you know that?"

He isn't going to stir up my imagination at this hour, is he? I'm exhausted and he's planting the seeds for a new concern? I'm about to go off on him when I notice the light blinking on our answering machine.

It's Jake. *I don't know what you two are up to, but if I find out this is about that goddamn porn house, you're in big trouble.*

"The porn house," I say. "We need to check it out."

My vision of somehow justifying new shoes and a jacket is fading fast.

I almost have the front door open when I notice Officer Davidson parked outside our house. "Why is he still here?"

"Maybe he's filling out his report."

"Or maybe he suspects we were part of the robbery and he's waiting to see if our accomplice shows up with the loot."

Brian shakes his head. "I'm going to take a shower."

Officer Davidson is still there even after I finish getting cleaned up.

"This isn't good," I say as I smooth out the crack in the drapes where I've been watching.

"He's probably wondering why we're still awake after you told him how tired you were."

I snap my fingers. "Exactly."

We turn off all the lights like we're going to bed then creep into the living room again to watch through the curtains.

Finally, at about seven-thirty, he drives away.

Dressed in sweats, we head out the front door, making a big deal about getting ready for a run. Brian stretches his quads, I try to touch my toes. Then we really run all the way to the robbery house. When we slip in through the sliding glass door, our fears come true. Everything has been cleared out.

CHAPTER SEVENTEEN

I try to sleep but it's useless. Everything we've been through has been for nothing. We have no evidence, Bonnie and Clyde are probably in the wind, and I'm scared to death that we've raised suspicion with the local police. It doesn't help that our pillows are in the back of the wrecked SUV and I'm trying to sleep on a rolled up beach towel inside a pillow case. I turn onto my back.

Does Officer Davidson really believe our story? When we show up at the police station will they put us in separate rooms and try to break us? Should I ask for a lawyer? I know on the TV shows I always assume the suspect is guilty the minute they lawyer-up.

The expense of an attorney gets me thinking about money. We're back to ground zero with these crooks but we still have rental fees and a hefty deductible to pay for the damage to the car. Our insurance rates will surely go up. I have to get a new drivers' license and cancel credit cards. (Only one set of cards was cut up, so does that mean they didn't take my purse?) I even anguish over having to replace our ratty blankets and buy new pillows. The jacket I lost is only four or five years old.

Totally agitated, I roll out of bed, my brain this close to sparking from all the activity. Brian sleeps like a baby of course. How do men turn off all their problems like that? I swear he'd sleep through a tornado, or at least until it tore the roof off.

I brew a cup of coffee, giving my machine an affectionate caress as I wait for the water to trickle through. My lower lip trembles at the thought that I'll have to put my sweet Keurig away for a while. I'll be buying instant coffee at Aldi's for the next few months until I dig us out of debt.

There's nothing like depression to kick up an appetite. I eat a bagel smeared with Nutella and when that doesn't work, I eat the creamy goodness right out of the jar with my knife.

By the time I nudge Brian awake at eleven o-clock, I'm nauseous from all the worry—and the chocolate spread.

I swear I could fall asleep in the car as he drives to the police station but it might be better to run through our story one more time.

As I grill Brian, my anxiety spikes again. He was sitting right next to me last night but he doesn't remember I told the cop we came home on Providence Road? I honestly don't know what goes on in a man's mind.

A couple years ago, I came up with a little game for Brian. We'd be eating dinner or riding in the car, I'd be talking and he'd be staring off into space.

"What are you thinking right this instant?" I'd ask.

I wanted him to actually consider what he was thinking about instead of listening to me. But his answer was always the same. "Nothing."

How could he be thinking of nothing? How did he ever get through school? Does he listen to other men at parties? Am I the only one he's tuning out? I swear if I could hook electrodes to his head I'd find out what was going on inside there.

At the police station, a different cop shows us the rental agreement that was retrieved from the wrecked car, Brian confirms his signature on the lease, and we sign a whole bunch of papers.

The officer says I can't get my purse or phone back because they are part of an ongoing investigation. I wonder how much of a stink I should raise but I'm glad I won't have to go to the DMV for a new license after all so I go for wimpy.

"Okay," I say as I hang my head like the helpless victim. "Whatever it takes to catch these guys," I add like the helpful citizen I am.

And we're done. The officer didn't even put us in separate rooms.

As we drive away, I'm giddy from lack of sleep. "I don't know why I was so paranoid this morning. Obviously, they believe our story. Why wouldn't they?"

"I can think of a couple reasons."

I refuse to buy into Brian's negativity. "All I need is a power nap and I'll be ready to kick some Bonnie and Clyde butt."

"No, we need to drop this, Rachel. I never should have let it go this far. We're lucky we got away with that bullshit story."

"I agree the stakeout was a bad idea, but I'm thinking of something safer."

"Like letting it go?"

"If there was just some way we could track their car."

I'm racking my brain for a solution when Brian pulls into Burger King.

"What do you think you're doing?" I ask.

"I'm starving."

"Well you'll just have to wait until we get home. We can't afford Burger King."

"Exactly," Brian says, giving me a raised eyebrow. "And we can't afford the car rental fee or the insurance deductible. That's why you need to forget about this."

He cruises on through the parking lot and back out onto the street. "What I do need is a new phone."

I get a sideways glance from him. He thinks I'm going to nix the idea but I'm keeping mum. Mostly because we'll need a cell phone for my next idea.

At the phone store, I'm definitely in Frugal Rachel mode. When the sales girl steers us towards the expensive iPhones, I herd Brian right on by to the off-brands.

"We're not getting a phone that has to be paid for in installment plans," I whisper. "It's bad enough we need to get the unlimited internet access."

"Maybe we don't," he says. "Let's just get a plain phone."

Has hell frozen over and it didn't make the news? Because I've never known Brian to take the cheap route on one of his toys in the whole sixteen years we've been married. But now that I'll need mobile internet access, he's willing to do without?

With phone in hand, we head for home. I offer to drive so Brian can play with his new gadget. Once he's busy pushing buttons, I slip in my idea.

"What about a tracking collar?" I say. "Instead of putting one on an animal to monitor their migration, couldn't we just hook it under a car somewhere?"

He actually takes his eyes off the phone. "Are you even listening to me?"

"You should take the surveillance camera back to Randy and see if he's got a collar."

"And what are you going to put this collar on?"

"Clyde's Escalade. We know where they live, too."

"You're assuming they're still at that apartment complex."

What a negative Neddy. I'm surprised Brian doesn't have ulcers.

"Just call him," I say.

Randy does have a tracking collar. Unfortunately, the collar is currently around the neck of a baby black bear somewhere in Ellijay. But here's the good thing. As soon as Brian mentions that he wants to put the collar on a car, Randy gets all excited.

"Dude! Do you think Rachel is cheating on you?" he says through the speaker phone.

"I'm right here, Randy," I say into the phone.

"Sorry. Sorry," he says. "So is it a drug dealer?"

"Something like that," Brian says.

"That's awesome!"

Before my very eyes, annoyed, sulking Brian transforms into proud, superhero Brian. His shoulders straighten, his head bobbles. I swear if I wasn't sitting right next to him, he'd adjust his package or possibly spit *and* fondle.

His swellage deflates a bit after he hangs up and I tell him he'll have to ask Madeline if he can borrow one of the magazine's collars.

"Oh, no you don't," he says. "I'm not calling in any favors with her just so you can get us in trouble again."

I display my shock facially. "This will be perfectly safe."

Brian displays his skepticism facially.

"Fine," I say. "I'll ask her myself."

"And what will you tell her you're using the collar for?"

"I'll tell her a coyote has invaded our neighborhood."

He strokes the stubble on his chin. "And how are you going to get the collar on this coyote?"

Good point. I'll have to go with something less threatening. "What about one of the wild turkeys?"

"You do understand that even if you were able to get a collar on an animal, you'd also have to get it back off and return it to Madeline in a timely manner or she'll take the cost out of your pay. Being grilled by the police is nothing compared to her."

Okay, I can't remember the last time someone was allowed to borrow anything significant from the magazine. Madeline has such a tight rein on the expensive stuff that some of us suspect it has all been lost over time and instead of Madeline replacing things like lenses and equipment, she keeps the garnished wages for herself.

That's doubtful. But I understand why she's so hesitant to loan stuff out. Getting a tracker on and off sounds close to impossible. And explaining how the device will be used is even more daunting.

"We should just sneak in and take one," I say.

Brian snorts so hard he practically blows snot. "Great idea! Why didn't I think of that?"

I know he's being sarcastic, but I decide to take his affirmation at face value and begin plotting how we can sneak into *The Good Life* and get a tracking collar.

The magazine office is not some bustling enterprise with rows of writers banging away on computers, phones ringing constantly, and coveted corner offices on the top floor of some high-rise in downtown Atlanta.

The Good Life is located in a shabby office park in Smyrna where the rent is cheap. In addition to the magazine, our particular building has an insurance agent, a holistic doctor, and two empty spaces.

Everyone on the staff works out of their home just like Brian and me. We send our data digitally and get paid the same way so there is seldom a reason to be in the office.

Thus, *The Good Life* is nothing more than two rooms: the front reception area where Madeline stands guard, and an inner office where Ray Jackson hangs out when he isn't golfing—excuse me—promoting the magazine. And of course, the magic supply closet is in a short hall right next to the bathroom.

I've worked at the magazine long enough to know that the keys to the front door and the closet are on one of those springy plastic bands that is worn on the wrist. When Madeline is in the office, the keys are in her drawer. When she goes to lunch, the band is snapped onto her wrist. I swear if the magazine ever goes under, she'll be a natural for bank security.

The trick to my caper is to catch Ray in his office while Madeline is at lunch. Surely he has a key too, even though I've never seen him use it.

This won't be as easy as it sounds because some days Madeline brings food from home and sits at her desk eating leftover lemon pepper cod and soggy sweet potato fries.

We figure that's what she'll do Monday, so we'll drive over Tuesday.

Back at Hamilton Farms, the neighborhood looks like a scene from *The Truman Show*. People we haven't seen in months are in their yards raking leaves, washing cars. When they see our car coming down the street, they all stop. My guess is they saw the police car in front of our house and can't wait for the details.

I mumble that they need to get a life but Brian snickers at the irony.

Ellie is on our front porch with Oscar. As we pull into the drive, she dashes over.

"What the hell's going on?" she asks. Oscar jumps up on the drivers-side door and rakes his claws down the side. A cash register bell dings in my head.

I give Ellie the abbreviated version, promising to elaborate over wine later.

She shakes her head as I wrap up my story. "Sarah got tired of waiting so she left a note on your door. She's going to be pissed that she missed out on this latest episode."

I look confused.

"She's flying to Chicago this afternoon for a business conference." She pauses until the light come on in my head. "The kids are staying with Ron?" she adds.

"That's right," I say. It's all coming back to me now. "Well, I'll fill her in when she gets back Wednesday."

"So what time should Joanie and I be back with the wine," Ellie asks.

This is what I like about my friends; they can turn a tragedy into a party.

"Five o'clock," I say.

160

The answering machine has messages from Gwen: *Please tell me you aren't still pursuing this porn house thing* and my mom: *Is everything all right?* I can only imagine the number of texts on my phone, now in police custody.

Ray's car isn't in the parking lot. I'm really disappointed because I had to buy a box of Krispy Kremes to get Brian to come along and he ate half of them on the drive over. (Well, I had a couple.) After about thirty minutes, Madeline gets in her car and leaves for lunch.

"I don't believe it," I say. "Now we've got to come back tomorrow."

My stomach is totally queasy from all the donuts. (And all the wine Ellie and Sarah and Brian and I drank last night.) I'm not sure I can handle a second day of this.

"Let's stick around," Brian says. "Maybe Ray will show up."

I check my watch. It's twelve-fifteen, so at one-fifteen Madeline will be back. At twelve-thirty, there's still no sign of Ray. At twelve-forty-five my anxiety level is at seven and my stomach is boiling with gastric juices. I decide another donut might quell the violence. It doesn't.

At five minutes to one, Ray pulls into the parking lot. I don't believe it. Brian is right again?

We don't have time for his gloating.

"Get in there!" I say.

I'm sorely tempted to follow Brian to make sure he gets it right, but I have my own task. I'll just have to trust him to keep his brain from slipping into power-saver mode for the ten seconds he needs to pay attention.

His assignment is to borrow the Nikon 2.8 10mm fisheye lens. I know, that's an expensive piece of equipment. How do I know? Because Brian owned one just like it until he was standing at the railing of a ferry heading to Mackinac Island and he dropped the lens into Lake Huron. (Let's not even discuss the fact that he hadn't used the lens in over a year so it shouldn't have even been in the carrying case.)

My assignment is to check out the lock on the front door. Yes, I know. Logically, I'd be the one to schmooze Ray and Brian would putter around with the door, but I'm not the photographer borrowing equipment. I don't really think Ray will unlock the vault to get me a printer cartridge.

The door is a piece of crap. We have better locks in our home. I know this for a fact because we had to pay a locksmith to change all the locks in case Bonnie or Clyde decide to come back for Brian's Packer Certificate. Plus, the office door itself is a joke. It's one of those with the big glass panel and the name of the business stenciled in gold and black. The grout around the glass is so old and cracked, I could push the whole pane out with one good shove.

Obviously, neither Ray nor Madeline feel threatened by a break-in. Why should they? If a burglar shined a flashlight into the office he'd see a battered metal desk with a big boxy monitor from the late 20th century. The metal filing cabinets along the back wall have seen better days, and the two chairs in the waiting area would be rejected by the Goodwill.

Beside Madeline's desk is a tired artificial ficus tree with a skirt of fallen leaves around its base. While I wait for Brian, I examine the bedraggled plant. It looks like Madeline tried gluing the leaves back on for a while, but each gust of wind that blows in when the door opens sends another fluttering to the floor. Evidently the cleaning crew avoids the whole mess because there is a distinct circle of dust where they stop vacuuming.

Once I have the lay of the room, I slip back out to wait in the car. When Ray comes out of his office to unlock the storage closet, I don't want him to see me snooping around.

Madeline pulls back into the parking lot and I duck down in the front seat. Then I scold myself for being so paranoid. Why shouldn't I be waiting in the car for Brian? He has a legitimate excuse for being there. I just hope he has gotten Ray to unlock the closet. If he hasn't, I'm going to withhold all affection for a month.

By the time he trots back to the car with the lens, I have sweated huge puddles under my arms. "What took you so long?"

"Ray's thinking about starting a second magazine about golf."

I make an unladylike nasal blart.

"Really," Brian says as though I need further convincing that Ray is an idiot. "He even asked me if I golf."

Swell. I can't think of anything more exciting than hanging out in country clubs across the country filled with preppy rich people dining on overcooked chicken breast smothered in some bland sauce.

"And what did you find out about the closet key?"

For a second I see that familiar blank expression on Brian's face. It's like in that robot movie where the red light blinks out in its eyes. But just when you think it's no longer a threat, the light comes back on.

"He keeps it in the very back of his middle desk drawer in a little plastic tray."

Brian rewards himself with the last donut. As an afterthought, he asks me about the front door.

"A piece of cake."

Okay, so it isn't as easy as it looks on TV. For the past two hours, Brian has tried to unlock our kitchen door with a credit card. Well, not a credit card. Ours were chopped to bits. But he found his old botanical gardens membership card in the junk drawer and is practicing with it.

Here's the thing though. Along the doorframe is a small strip of wood, so to get a credit card to the latch, you have to ziggity-zag around this doorstop. After many failed attempts, Brian decides to circumvent the doorstop by prying it away from the frame with a putty knife so the card can slide straight to the latch. He succeeds in popping the lock and calls me over to witness his triumph.

I should have been paying closer attention. It's all my fault.

"Look at the doorstop!" I bellow. "There's a big groove in it. Don't you think Madeline will notice?"

Brian presses the wood to close the gap. "I'll have to bring some glue." He pushes on it harder. "And maybe some caulk."

Whatever. Tonight we drive to the magazine office as soon as it gets dark.

Brian's sweaty hands make a perfect entry a little shaky, but we get inside, find the key in Ray's desk, and head down the small hallway to the hallowed closet.

I must admit I'm as excited as the explorers must have been when they found King Tut's Tomb. I have visions of golden crowns and precious stones, or at least shelves of expensive telephoto lenses a foot long, and lots of fancy strobes. What I see is copy paper, printer cartridges, and file folders.

Surprisingly, there is no supernatural blue light radiating from the tracking collars or the remote cameras. In fact, it takes quite a bit of rummaging to find the stupid things. They're in a box labeled PARTY SUPPLIES. Very clever, Madeline.

Brian thinks we should immediately drive home to celebrate our first *real* B & E. On the other hand, I think we should drive immediately to Bonnie and Clyde's apartment. He sulks from the passenger seat while he reads the instructions on activating the collar while I drive to the apartment complex.

We have no idea which is their apartment, or even their building, but I'm hoping that with dumb luck we might spot their

Escalade and use deductive reasoning or extra-sensory perception to triangulate the apartment from the positioning of the car. We can't have them staring out their window or smoking a cigarette on the front stoop while Brian does his thing.

We park at the rental office in front then wander around the various parking lots for a good thirty minutes, trying to look like we belong. As we come around the corner of a unit in the back of the complex, we spot a U-Haul backed up to a rickety wooden stairway. A guy is carrying an armchair down the steps.

Right next to the U-Haul is the Escalade. How can we have such bad luck? Brian's going to attempt to crawl under the Escalade while some cretin is moving? I don't think so.

A woman scurries down the stairs with two cloth travel bags but instead of putting them in the van, she opens the back of the Escalade and tosses them in.

"Holy shit!" Brian hisses in my ear. "It's Bonnie and Clyde."

"And they're moving," I whisper back.

When Clyde passes under the security light, I get a better look at his face. He's dark-complected and has dark hair, but he doesn't really look black. More Hispanic maybe, but as I watch him lug the chair up the ramp and into the back of the truck, I'm thinking that's not right either.

I'm sure Brian would call it a coincidence but I prefer to credit our excellent timing to my superior women's intuition. There is no doubt in my mind that if we'd shown up an hour later, those two would have been long gone.

Regardless of my skills, we still have the problem of how Brian is going to shimmy under their SUV and latch the tracking collar to an axle while they tromped up and down the stairs with their belongings.

"I'll be right back," he whispers before he ducks behind the building next to us. I don't see him again until I notice rustling in the holly bushes in front of Bonnie's building.

How clever of the apartment owners to plant those barbed shrubs from hell to keep undesirables from breaking into first floor apartments, or peeping in windows. I know first-hand how painful spiny holly leaves are.

I skitter across the parking lot like a commando in Afghanistan and position myself behind a van where I can get a better look at the situation. I must not have been as stealthy as I thought because Brian waves and signals me with a thumbs up. Then he points to the stairs.

My job is to give him the all clear.

Clyde struggles down the steps with the lead end of a mattress this time; Bonnie's at the back, but she isn't doing much more than keeping the mattress upright because it bounces down each step. She's got quite a head of blonde hair that probably looks great all tousled and piled on top of her head. Right now it looks limp and dirty.

"Next time I see Bobby," she says in classic white-trash Southernese, "I'm gonna kick him in the balls."

"He said he *might* be able to help," Clyde explains to her. His accent is definitely not Southern. More like Indian or Pakistani, the short clipped words, the careful enunciation.

At the bottom of the stairs she actually has to lift the mattress and turns to aim it into the truck. Holy cow, she's bigger in the chest than Sarah.

"He's your brother," she snaps as she pushes the bed up the ramp.

"Yes, but perhaps something has come up."

I'll bet. Bobby's probably standing on a corner selling drugs, or stalking some poor defenseless woman.

"Well, I'm not helping you unload. All this shit can just sit in the truck until he can get his ass to Jonesboro."

Is this a golden moment or what? I get a good look at both of them. I find out they're moving to Jonesboro, and Clyde has a brother named Bobby. I just wish Bonnie would get pissed enough to call Clyde by his name.

Once in the truck, Clyde gives a mighty pull and the bed disappears inside with Bonnie still clinging on. This seems like as good a time as any. I raise my arm and drop it like a flag.

Brian slithers out from behind the bushes on his belly, down the curb and to the far side of the Escalade. Then he rolls onto his back and scoots under the chassis.

I wish I'd learned some clever bird calls, or Indian tweets to let him know when he can slid back out. But it really isn't necessary. Bonnie bitches as she stomps back up to their apartment. I can't really make out what she's saying now that she's turned around but I think either she broke a fingernail or dislocated a disc.

When the apartment door slams, Brian wrangles back out from under the SUV and darts for the safety of the van. Together, we run back to the entrance of the apartment complex and hop into the Jeep.

It isn't until we're out on the street that we both whoop with glee.

Do all men think any little thing they do is monumental? Sure, I understand if he removes a brain tumor, or nails shingles on those really steep roofs, but come on. All Brian did was crawl under a car and snap on a collar. He crawls under our cars all the time to change the oil, so what's the big deal?

But all the way home, he cannot stop boasting about how stealthy he was and how much danger he was been in. For the tenth time he reminds me how he crawled on his belly like a CIA operative, then he grips the steering wheel and lifts himself up like he's making more room for his expanding manhood.

I decide I better change the subject before he expects me to lean over and relieve the tension.

"I wonder if they've found a new storage place in Jonesboro, too. Although I guess it doesn't matter. I'll be able to keep tabs on them."

"As long as they're in the Escalade."

Leave it to Donny Downer to find the flaw. If Bonnie and Clyde use a stolen vehicle, I won't know where they're taking the goods.

"Yeah, well, sooner or later they'll go by with the Escalade," I say. "Then we've got 'em."

We don't discuss how much more difficult it will be to track these two in Jonesboro rather than two block away. That would ruin the glow of the adventure.

It isn't until Brian gets in the shower that he realizes he's been wounded in action. He comes out of the bathroom wearing a towel and asks me if there's anything on his back. He has about a two-inch scrape that's red but doesn't look like it even bled and another little bitty scratch on the back of his left elbow.

I get out the antibiotic cream to dab on his injuries. There's lots of hissing and moaning like I'm digging out a bullet with a nail file, but I let him carry on. We're back in the crime-fighting business, that's all that matters.

Once he's out of mortal danger, I run my hands up his bare chest. "You really were brave tonight."

His towel jumps in front. A familiar gleam flashes in his eyes and the next thing I know, I'm flat on the bed giggling while he kisses my neck.

Interesting note here: He doesn't scream out once when I claw at his back.

CHAPTER EIGHTEEN

I wake up to birds singing, flowers blooming, and colorful butterflies cavorting overhead. Not really, but I'm feeling pretty damn good this morning.

I nestle my head deeper into my new bed pillow that I got at a two-for-one sale; plus I had a $5 coupon. All is well in my world.

We haven't heard anything more from the police since we filed our report on the stolen rental car Sunday. One of the things on my to-do list this morning is call the police station and see if I can get my purse and phone. I'm dreading the call to our insurance agent about the damage so I won't be pushing for the police to release the car.

Have you ever read Janet Evanovich? Her character Stephanie Plum wrecks cars all the time but I never read about her insurance premiums skyrocketing.

Brian successfully downloaded the app to follow the tracking collar so everything is cool with that. I even checked it when I got up to go to the bathroom in the middle of the night. The blinking dot was stationary somewhere down by the airport. I feel so good, I might make pancakes for breakfast.

Next to me, Brian stirs, rolls over, and gropes for a breast. I'm a little surprised. The way he groaned last night—the cords in his neck looked like something from the Crypt Keeper—I thought he'd be good for a week.

His hand is just heading south of the border when my cell rings. I check the caller ID.

"It's Gwen."

"Don't answer," he says, twirling a finger through my pubes as an incentive.

"But if I don't answer she'll just call mom to see if we're out of town and then mom will call to ask why I didn't tell her we were traveling."

My mother likes to worry that I'll die in a fiery crash so she can tell her bridge club ladies that she had a bad feeling from the moment she awoke.

I answer.

Gwen sounds excited. "Jake just got a call. They've got a search warrant."

She can barely finish before I whoop out a cheer. "Fantastic!" I decide to be gracious even though her husband is a douche. "Tell Jake congratulations."

"You dummy," she says. "The warrant is for your house."

"What?"

Brian snatches his hand away and sits up. I cover the mouthpiece and tell him the good news.

"What?"

I nod and get back to Gwen. "What if we're not here?"

"Are you crazy?" she whispers. "You watch CSI. If they have a warrant they can use one of those battering rams to bust through the front door."

Oh, yeah.

Gwen hangs up without another word. Did Jake just walk into the room? If he's still at home, we have about twenty minutes before the cops get here.

Brian and I fly out of bed like the sheets are on fire. What should we do? Just sit and wait for the cops to show up? Will they pull up with sirens blaring? This is going to get tongues wagging in the neighborhood.

"I can't believe this is happening?" I say around my toothbrush. "What evidence could they possibly have?" I spit out my toothpaste. "What do they hope to find in our house?" I wonder if I should give the toilets a quick swab with a cleaning brush.

"Well for one thing, they can confiscate your laptop with all those pictures from the robbery house."

Eeks!

"And my new phone is currently running a tracking app on some strangers' car," Brian adds.

"Holy crap! We need to hide them."

"You can't hide stuff from the police. They look behind ceiling tiles and in toilet tanks."

"You're right," I say. "I need to take that stuff and get out of here."

"You!? Why not me? I'm the innocent one here. You're the mastermind who got us into this mess."

My how quickly the tables turn. Not three minutes ago he was hot to trot.

I'm tempted to play the 'woman' card; the helpless female who is much more delicate than a man. But that will only come back to bite me later.

"Why don't we draw straws for who stays?" I suggest.

He sighs and shakes his head. "I'll stay."

I take back every unkind thing I've said about him. He's a true gentleman and a hero.

Then he brings up a frightening scenario. "How much do you think bond will be if they arrest me?"

"There's no way they're going to arrest you. This is just Jake being an asshole."

"I really don't think he could bullshit a judge into signing a warrant just because he doesn't like you."

The reality sinks in. Brian could be arrested. We have no savings. I already tapped into our 401k last year when we needed a new washer and dryer. My parents don't have that kind of money. I don't think Jake's going to let Gwen post bond.

Time is ticking.

I grab a clean pair of yoga pants from my drawer. Brian puts on a pair of cargo pants and cinches them tight with a belt. Really? Is he worrying about a gang rape at the Batesville Police Department? Those six episodes of *Oz* must have left quite an impression on him.

He sits on the bed to put on his socks. "You need to go see Keisha immediately."

I pull a tee shirt over my head. "We don't need a lawyer."

"You don't. But what about me?"

My look of exasperation does nothing to change his glare. He's also giving me the up and down clothing inspection.

"Fine," I say, raking off my yoga pants. ""I'll go talk to Keisha."

I dig through the closet for an appropriate lawyer outfit, something that looks businesslike but screams poverty.

"And what do you suggest I tell the police?" Brian asks.

"I think you better stick to the truth."

"The truth? After we lied?"

"People always lie to the police. They expect it."

"We left the scene of a crime! Don't you think that makes us look just a little bit guilty?"

"Do the best you can," I say, then wiggle my fingers. "Give me your phone."

"What if they ask me where you are?"

I turn on his phone and open the new app.

"Tell them I went to the grocery store," I mumble as I zoom out on the map that's supposed to show me the location of the collar.

"That's convenient," he says.

The dot is blinking along the downtown connector. They're on the move. Probably staking out a new target. Or Bonnie is looking for Bobby to take care of business with a pointy-toed shoe.

"Are you even listening to me?" Brian asks.

I huff out a breath. "Tell Jake if I'd known he was coming I'd have stayed home and made the troops a breakfast roll."

He turns the tables by getting snippy himself. "What are you doing?"

"Hey. You went to all the trouble to put the tracker on the car. I'm just making sure it isn't in Canada."

"Get going. You can check the tracker later."

I run for the stairs, taking a quick glance out of my office window to see if the police are already sitting at the curb. The coast is clear.

In the kitchen, I shove my laptop into a shoulder bag. I'll ask Keisha what I should do with all the evidence we've gathered. Then she can go to the police station or do whatever lawyers do to get Brian out. He should be home for dinner.

Should I get something out of the freezer?

The GPS in my Cooper takes me to a high-rise in Buckhead that's all mirrored-glass and granite. Keisha has come a long way from our days of campus activism. I feel a moment of trepidation, wondering how much her firm pays for their lease. But I comfort myself with the knowledge that friendship runs deep.

Keisha was the first woman to raise my consciousness about the disparity between blacks and whites. She and I worked together on the campus newspaper for two years, trying to raise awareness in a Southern city. Yeah, I know. What were we thinking?

It all started when Brian and I were hanging out in Piedmont Park the year Freaknik exploded into a free-for-all. Black college students from all over the country congregated for a spring break weekend of debauchery—just like students do every year in Ft. Lauderdale, Daytona, and Panama City Beach. The difference was the city of Atlanta wasn't prepared for the thousands of cars clogging Peachtree Street, their stereos blaring, and scantily-clad girls sprawling on hoods. Or that all of these revelers were black.

With cameras dangling, Brian captured the essence of the experience while I interviewed students about where they were from and why they had come. Just like with the music festival, Woodstock, most of them had heard about it through the grapevine and it mushroomed into this gigantic event.

I also interviewed the locals: city workers and angry residents who didn't appreciate the disruption in their lives.

I first spotted Keisha in a face-to-face confrontation with an Atlanta City cop. He told her to 'go back home and take her colored friends with her.'

I swear I saw steam erupt from her ears.

"The First Amendment," she bellowed so everyone around her could hear, "prohibits interfering with the right to assemble. And I quote: Congress shall make no law—"

"One more word out of you," the cop said, "and I'll arrest you right now."

She had the balls to remind him that the First Amendment also protected her freedom to speak. I swear the cop had his hand on his gun when Brian moved in close and took pictures of the confrontation.

Keisha and the cop were kind of at a stalemate, still glaring at each other, nostrils flaring, when a loud roar echoed across the park. Something was going on down by the lake.

The microphone on the cop's walkie burped out something and after pointing a finger at Keisha, he took off towards the new disturbance.

Back at the newspaper, Keisha and I put together a montage of images comparing white girls in bikinis on the beach with black girls in halter tops and short-shorts dancing in Piedmont Park; white girls in wet tee shirt contests at a beach bar and black girls wearing see-through tops while riding on the back seat of a convertible on Peachtree Street. We even had a shot of girls in New Orleans baring their breasts for a strand of cheap plastic beads. Interspersed with the pictures were quotes from Atlantans on those 'heathens' and how 'disrespectful' they were. Even though we didn't get much local recognition for our exposure of the racial bias, we got a couple reprints in the national media. I thought I was on my way to greatness. I wasn't.

Since I don't have an appointment, I have to wait over an hour to get in to see Keisha. The tracker is blinking in Cartersville, north of Atlanta. Are Bonnie and Clyde casing a joint?

I'm in the middle of Googling jewelry stores and pawn shops when the receptionist announces that Keisha will see me now.

After hugs and kisses, I sit in a plush leather chair opposite my old friend. I dig into my purse for a dollar bill and slide it across her desk. "I need some advice."

She picks up the dollar. "What's this?"

"I'm retaining you as my attorney. The dollar is for client/attorney privilege."

"I always said you watch too much TV," she says as she smiles and hands it back. "My standard hourly rate is $300. Because you're a friend, I'll give you the first hour free. If I decide to take your case, you'll need to sign a contract. That will guarantee confidentiality."

Turning sullen or defensive is a waste of time. The clock is ticking. I tell Keisha all about the porn house, the robbers, renting the SUV, and it being stolen. I don't bother to give her the full Gilbert

176

and Sullivan performance of being dragged out of the car, and I decide she doesn't need to know about my breasts hanging in the breeze.

"How could someone just sneak up on you like that?" she says. "Were you both asleep?"

I roll my eyes and wave limp hands in the air. "We were distracted momentarily."

"Some stakeout."

"Yeah, well the police came to our house this morning with a search warrant. I'm pretty sure they took Brian to the Batesville Police Station."

I dig into my shoulder bag and pull out the laptop. "There are a few more things you should know."

My fingers massage the cover as though I might be able to magically lessen the severity of taking pictures in a house we broke into.

The first hour is well over by the time I show her the pictures of loot, the notebook pages, the map. I'm hoping she can negotiate with the police: our evidence for Brian's release.

Keisha isn't so sure. "You have no pictures of the suspects either in this house or at the scene of a crime. These pictures look more like inventory shots." She gives me a solemn shake of the head. "You better resolve yourself to the fact that Brian will be spending at least one night in jail."

"What about bond?"

"That's up to the judge. Since robbery is a felony, bail usually starts at ten thousand. It will depend on whether the police charge Brian with all the robberies. Multiple felonies jack up the bail quickly. Whatever the judge decides, the bondsman will expect ten percent from you."

I actually get a little misty-eyed, not about Brian in the hoosegow, but how I'm going to come up with all this money. "So it'll cost me at least $1000 to get Brian out. You're going to charge me $300 an hour. We have a $1000 deductible on our car insurance which has to pay for the rental damage, I had to pay a locksmith to change all the locks on our doors," I know I'm talking faster, and my voice is rising, but I can't seem to reign in the hysteria. "Brian's camera was trashed. The police have my purse and my phone."

"Okay, okay!" Keisha holds up her hands. "I'll see what I can do. But I'm not working pro bono, and I'm not compromising my clients who pay full price. Hopefully this is just a misunderstanding and I can wrap it up quickly. I'll look into the charges tomorrow."

"Tomorrow!?"

Oh, boy. There are going to be some major repercussions from this.

"It usually takes 72 hours from the time of arrest until the plaintiff can go before a judge for a bond hearing."

Three nights in jail. That's grounds for divorce right there. I know he wore his belt but they will surely take it away so he can't hang himself. Do the Batesville police even arrest that many violent lunatics?

"Because your vehicle was used in the commission of a crime, the burden of proof will be on us to produce an alibi. Yours is that supposedly you were in a park at the time. Let's hope they don't find any evidence to prove you wrong."

Yeah, me too.

"And don't go home until you hear from me," she adds. "I don't need you getting arrested as well."

Don't go home? These shoes are killing me, and if I sit down one more time, that back seam is going to pop.

The last thing Keisha says is "stay out of trouble."

CHAPTER NINETEEN

I sit in my car in a parking garage staring at the blinking light on Brian's phone. Bonnie and Clyde are still in Cartersville. They're definitely staking out their next hit because I distinctly heard her say they would be unloading the furniture in Jonesboro. Maybe Clyde's brother Bobby lives in Cartersville. I hope he has insurance because Bonnie's lookin' for a rumble.

There's another reason why I'm just staring at the phone. I can't remember anybody's phone number. They're all in my phone at the police station. Keisha said I can't go home but what am I supposed to do for clothes? Where am I going to stay tonight?

Even if I could afford to stay at a motel, I have no ID to cash a check, no debit card to get money from an ATM. No credit cards to charge.

I can hang out in Sarah's driveway until she gets home, but I can't wear her clothes. I've got to take a chance and sneak into our house.

I park on the next street over and cut through the Bradford's back yard. Hopefully Lisa isn't playing hooky—and nooky—today. The moment our garage door starts to open, I worry that the police have some kind of monitor on it that will beep and let them know someone is at our house. I run to the button and close the door.

The kitchen cupboard doors are all open, food boxes and dishes clutter the counters. The silverware drawer is on the table, cleaning products have been taken out of the cupboard under the sink and are on the floor. At least the police didn't dump a canister of flour all over the place. In the living room, furniture cushions have been raised and not completely returned, the sofa has been pulled away from the wall. The urge is strong, but I can't take the time to straighten up. And if the police come back, I don't want them to know I was here.

I dash upstairs to pack a bag. The bedspread and covers are pulled off and the mattress is askew. Our drawers hang open. I shrug out of my blazer and unbutton my blouse. I wriggle out of the skirt that's been cutting into my waist and leave it in a pile on the floor. Underwear, sweats, some comfortable tee shirts are crammed into a duffel. I start to zip the bag shut when I glance at my 'attorney' outfit strewn around the room. I may actually need these clothes again. I lay the hastily folded ensemble in on top of the other clothes.

My next mission is money. I know I stashed a twenty in a jacket pocket one day when Sarah and I were out for lunch and she offered to pay. Thank god it wasn't the jacket I left in the car.

I paw through old reading glasses and half-empty bottles of personal lubricants in the bedside drawer, looking for our safety deposit key. I'm not even sure why. Then I wonder if Brian has any mad money in his office.

I stand in the doorway, amazed. You can't even tell his room has been searched. He has a wooden bowl with a lid that he got in Costa Rica. I find a little over three dollars in change. Next I try the souvenir Bento box he got in Japan and hit the jackpot: two twenties folded up and hidden under some wrapped candies that have turned white.

A quick glance out his window to see if the police are pulling up out front, and I'm on my way out. I stop at the phone in the kitchen to page through the caller ID memory and get Sarah's number. I see the light blinking on our answering machine. Brian? No such luck. It's Jake. *Don't make me issue an arrest warrant on you. Come on in.*

I'm never going to Gwen's house again. Ever. Of course, after this, I may not be invited.

I consider getting another book of checks out of the junk drawer but what's the point? Writing a check to pay Brian's bail and having it bounce will do nothing to further our pleas of innocence.

Speaking of bail. I scan the stuff we got at our wedding that the police have thoughtfully left on the dining room table. All of the silver is plated. No one wants Crystal d'Arc drinking goblets. I wonder if any of this is worth taking to a pawn shop. I also wonder if I'll be able to take out a second mortgage on a house that isn't even worth what we're paying on the first mortgage.

Depression gets the better of me and I yank open the refrigerator door. The bottle of wine I thought was in there is gone. I take Brian's last two beers and head out the back door. I slug down the first beer the instant I get back in my car.

Then I call Sarah.

"I guess I missed all the excitement Sunday," she says when she answers.

"Yeah, and it's getting worse by the minute. Can I spend the night?"

"O-kay," she says. "I have to pick up the kids at after-school by six, then stop to get something for dinner. We should be there by seven."

"Have you got any wine?" I ask.

At the bank, I pick through the contents of our safety deposit box. There are actually two $50 bonds from my college graduation still in the cards. They won't do me any good since I have no ID. I flip open a few more cards and discover someone named The Farmington's gave me $50 in cash. I have no idea who they are but I'd put them on my Christmas card list if I had one.

While I sit in Sarah's driveway waiting, I drink Brian's last beer. Some people might get despondent over his situation, or experience some remorse over getting him into all this trouble. Mostly, I just feel a fullness in my bladder.

Sarah and the kids show up at seven as promised; and she's got a big bag from Wendy's in her hand. My heart cries out with joy. We all trundle into the kitchen. She pulls out two wrapped hamburgers while she instructs Tyler to get silverware for him and Courtney. I wish I'd known where she was stopping. I would have asked her to get me the double cheeseburger with bacon.

The kids snatch up the burgers.

"Hang on," Sarah says, then reaches back into the bag and pulls out a side salad. She hands it to Tyler.

No.

She reaches back into the bag and produces another salad which she gives to Courtney.

No.

And here's the weirdest part. Neither of the kids complain. They just grab the salads and their burgers and scurry to the family room. Tyler turns on the TV while Courtney glops dressing on her salad.

"Don't forget," Sarah calls to them. "Homework at 7:30."

I can see the writing on the wall so I grab a bottle of merlot from her wine rack and paw through a drawer for a corkscrew. I glug a tall one while Sarah lays out our dinner. Chef salads.

NOOOOOOO!

"I got the apple pecan chicken and the Asian cashew chicken," she says. "Which do you want?"

I slug down a big gulp and take the Asian.

There's only so long Sarah will continue being patient. She keeps giving me these looks with the raised eyebrows and the too-big smile; that 'no judgment here' expression. It's reassuring to know that I can tell her anything.

We carry our salads into her dining room where kids can't hear, and around big mouthfuls of lettuce, I tell all that has happened:

staking out the jewelry store, renting the car, even the part about how we ended up without our coats.

"Damn," she says with a giggle. "You guys are acting like kids again."

"I can't help it. There's something about adrenalin that they never told us in biology class."

So far, I've been entertaining Sarah with my story like it's a joke. But I take another slug of wine to fortify myself because it's about to turn ugly. Sure enough, when I get to the part about the car crashing into the store, her mouth flies open.

"Oh, Rachel," she whispers with such condemnation in her voice that I feel ashamed.

Her reaction hits a lot harder than Keisha's brusque assessment of how bad the situation is. When your best friend thinks you've screwed up, you've really screwed up.

Tears well up in my eyes, my bottom lip trembles when I get to the part where Brian is currently in jail. Sarah blows out a breath, unable to even respond.

"I can't believe I've gotten us into this mess," I say, and for the first time, I really feel bad. "Why couldn't I just mind my own business? How did I get so obsessed over something so stupid?"

"I can't believe Brian helped you break into your office."

I use a Wendy's napkin to blot my eyes and blow my nose. "I've got to catch these guys to prove we didn't do it."

"I think you should follow your attorney's advice and stay out of trouble."

"Too late," I say as I drain my tumbler of wine.

Bringing her up to date reminds me that I haven't checked on Bonnie and Clyde lately. Are they back in Jonesboro? I fish Brian's phone out of my pocket and turn on the app.

"Holy crap! They're in Chattanooga."

"Who?"

"Bonnie and Clyde!" I jump to my feet like I'm going to dash out the door. Instead, a wave of wine drunkenness sends me reeling and I drop back into my seat.

"You are NOT going to Chattanooga," she says. "You're smashed. And I don't know why I need to remind you, but your purse is at the police station. You don't have a driver's license."

The tears start again. "How else am I going to get the evidence I need?"

* * *

Traffic is light since I'm driving north, away from Atlanta. I waited until Sarah left for work this morning, then scribbled a note that I'd see her soon. I laid in her guest bed last night thinking out my strategy for hours.

I've got to locate Bonnie and Clyde, find some kind of proof that they possess stolen goods, and get Brian out of jail.

I have one hundred thirteen dollars and forty-nine cents. That's for gas and food. I have no idea how long it will take for me to get these two busted but I certainly can't afford a motel. I borrowed a blanket and pillow from Sarah. If I tilt back the passenger seat in my Cooper, and I can find some place that looks safe besides the front of a police station, I should be able to get a little sleep before my first stakeout tonight.

Sarah had a huge bag of baby carrots and a family-sized tub of hummus in her fridge. I scooped some dip into a plastic container, made three sandwiches out of gluten-free, twelve-grain bread and almond butter—naturally there was no jelly—and packed four bottles of water into a soft-side cooler I found in her pantry.

What I didn't find in her pantry were any crackers or cookies or chips. How does a woman with two kids not have some junk food? No Twinkies or Fiddle Faddle. Okay, I found a box of cereal but it was plain Cherrios. (I've been known to go through a big bowl of dry Cinnamon Toast Crunch while watching a movie.) I passed on a bag of unsalted cashews. At the back of a cupboard, I found two candy canes; no telling if they're from this past Christmas. When I get desperate enough, they'll taste delicious.

The sky turns from black to gray around Cartersville and the sun is up by the time I get to the Tennessee state line. I pull into the welcome center and check the tracking app. Bonnie and Clyde's car is on the east side of Chattanooga. The blinking light hasn't moved since I checked it an hour ago. They're probably sleeping in, resting up for a big caper tonight. Or they stole a vehicle last night and absconded with a cache of jewelry or high-end TVs.

Exhaustion has got my eyes scratchy; every time I blink I'm sure they will stay closed. I crank my seat back for a quick nap but the moment I close my eyes, my heart ramps up again with all this anxiety. I squeeze my eyes tighter and take deep cleansing breaths but it's no use. My body is tired but my brain is too keyed up to leave me alone.

I should do a quick drive-by to check Bonnie and Clyde's location at the very least. Is it an apartment complex? Are they doing surveillance on their next target? Once I have a bead on what they're up to, I'll find someplace where I can hang out all day. A mall? A coffee shop? Nothing's going to happen until tonight at the earliest. They pulled the jewelry store heist a week ago. But now that they are in virgin territory, they could pull a robbery tonight.

What wishful thinking. I'm assuming they've found a new apartment, and some place to stash their stolen goods, and they're ready to start another crime spree. Yeah, right.

How long can I live in a Cooper? How far can I stretch a little over a hundred dollars? My strategy isn't as sound as it seemed last night after drinking all that wine.

The Escalade is parked at a motel that advertises daily and weekly rates. A U-Haul trailer is parked in the back of the lot; I assume it's theirs. Are they staying here while they look for an apartment? Or are they moving on soon? What happened to moving to Jonesboro?

I need to check the local newspaper for recent robberies. Maybe they hit a jewelry store and Bonnie has the goods in her purse. What better place to search the news than a library? My GPS takes me to a crappy little branch in a rundown shopping center but it has what I need. There's nothing in yesterday's or today's paper about a smash and grab or a break-in at an upscale home.

Now what? I'm tired of waking up the phone every ten minutes to check the tracking app. I've got nothing else to do so I fiddle around until I find a setting for vibrate alert if motion is detected. Fantastic! Of course, now I have even less to do until tonight.

The armchair in the library is comfortable; it's nice and warm inside. I pick up this morning's paper again and read the gossip column and the funnies. The next thing I know, the librarian is nudging me on the shoulder.

"Are you alright?" she asks. What she really means is there's no sleeping in the library.

I apologize, hastily return the newspaper to the shelf, and leave.

I'm starving and I've already eaten one of my delightful gluten-free sandwich. I can't make myself eat anymore carrots. Where can I find free food without digging through trash bins outside fast food restaurants?

Costco.

They always have people doling out samples. And it's conveniently located on the east side of town so I won't burn too much gas.

I've never seen a parking lot so full. Do people come from the tri-state area to shop here? I get one of the last parking spots way in the back.

My normal routine is to get my Costco buyer's card out and have it in my pocket so I can glide right past the guy at the door. But since I don't have my purse, I don't have my card. I'm thinking through my options when I see the mob at the entrance. People are flooding in like it's Black Friday at Walmart.

I get a grocery buggy even though I don't intend to buy anything. I've got to look the part. And there are so many of us squeezing in, the checker guy has given up. He knows the cashiers check the cards again at the end so he's mostly nodding and smiling.

Once safely inside, I dodge other shoppers as I push my cart down one of the main thoroughfares of the warehouse. Nearly each aisle has a worker doling out some kind of food sample. How did I get so lucky?

I taste fruit drinks, and yogurt, and granola as I work my way to the deli section in the back. I beat a pregnant woman to the last little cup of spicy chili. She gives me an icy stare but she should be grateful that I've saved her from heartburn and indigestion later. Now and then I put a case of ketchup or a year's supply of oatmeal in my buggy to look like a serious shopper.

At another kiosk, a woman is slicing a giant rolled tortilla filled with something that looks yummy. When she gets to that last slice of bunched up tortilla she starts to throw it away.

"I'll take that!"

She startles like I'm some kind of phycho so I give her a smile and hold out the paper napkin with a pristine slice on it. She plops the butt on my stack.

At the back of the store, I see stacks of fruit trays, meat and cheese trays, cookie trays, and shrimp platters. That's when it finally hits me. This is New Year's Eve day. Everyone is stocking up for a big bash tonight.

How depressing. Brian is either spending New Year's Eve in jail, or he's alone in our house with nothing but rice cakes and flavored water.

Who am I kidding? If he's at home, he's already made a run for beer, take and bake pizza, and the family sized pack of double-stuffed Oreos. I've tried calling the landline twice but haven't gotten an answer so I'm pretty sure he's in jail.

I will be spending New Year's Eve hunkered down in my Cooper trying to stay awake while I keep an eye on Bonnie and Clyde.

After I make my rounds to every sample stand in the store, I take off my jacket and start again. When a woman dishing out tiny morsels of crab cake sees me for the third time, she pinches her face and squints at me. I snarl right back and take two just to show her who's boss.

My phone rings. It's Keisha. I hope this is good news because I want to go home and take a shower and sleep in my own bed. And I'm sure Brian wants to get out of jail.

"Are you being straight with me?"

Wow! She sounds mad.

"About what?"

"Everything! The surveillance, the robbery . . ."

"Yes," I insist, adding a bit of my own indignation at being called a liar. Then a dizzy kind of nausea makes me feel light-headed. "Why?"

"Because when they searched your house they found a piece of jewelry in your closet. It still had the tag on it from Charles Martin and Associates Jewelry store."

That woozy feeling turns into a wave that almost knocks me off my feet. I stagger into the furniture department and slump into an armchair. I can't even speak.

"That's a big nail in Brian's coffin," Keisha says. "They also have closed-circuit video of you and Brian in the store taking pictures of the jewelry in the glass cases. The guy at the jewelry store says he suspected you from the very beginning. Said you weren't the typical Charles Martin shoppers."

My lips get tingly and I lose the feeling in my fingers. I think I'm going to throw up crab cakes and Go-gurt. Still holding the phone to my ear, I lean forward to put my head between my legs.

"I gave them your laptop like you asked, but they're not buying that you were merely documenting your surveillance. All the pictures of TVs and stereo equipment, and the map that shows all the recent break-ins—"

"Stop!" I yell. I straighten up, no longer feeling faint. I'm mad. "I told you that was from the porn house."

A quick glance around shows that I'm gathering an audience.

I lower my voice. "We were getting evidence."

"The police don't see it that way."

I sputter for an instant while I turn away from an elderly woman who has taken a seat in the chair next to mine so she can hear better. I cup my hand on the phone. "Surely we have alibis for the other crimes."

"Right now the police are only charging Brian with the robbery at Charles Martin. They're calling it a copycat crime."

"Did the police check out the porn house?"

Oh, great. Here comes an employee.

Interesting observation. If I needed help with a computer printer or wanted to buy a bass boat, I wouldn't be able to find a store worker for love or money. But I sit down in an armchair for just a minute—and use the word porn in a sentence—and right away some guy in a red shirt trots over to ask if I need assistance.

I abandon the armchair and head for the small appliances aisle.

"Yeah," Keisha says with a laugh, but I can visualize the derision on her face. "They found all kinds of fingerprints at the porn house but only Brian's can be identified. They're talking about adding breaking and entering to the charges."

"The sliding door wasn't locked," I argue. But of course she knows how we really got in.

"Were you invited into the house?"

"It's vacant."

"Whatever," she says, dismissing my lame argument. "There's nothing in there. Oh, but they did find a different set of fingerprints on the outside of the kitchen windowsill. I assume those are yours."

I moan as I massage the tightness in my forehead. The shit just keeps getting deeper.

"There's certainly no evidence to continue searching for this mysterious couple."

"Hang on," I say. "Let me think."

This is all coming at me too fast. I can't even compute what she has said. I stare at my reflection in the one style of toaster available at Costco. My cheeks are pasty, my eyes are bulging. Then a revelation hits me like another wave.

"We're being framed," I say.

"What are you talking about?"

"We're being framed by the robbers. I told you they came into the house and cut up our credit cards. What better way to get the heat off them than by setting someone else up?"

"That's pretty far-fetched," Keisha says. "And you know your brother-in-law better than I do. Cops like him aren't interested in theories. They love facts. And the fact is all this evidence is going to make getting Brian out harder. The judge will certainly set a higher bond."

"Keisha. Listen."

"No. You listen. There's an arrest warrant out on you. You are a fugitive. If you want to help Brian, and your case, you need to turn yourself in." She takes a breath to calm herself and blows it in my ear. I think she believes me but I can't be sure. "They'll be more inclined to believe you if you do."

"But then I'll have to pay bond, too." I know I sound like a fussy child but I can't help it.

"You should think about that next time you want to play amateur detective."

I'm desperate for a way out of this madness. "What if Brian met with sketch artist?"

"Can you hear yourself? You're in denial. Even if they got an arrest warrant, they surely wouldn't find anything to incriminate this Bonnie and Clyde. You said they were using a separate location to warehouse the stolen goods. Now turn yourself in."

"I can't. I'm in Chattanooga."

"Have you lost your mind? You've crossed a state line."

It's almost five o'clock when I mosey over to the televisions. Surely one will be turned to a Chattanooga news station. I just want to double check that there have been no robberies in the last couple of days.

Just an FYI here. The sales people in the electronics department must work on commission because they will NOT leave you alone, especially when you ask one to change a channel.

The teasers at the top of the hour are about a fire at an apartment complex, a shooting somewhere in downtown Chattanooga, and a forecast of rain. I escape the pushy sales guy by saying I'll have to talk it over with my husband and wander back to paper goods again to return the twelve-pack of paper towels in my cart, and to snag one last brownie sample for dessert.

When the announcement comes on that the store is closing, I scurry to the restroom before I'm turned out into the cold. I am literally the last customer to leave. The guy at the door who inspects receipts gives me the stink eye since I have no cart filled with cases of coffee creamer or party platters.

Outside, it's not as cold as I feared. If it's going to rain tomorrow that means a warm front is coming through. Lucky me. I zip up my jacket and head for my lonely Cooper out at the far end of the deserted parking lot.

With each step, I strengthen my resolve to find Bonnie and Clyde. Brian will never forgive me if he goes to prison.

CHAPTER TWENTY

Once I get in my car, I check the monitoring app again. I know, I've set the phone to vibrate if there is movement, but now I don't trust it. I can't believe the car hasn't gone anywhere all day.

Was Clyde under the car for some reason and found the collar? In a panic, I drive back to the motel. The Escalade is still in the lot. Maybe they stole another car for a robbery and they're using it? That doesn't make sense because the Escalade is the pickup vehicle. I'd love to go listen at their door to see if there are any shenanigans going on inside, but I don't really know which room is theirs.

I drive to the far end of the parking lot to wait and watch.

By nine o'clock, all of my Costco samples have worn off and I'm starving. At this rate, I'll have eaten all my food supply before tomorrow. I vow not to eat another sandwich until midnight. That way, technically, it will be Saturday. Whoopie! I'll ring in the New Year with an almond butter sandwich.

In the meantime, I unwrap one of the candy canes I found at Sarah's and suck on it. The sugar gives me a short burst of energy, but by ten o'clock my eyes are drooping. If I could just catch a quick nap—

My solution is to stick the phone between my breasts. Surely I will feel it vibrate and wake up. Then I crank my seat back, snuggle my head into Sarah's pillow and pull her blanket up to my chin.

I'm having this erotic dream about Brian tickling me all over with a giant purple dildo. I'm just about reach orgasm central when I jerk awake. Disoriented, I clasp my vibrating bosom and pull the phone out. Then I sit up, and with bleary eyes, I scan the parking lot. The Escalade is gone.

According to the tracking app, they are heading west on Interstate 24. My stomach wrenches into a knot. What if Bonnie and

Clyde were sleeping all day to prepare for some marathon cross-country drive tonight?

I play Brian's calculating game: If my car holds 12 gallons of gas, and it can get about 30 miles to the gallon, I can follow them for 360 miles before I have to refill. I topped off at Costco earlier, so I'm down to seventy-two dollars and eighty-one cents. I'll need more than half of that to fill my tank again . . . when I have to turn around . . . and admit defeat. Damn it!

I've got myself worked into a pretty good depression when the blinking dot turns off the interstate and moves north on a city street. Hot diggity. Maybe I'm on to something. I step on the gas.

The Escalade is just ahead when it turns into the parking lot of a cowboy bar on the outskirts of town. It must be a popular spot because the original building is old weathered wood, but then two more sections have been added on with newer rough-hewn siding. The neon sign reads *Buck's*. The B is wearing a cowboy hat.

The parking lot is packed. I can only imagine all the boots and Stetsons inside. Everyone wants to party on New Year's Eve.

Clyde circles around until he finds a parking space relatively close to the front entrance of the bar, then turns off the engine.

I can see Bonnie as a line-dancing kind of girl, but Clyde? I suppose he could be here just for the drinking. Maybe while Bonnie's out on the dance floor kickin' and stompin', Clyde hangs out at the bar and flirts with the waitresses. I can't imagine there are any customers in there with Rolex watches or diamond bracelets.

Since I don't want them to spot my Cooper, I park in the last row. It isn't really a parking space, but hey, it's a Cooper. I can wedge this baby in anywhere.

I wait for them to go into the bar, but they don't. After several minutes I get out to have a closer look. My knee pops as I crouch down and creep between cars.

Bonnie and Clyde are just sitting inside the car. Are they arguing? She's telling him not to grab any asses and he's telling her not to shake her booty at other men. That doesn't seem to be the case because they're both just staring at the front door. Maybe they've already had their fight. So why not get out and go inside?

After crouching for about ten hours—okay so it's about five minutes—I duck-walk back to my car. I'll be able to see what they're doing from here and I can at least sit.

It doesn't take long to realize this is the stakeout. Okay, so the bar takes in a ton of cash and somehow Clyde has found out that the man or woman in charge of closing out and taking the money to some drop box is an easy target. But why get here at twelve-fifteen when the bar doesn't close until two?

Around one o'clock, a man and woman burst out of the front door, laughing and clinging to each other for support. She's got her arm slung around his neck, pressing her tits on him. His arm is down her back and firmly planted on her butt. My guess is they just met on the dance floor an hour ago, she bumped to his grind, and now they're on their way to someone's apartment. If they don't crash on the way, they'll be having sloppy drunken sex soon.

After a while, two rather hefty girls come out. One of them is gingerly making her way across the asphalt like her boots have worn blisters on her feet. I imagine that they both came with high hopes of meeting a couple guys who'd get drunk enough to take them home and make them feel like 'real women' even if it's just for an hour. They're better off going home alone.

Next is a lone guy with a beard that doesn't quite disguise his baby face. He stares at the ground as he passes the Escalade. Afraid of a confrontation? He probably spent the whole night sitting at the bar, facing the mirror instead of the crowd, and nursing a beer.

This is getting really boring. I decide I deserve a break so I reach into the cooler for my celebratory second sandwich. The almond butter has further dehydrated to the consistency of jerky and the bread is stale.

I'm licking my fingers when I see a single girl stumble out of the bar. At the doorway, she fishes into her purse for her keys, pulls them out and immediately drops them. Her blue jeans are so tight she struggles to lean over, then once she snatches the keys, she stands too fast and wobbles on her feet.

"Atta girl," I say when she manages to stay upright.

She steps off the low curb with a jolt, and suddenly Bonnie swings out of the Escalade.

"You son-of-a-bitch," she yells at Clyde and then slams the door.

Drunk Girl startles from the outburst.

Bonnie rounds the front of the Escalade, wobbling on high heels—are those the Louboutin's I tried on in the bedroom?—and starts for the door. Then she turns back to the car.

"I told you I don't do that," she yells.

She's wearing a short skirt and ratty fake-fur jacket, one of the standard white-trash uniforms.

Drunk girl gets a goofy grin on her face. Looks like she's been there before, too.

I slip out of my car to get a better view of the action. These two are impressive.

Clyde runs his window down. "Come on, Baby," he calls. It doesn't quite ring true in that accent; not like a Southern man with his soothing drawl.

By now, Bonnie is getting close to Drunk Girl. She's got an attitude but she's also staggering. One of her heels tilts dangerously to the side. If she trashes those Louboutins I might cry.

"I hate men," she mumbles. "They're always wantin' that dirty stuff." She looks right at drunk girl. "Ain't they?"

Drunk Girl nods but keeps walking. Evidently she's smart enough not to get into a donnybrook between these two.

Bonnie plants her feet and half-turns back towards the Escalade.

"Fuck you!" she yells.

Then she swings her purse toward the car like somehow it will reach all that way and whop him in the head. Drunk Girl snickers. But Bonnie lets the forward motion of her purse continue until it comes all the way around and smashes right into Drunk Girl's face.

Drunk Girl flies backwards and hits the pavement like a bale of straw. Her keys go flying out of her hand. And miraculously, Bonnie is no longer drunk. She sprints to where the keys land and swoops them up.

What she doesn't know is that Drunk Girl is not out cold. In fact, she sits up pretty darn fast, pulls her purse into her lap, and digs deep. In one fluid movement, she produces a gun and rolls to her knees. She steps out with one foot to anchor her position and fires. Bonnie grabs her arm like she's been shot and dives for cover between two cars.

Clyde leaps from the Escalade and fires two shots at Drunk Girl. She actually tries to wheel around before she loses her balance and tumbles to the pavement. Her gun clatters to the ground.

I'm so stunned I gripe the antenna base of the car I'm hiding beside. This is like something out of a crime show. My stomach gives a funny lurch, but that almond butter is anchored in there like cement so I don't think it's coming back up.

The gunshots sounded like cannons. I'm sure everyone in the bar must have heard it and will come pouring out any second. Naturally, they don't because the music inside is blasting and everyone's too drunk to care.

Clyde doesn't bother to check on Drunk Girl but he does take the time to kick her gun under a car before he runs to Bonnie's aid. (He must watch the same shows I do.)

Bonnie comes up swinging and manages to tag him in the chest with her purse. "She shot me!"

"Yeah, well you kinda had it coming," I mutter as I watch from the safety of the other side of a car.

"I am amazed," Clyde says as he attempts to get Bonnie's jacket off. "Why do so many women carry guns?"

Bonnie swats at him and shrugs out of the jacket. "Because of numb nuts like you."

There's blood on her sleeve and a tear in the fabric. I'm guessing it's a cotton/Spandex blend the way it clings to her curves. Clyde parts the tear to have a look at the wound.

"It has merely grazed the skin," he says.

"It hurts like hell!"

"I can imagine," he says, nodding, nodding, nodding in contrition.

"Let's get out of here," she says and tries to pull her arm free.

I glance again at the front door. Why isn't anyone coming? I need to get back to my car to call the police but I'm scared shitless that Clyde will see me and shoot *me* in the back.

He keeps a pretty good grip on Bonnie's arm. "What about the car?"

"The Car!?"

"You have gone to much trouble. I believe we should take her car as planned."

Bonnie blows out an exasperated huff. "I guess. But I'm driving." She keeps a firm grip on the keys. "You said I could do this one."

Holy crap! They're arguing over who's going to pull off their next heist. I'm guessing it's going to be a smash and grab.

"First, let me fix this." Clyde tears the rest of her sleeve off and gently ties it around her wound. Isn't that touching? Although that Spandex won't absorb much blood.

"What about the girl?" she asks.

They both stare down at Drunk Girl. She hasn't moved so I'm guessing she's dead. Still no sign that the almond butter is coming up. Clyde squats and presses a couple fingers against her neck.

"She is alive."

"Shit," Bonnie says. "I guess we better take her along. She's seen my face."

She raises her good arm and aims the key fob in different directions until a car in the next aisle beeps.

"I do not want her in the Escalade," he says. "If she regains consciousness, she may attack me."

"Yeah, yeah," Bonnie says. "Get her up. We'll put her in the trunk."

While they're busy piling Drunk Girl into her own trunk, I scurry back to my car. I open the door, get in, and at the same time Clyde slams the trunk closed, I pull my door shut.

He sprints back to the Escalade while Bonnie starts up Drunk Girl's car. It's a no-brainer. I've got to follow Drunk Girl's car.

My hand shakes as I dial 911. When an operator answers, I'm so scared, I drop the phone.

I grope blindly along the floor mat while pulling out of my parking space to follow Bonnie. No sooner am I out on the street than I see Clyde turn left. Bonnie continues straight. What the heck? I thought they were on their way to a heist.

I find the phone and the operator asks me again what my emergency is.

"I just witnessed a shooting at Buck's bar!" I shout into the phone. "They stole her car. She's in the trunk!"

"Ma'am," the operator says. "Please calm down so you can tell me what happened."

Didn't I just do that?

Okay, okay, she's right. I need to be a good witness, not a hysterical one. I take a deep breath and start again.

"I was in the parking lot of Buck's bar when I saw a man shoot a drunk girl and steal her car." I know that isn't exactly what happened, but it's more efficient. We can work out the details later.

"What is the address?"

"I don't know. I'm not from around here." I look around at non-descript body shops and closed fast-food restaurants. "I'm coming to a light, I'll give you the cross street."

"I thought you said you were in the parking lot," the operator says.

"I was, but now I'm following the car. There's a girl in the trunk! He shot her!"

"Yes, Ma'am. Stay calm. Tell me when you see a street name."

"Okay, here it comes. Holly Street! We just crossed Holly Street on East Third Street."

"Okay, ma'am, I have your location and I am dispatching the police. Can you tell me the make and color of the car?"

"I'm pretty sure it's a grey Honda." Thank god those people use an H as their logo instead of some swirly symbol.

'Good," the operator says. "I need you to stop following the car and let the police handle it from here."

"But she'll get away!"

"She? I thought you said a man stole the car."

Ahead, Bonnie speeds up. There are no other cars on the street. Of course not. We're in some seedy part of town, not city center. The way she's driving, I'm afraid she may have spotted me. I roll my window down to listen for sirens. Nothing.

"Ma'am? Is it a man or woman driving the Honda?"

"Shit!" I scream without meaning to. "She just ran a light!"

I'm sure Bonnie knows I'm following. I look both ways. No one's coming. I run the light.

"She just ran the light at something Knob Drive. I couldn't make it all out."

"Aren't you sitting at the light?"

Oops. "Uh, it turned green. I'm still following the Honda."

"Ma'am, you need to stop the pursuit immediately."

Bonnie's tires squeal as she turns left. I have to drop the phone into my lap to make the turn. We drive one short block and Bonnie skids sideways into another left turn. She barrels down a quiet residential street. Ahead, I can see an intersection. I've got to get the name of this street.

Without stopping at the stop sign, Bonnie flies across the intersection. I hit the brakes long enough to get a look at the street sign.

"Orchard Knob!" I yell into the phone. "We just went back over Orchard Knob."

There's a slight zigzag in the road. I speed up through the intersection, make the maneuver, and drive into a cloud of dust. We're on a dirt road. It's so thick I can barely make out Bonnie's tail lights. Then they're gone. Did she turn again? It's still pretty dusty which makes me think she didn't. I'm looking to the left and right for anyplace she may have turned off when these bright lights beam through my back window.

Some huge monster truck is following me. I drop the phone again and grip the wheel with both hands because he is coming so fast, I'm sure he's going to ram right into me. If he hits me, I'm sure my poor little car will collapse like a paper bag.

I'm so freaked out, watching it get closer, that I'm not paying attention in front. I slam into the back of the Honda and my airbag punches me in the face. For a split second, I'm pinned to the seat but then my head bobbles forward as the airbag deflates.

I swing wildly at the bag because I can't see anything. What is happening behind me? What about Bonnie? What about the poor girl in the trunk??

Finally I punch the airbag down enough that I can peer over the top. I'm stunned. The Honda is gone leaving behind a cloud of dust. The bright lights are still beaming into the back of my car. The driver of the monster truck walks in front of one of the lights, casting a shadow for an instant. I turn around just in time to see my back window blow out. The impact of the airbag has my ears ringing, but I'm no dummy. Someone just shot at me. I slip out of my shoulder harness and fall to the side.

From the corner of my eye, I see someone coming up alongside my car. Fear has got that almond butter in my stomach determined to get out. My hand scrambles to hit the release button on my seat belt, but I'm so scared I can't make it work. What am I going to do if get free? Crawl out the passenger door and get shot as I try to run away?

I distinctly remember seeing the car's logo while the guy was standing in front of the headlight. It's some kind of shield with a wreath or something around it. That's Cadillac's logo. That's the Escalade and Clyde is stomping up to my door to finish me off.

CHAPTER TWENTY-ONE

It's funny how your mind gets stuck on the craziest things. In the few seconds it takes Clyde to get to my car door, I think about how proud Brian would be that I knew it was the Cadillac logo. From now on, I'm going to memorize every car manufacturer's logo so when Brian asks me what kind of car beat me to the parking space at the grocery store, I'll be able to tell him, 'It was a Toyota.'

Of course, once Clyde yanks open my car door, I realize that 'from now on' will be the next three seconds. I guess he's going to shoot me at point blank range to make sure I'm good and dead. What a mess that's going to make. But then I don't suppose my car will be worth fixing. The front end is pretty much toast.

I wish I'd told Brian I loved him more often. Neither of us is big on the mushy stuff. Other than right after sex, I don't remember Brian ever telling me he loves me either but I know he does.

Clyde reaches into my car but I don't see the gun. Instead, he turns the steering wheel which really has me confused. He may be saying something but my ears are still ringing. The next thing I know, my car is moving. I try to sit up and grab the steering wheel for support. I look out the front window and see a telephone pole right in front of me. My head bangs the steering wheel on impact and I tumble back into the passenger seat.

I must have passed out because the next thing I remember is a light shining in my face.

"Lie still, ma'am," someone says.

So what do I do? I reach a hand out to grip the steering wheel and sit up.

'Ma'am. Ma'am!" the stern voice says. "Please don't move."

"What happened?" I ask.

I raise my hand to block the laser beam of light that is boring a hole in my left eyeball. I squint against the light too, and that makes my forehead crease and that's when I feel wet stickiness. I hope he doesn't tell me to keep my hand down because I immediately reach up to see what's on my face. I feel a lump and come away with blood on my fingertips.

My brain isn't functioning at 100% yet, but I remember something that I think is important.

"It isn't Drunk Girl," I say, "It's Dance Girl."

The flashlight lowers and I can finally see who is behind the voice. It's a policeman.

"An ambulance is on the way," he says. "Please remain in the car until the paramedics arrive."

He's not being as bossy this time, so I decide I'll wait. (I don't really think I can get to my feet yet anyway.) My lips are tingly and one of those old-fashioned hand drills is boring out from the inside of my scull. I touch my forehead to see if the bit has poked out yet, but it hasn't.

The scream of an ambulance finishes the job and my head explodes with pain. I lean back against the headrest and close my eyes. I'm done with this.

Paramedics hustle over to the car and gingerly get me out and onto a stretcher. An alarm bell goes off as they raise the folding cot.

"Stop," I mumble, holding out my hand.

They don't.

I try to be a little more forceful.

"Wait," I murmur as I reach out to the policeman. "Dance Girl. You have to find Dance Girl."

"Yes ma'am," he says, and I swear he sounds just as condescending as Jake.

Okay, that's it with the weak girly voice and the pounding headache.

I suck in a breath and yell "Everybody stop!"

Believe it or not, they do. I raise up on my elbows with some authority. "I saw a girl get shot and dumped into her car. A gray Honda. I ran into the back of the car and then Clyde shot at me."

"So you know the man who was driving the Honda."

"No, Clyde was driving the Escalade. Bonnie was in the Honda."

The officer makes a big deal of turning in both directions to look down the deserted road.

"Yeah, yeah," I say. "I know they're gone. But they were both here. I slammed right into the Honda." I cup my hand over my mouth in horror. "I hope I didn't kill Dance Girl."

The paramedics inch the stretcher towards the back of the ambulance. The policeman stands where I can see him and slowly directs his pointed finger to the right.

"Your car hit a power pole," he says.

"No. That's just what Clyde wants you to think." I flop back down on the stretcher and press my fingers against my temples. I've got to get it together.

One of the paramedics puts a blood-pressure cuff on my arm. The other pulls my eyelid up and shines a light inside. I'm sure they're trying to determine if I have a concussion so the fastest way to get them to back off is to sound intelligent.

"My name is Rachel Sanders. This is Friday. The road we're were on was . . . was . . . Orchard Knob! It was Orchard Knob!"

The police officer nods his head, reluctantly. I glance at the two paramedics. One of them shrugs.

"You've got to send someone to Buck's tavern or bar or whatever it's called."

"Yes, ma'am," the cop says.

We're back to condescension again?

The radio on his shirt crackles. "Base to seventy-seven."

The officer twists his head to the side and presses the button on the radio. "This is seventy-seven."

"We've got blood in the parking lot of Buck's Bar and Grill on Palmetto Street. CSI is in route."

"That's it! That's her blood."

"Dance Girl?" the cop says.

"Yeah." But something's not right. That's not her name. Why do I keep saying Dance Girl? "It's her vanity plate!" I sit up on the stretcher, reach out and actually grab his shirt. "It says DANCGRL." I spell out the letters.

"Are you sure about that?"

I let go of his shirt and realize his name badge has been digging into my palm. It says DANIELS. I nod too hard and my head throbs. "I'm positive. . . Officer Daniels."

He calls in a BOLO on the stolen car while the paramedic swabs the blood off my face. He says he doesn't think the cut on my forehead will need stitches. I push his hand away to talk to the cop again.

"Tell them they're going to rob some kind of store," I say while he's still talking into the radio. "It'll be a smash and grab. That's why they stole the car."

Daniels takes his thumb off the call button.

"And how do you know that?"

"I followed these criminals from Atlanta."

He gets back on his radio but there are no reports of a robbery.

"The Escalade!" I hop off the stretcher before the paramedics can stop me, and race to my car. I squat down and fumble around on the floor before I find Brian's phone under the seat. I back out of the car with a victory smile on my face and turn to find Officer Daniels in the classic shooter-stance with his gun aimed at me.

I raise my hands and show him the phone. "I've been tracking their getaway car. That's how I found them here." I lay the phone on the ground and take two steps back, throwing my hands back into the air. I know, it's a bit dramatic, but I see it all the time on television. I never dreamed I'd actually get to do it.

Daniels can't figure out how to get to the app so I finally put my hands down and go help. The map comes up; the blinking dot isn't moving.

"They're probably at the crime scene right now," I say. "She wanted to do the actual smash part but he must be helping with the grab."

Before Daniels can call in the address, his radio crackles. An APB comes through for a burglar alarm going off at a business. It's the address on the phone app. The operator says cars are enroute.

"Tell them to look for the Escalade," I say.

His jaw juts out and he blows an exasperated breath. "Ma'am. Would you please let me do my job?"

"They're moving!" I snatch the phone out of the officer's hand. "The robbery is already over. The Escalade is on—" I use my fingers to enlarge the map, "Knowles Street. That's where they need to go."

Poor Daniels probably hasn't had this much excitement since he joined the force. He's young, naturally. That's why he's working the graveyard shift. And I seriously doubt if he's married. He does *not* know how to take directions from a woman.

He requests more backup for the Escalade. Less than a minute later, a call comes through that an officer is at the scene of a smash and grab.

"I've got a gray Honda, plate DANCGRL, driven into the front of Maxwell's Jewelry Store."

"Look in the trunk!" I yell into the radio.

Daniels bares his teeth at me. I step away but not so far that I can't hear what's happening.

"Holy shit!" the call comes back. *"We've got a body."*

"In the trunk?"

"Negative. In the driver's seat."

That report has both Daniels and I flabbergasted. My eyes roam without focusing while I try to compute what is happening. "Did they put Dance Girl in the driver's seat to make it look like she was driving?"

Daniel's jaw tightens. "I thought you said she was shot."

"She was! Clyde knows the coroner will figure it all out. But in the meantime, you guys think you've caught your suspect so you won't look further."

He gives his ear a tug as he thinks it through, then pushes the button on the radio.

"Roger that," he says. "Any sign of the Escalade?"

"Negative."

I glance at Brian's phone. The Escalade is still on Knowles Street. Is Bonnie bleeding again? Did her first smash and grab shake her up? Is she arguing with Clyde about having to move a dead girl's body?

I start to blurt the address again but Daniels holds up a finger and I'm pretty sure if I don't keep quiet, he will shoot me. Instead I turn the phone around so he can see.

"The getaway car is still on Knowles Street," he says into the radio. "Anybody there yet?"

"Coming up on the 200-block now," an officer reports.

I squeeze my fists and squeal like a kid. This is going to be so great when I tell Jake how I had to go all the way to Chattanooga to catch a couple thieves that he should have collared a month ago.

Even Officer Daniels has relaxed his shoulders. His chin tilts up as he waits for the report that either the perps have been apprehended or that a car is in pursuit.

My victory dance loses some momentum because it's taking so long to hear back. The smile on Daniel's face fades. Something is wrong. They could have driven past the Escalade twice by now.

My stomach is so over all of this that it only makes a half-hearted attempt at a lurch. Did we send an officer into a trap? Did Clyde leave the Escalade and ambushed the policeman when he got out to investigate?

When he can't wait any longer, Officer Daniels presses the button on the radio.

"Are you in pursuit?"

"Negative. No sign of an Escalade. I'm turning around for another pass."

"No way!" Daniels barks. "I'm looking right at the tracking location. It should be right in front of you."

"This is an industrial area. There aren't any parked cars. Hang . . . hang on. I see something."

I hold my breath, expecting to hear gunshots come through the radio. A moment later, the officer comes back.

"I've got your tracking collar. It was in the middle of the road."

Damn it! They've gotten away again? My picture in the paper holding a certificate for Citizen of the Year fades. Wild sex with Brian when he gets released will not be happening any time soon.

Daniels looks just as disappointed.

"Don't know if it's related," the officer says, *"but I've also got a Georgia license plate, could have been tossed into this vacant lot."*

"Roger that," the call center operator says. *"CSI is on their way."*

So Bonnie and Clyde have pulled of another robbery and are on their way to Alabama or South Carolina. We don't even have a plate on the Escalade. I have no proof that this robbery is in any way connected to the robberies in Atlanta. I'm screwed.

"Come on," Daniels says, sounding every bit as disheartened as I feel. "Let's head to the station and fill out the reports."

He's helping me into the back seat when his radio sputters.

"We've got another body. This one's in the trunk."

CHAPTER TWENTY-TWO

Two bodies? My brain overloads. I can hear alarm horns blaring just like in <u>China Syndrome</u> when Jane Fonda and Michael Douglas wait for the nuclear power plant to implode.

If there's a body in the trunk, then whose body is in the front seat. Bonnie's?

I whirl around. "Are they dead?"

Daniel's has already turned away from me. "What's the status on the 10-54s?"

"The driver is unconscious. EMTs enroute. I think she banged her head on the steering wheel at impact. The airbag did not deploy."

"And the girl in the trunk?"

"Anderson is assessing."

A horrible thought crosses my mind. What if the coroner ascertains that the girl was alive from the gunshot wounds but died because I rear-ended the car? Could I be charged with vehicular homicide?

I hear shouting in the background. Has Clyde been lurking somewhere and he just jumped somebody?

"We've got a pulse. EMTs have arrived."

A screech erupts from deep inside me. I literally leap at Officer Daniels and throw my arms around him. He doesn't know whether to pull his gun or hug back. He settles for a nervous giggle and gently removes me from his person. Then he holds the back door and I climb into the patrol car. I lean my head back, closes my eyes and sigh. I know, it's not a perfect ending. Clyde is still out there somewhere. But the police have Bonnie. They'll be able to get her fingerprints and link her back to the robbery house. Maybe even at some other crime scenes, or on some stolen goods: like those Louboutin heels.

When I get to the police station, I'll call Jake and get his sorry ass busy communicating with the Chattanooga police. Surely, Brian will be released sometime later today. I need to call Keisha and give her the good news.

I chew at a piece of dead skin on my lower lip, wondering how I'm going to get home. The Cooper is toast, and even if I could drive it, I've got a pretty good idea that the police will impound it as evidence in the crime.

It doesn't matter. I feel great. I inhale deeply and blow it out. My mind drifts. I'm so tired.

"Car seventy-seven. Be advised, the driver of the Mini Cooper, license plate Delta Alpha Bravo 774 has an outstanding arrest warrant in the State of Georgia for felony robbery. Use caution."

My eyes fly open. Officer Daniel hits his brakes and swerves to the side of the road. I'm juggling between the shocked 'big O' mouth like I can't believe what I'm hearing, or the sheepish grin. His tires squeal and the car rocks to a stop. He swings around, bracing his arm on the back of the seat.

I go for the grin and the shrug. And throw in the girly finger wave for good measure.

* * *

Daniels hasn't made a peep the whole way to the police station. I know he's disappointed. I'm sorry that his impression of me has been tainted by such a silly thing but I don't think he wants to hear any excuses right now. I'm going to at least wait until that throbbing vein in his neck simmers down.

He yanks open the back door of the car and I step out. He won't even make eye contact with me. I tilt my head slightly to get another look. Bummer. The vein is still pulsing. At least he doesn't cuff me, or march me into the precinct at gun point.

Surprise, surprise. Everyone in the station is standing at the front to get a look at me. I can't believe they think I'm a robber. I just saved a girl's life. I broke up a theft ring.

Daniels escorts me to an interrogation room, tells me to have a seat then shuts the door. There's no reason to check it. I'm sure it's locked.

Exhaustion gets the better of me. I fold my arms on the table, lay my head down and conk out.

I have no idea how long I sleep. The change in air pressure when the door opens snaps me awake. Either that or it's the anger radiating off Detective Napier who barges into the room.

He's got a gut just like Jake, his sport coat looks like it hasn't been to the cleaners in months, and his eyes are bloodshot. Evidently, Chattanooga police don't have much crime in the middle of the night. Or New Year's revelers have kept everyone jumping. He scrapes the chair out opposite me and sits with a growling sigh.

"You and your buddies were busy this morning."

"They aren't my buddies. They're thieves."

He slaps a notepad onto the table and clicks open a pen.

"Why did you decide to turn in your partners? Did they cut you out of this last heist?"

I speak slowly since he looks a little punchy. "They aren't my partners."

"No? You keep calling them by name."

"Hello. I call them Bonnie and Clyde. You know, like in the movie?"

"Well, your buddy Bonnie rammed her car into the front of a store doing forty miles an hour. And the Honda's airbag was missing."

"So I heard. What about the girl in the trunk?"

Finally, Napier stops acting like an asshole and even looks a smidge contrite. "She's in the hospital."

"She's still alive?!"

Relief washes over me. At least I won't be charged with vehicular homicide. Yet.

"Just barely. Loss of blood, internal injuries. She's in a coma."

"Good thing I kept insisting you check the trunk, even though no one wanted to believe me." I give my head a little bobble.

"Yeah, you're a regular hero." He writes something on the notepad. I'm not real good at reading upside down but I think I see the word 'smartass.'

"Any prints on the car trunk?"

He stops writing and drops his pen. "Oh, no. I've got me one of them amateur crime solvers."

I shrug. "I've watched <u>Police Academy</u> a few times."

Napier doesn't see the humor in my dig. I'm not even sure why I'm trying to antagonize this guy. But now that Bonnie is in custody, my snark level is on the rise again.

"Your car is in impound and will remain for the duration of our investigation," he tells me. "Mansell County Sheriff's Department is sending a deputy to take you into custody on your outstanding warrant."

"I had nothing to do with any of those robberies."

He holds up a hand. "I'm going to let Batesville PD straighten all that out. I've got enough to keep me busy here for a while." He points a finger at me. "But if we find out you had anything to do with this robbery, we'll issue our own arrest warrant."

It's almost one in the afternoon when a deputy finally comes to get me. Not only are they keeping my demolished Cooper, but also Brian's new phone, the tracking collar, Sarah's blanket and pillow, and the soft-side cooler. They graciously return my seventy-two dollars and eighty one cents.

214

I'm starving. All they gave me last night was a bottle of water and earlier this morning, a sausage biscuit from Hardee's. I ask the deputy if he'll stop for burgers—I even offer to buy his lunch—but he doesn't respond.

My only recourse is to fall asleep in the back seat of deputy's car. The deputy's voice wakes me when he calls the Batesville Police Department to let them know he's coming in.

I walk in with my hands cuffed in front. Jake stands in the front lobby to catch the moment. He even claps for the deputy who has brought me in. I'm sure he's trying to draw attention to the desperate fugitive I am, but I take a bow and nod to everyone.

"You're very welcome," I say in a loud voice. "I'm only sorry I couldn't be instrumental in arresting BOTH felons who have committed numerous crimes in Atlanta. And even though you do not know the poor victim who lies in a coma fighting for her life, it warms my heart that you care."

Jake's face slowly shrivels into a prune as I turn the tables on him.

"Take her back to booking," he snarls.

A uniformed Batesville cop grabs my arm and tugs. I twist back to my audience. "I'm only sorry Detective Haggarty didn't handled this situation a month ago when I first told him about it. That young lady never would have been shot—," I manage to make eye contact with Jake. "—twice."

The policeman jabs me in the back to get me moving.

"Touch me again and I'll have you charged with assault."

He lets go and holds his hands up where everyone can see it. Although most of the people in the room are back shuffling papers and talking on telephones.

"I want to speak to my lawyer," I yell. "Keisha Randall."

I'm back in a locked interrogation room, nursing another bottle of water, when Keisha finally calls. As a female officer escorts me to the phone, I repeat my mantra 'Be nice, be nice.' There's no point in wasting time bitching about how long I've been waiting. If I go off on Keisha she's just going to bill me for the time.

"Well, Wonder Woman," she says, "Looks like you got lucky. The finger prints from the woman who drove the car into the business in Chattanooga match prints found in your neighborhood robbery house."

I slap my hand on the desk so hard the female officer jumps. "Finally, we're getting somewhere."

She sounds upbeat, even—dare I say it?—happy. The last time we talked, she was so livid I'm sure she was looking for a way to distance herself from Brian and me.

"The investigation has also produced surveillance footage from the car dealership. They've got some good video of you and Brian getting dragged out of the Toyota and being held at gunpoint."

I cheer and pump my fist in the air. Now I get it, the reason she's so stoked. She's going to take this to the media. In fact, she probably already has, while Brian is still incarcerated. I'm already thinking of changes to the article about our experience. And I've got the perfect opening line. 'Our government came up with a catchy phrase: *See Something. Say Something.* But it doesn't always work out the way it should.'

"Yeah, well," she says, and I know she grinning. "The video is a kind of a double-edged sword. It'll undoubtedly get Brian released, but I'm pretty sure someone's going to leak the section where you're standing with your arms up and your boobs hanging out. Don't be surprised if it ends up on YouTube."

Gulp. I forgot about that part. My mother will be mortified. My neighbors will all look at me with that knowing nod—'I've seen her naked.' Shit! Jake and the rest of the precinct have probably watched it a hundred times. He'll be the one to leak it. Is that why he was clapping?

"The case against you and Brian is crumbling fast. I suspect your brother-in-law is just dragging this out as a personal vendetta against you, so don't do anything to piss him off."

Too late.

"I've got a client coming at four and then I'll be down to get you both released. Hopefully, they'll have the suspect's real name and something on 'Clyde'."

By the time she gets to the station, my idea for a single piece on our adventure has grown to a six-part series. On my last bathroom break, I convinced Sherry—Officer Rogers—to give me a couple pieces of paper and a pen. I promised not to inflict any paper cuts that would lead to my bleeding to death. (It's a good thing she doesn't know what I'm outlining or she might have refused.)

A Detective Baker escorts Keisha into the interrogation room and then sits across from us. I'm surprised that she doesn't want to speak with me alone, but then she must have her reasons.

"So," she says, taking a moment to drag papers and a notebook from her Gucci briefcase. "Let me catch you up on a few things, Rachel."

I turn to face her. Knowing Keisha, this could be the beginning of a mini-drama and I want to play the part of the attentive victim well.

"The suspect that you tracked to Chattanooga, and witnessed bashing a defenseless woman in the head, is Caitlyn Pritchett. She's a longtime resident of Lawrenceville. No priors. Not real bright. She's tried to get her GED twice."

At this point, I think my only role is to nod or shake my head at the appropriate time. But then Keisha sets her notes down and turns to the detective.

"Of course, the Batesville Police Department already knows all this."

My mouth flies open in shock as I turn to him as well. At least he has the decency to look guilty.

He clears his throat. "We're just trying to get all our ducks in a row," he sputters.

Keisha mumbles something about what he can do with those ducks.

She picks up her notes to continue with me. "Chattanooga PD is holding Caitlyn on counts of kidnapping, attempted murder, and attempted robbery. I spoke with a Detective Napier. Who, by the way, told me that he sent his report to Batesville PD at noon."

She pauses for me to deliver my line. "Noon! It's almost five o'clock." (Damn, we're good.)

Then she glances over at Detective Baker. "You might want to see if it's still in your fax machine."

"Because this is Ms. Pritchett's first run-in with the law," Keisha tells me, "she's understandably nervous. Napier figures forty-eight hours locked up should be enough to get her talking about her partner."

I guess the chief, or a lieutenant has been watching or listening behind the 'mirrored' window because he bursts into the room to inform Keisha that I'm free to go.

"And Brian Sanders?" she asks.

"He's on his way up."

Keisha and I are waiting in the squad room when I see an officer come in with Brian. My heart does a little flip-flop when I see him. It's only been two days, I don't know why I'm getting so emotional, but my eyes well up with tears.

When he gets closer, he gives me that boyish grin that has been known to leave me breathless—and it does. I grab him tight and squeeze hard. It feels like we've been apart for weeks. A familiar poke in my crotch lets me know he's glad to see me, too. I pull my head back to chuckle and he latches onto my lips like a Casanova. My body heat shoots up to incinerate.

"Save it for the backseat," Keisha says before turning to speed-walk out to the parking lot.

She's got to take us home since neither of us has a car at the station and I know her time is my money so I hustle to catch up, pulling Brian along by the hand. We're dropped off with an admonition not to ever call her again unless we're prepared to pay then zooms away in a flutter of leaves.

We get inside the front door before Brian mashes me against the wall. "God what a nightmare."

He kisses my neck and I press my palm against the prominent bulge in his pants. When he wraps his arms around my waist to pull me closer, I get a whiff of what two days in lockup smells like: a wet sheep dog that has rolled on a carcass.

I casually lean away and can't help but notice the good china all over the dining room table, and the torn-up living room. I already know what the kitchen looks like.

Brian catches me looking. "Oh, no you don't. First things first."

He tries backing me up the stairs but that's only going to get one of us killed, or paralyzed. I turn and race up the steps. "How about a shower first?"

At the top of the stairs, he ducks his nose under his arm. "Whew!"

"Yeah." I make an exaggerated wave of my hand in front of my nose to show it's not really that bad. He's not buying my joke.

"Hey, next time you go to jail and I'll get the attorney."

"I'm really sorry."

That grin of his is back. "Show me."

Once I have him lathered up good, I use my fingers to roam through the hair on his balls. "Looking for cooties," I say and he smiles.

I figure I'll give him some personal attention with my mouth but after a few strokes he hisses. "Bed. Get to the bed."

The bellow that he roars when he comes might have a smidge of anger in it for being dragged into this whole mess.

I snuggle into his arms and enjoy a deep breath now that he has washed off the stress sweat.

He even gets the deluxe backrub with massage oil until he falls asleep. I curl up next to him and revise my New Year's resolution. I will never, *ever* do anything like this again.

CHAPTER TWENTY-THREE

We spend the day after New Year's Day lounging in bed in a state of wedded bliss. That means he doesn't nag me about the mess I got us into, and I let him play with my chi-chis during the morning news.

Once we fooled around yesterday, Brian slipped into a coma and I spent a couple hours cleaning up the mess the cops made when they searched our house. I even dusted the crystal before I put it away and I didn't find one bug. (I'd love to call Gwen about that but I doubt if she wants to talk to me since I've outed her husband as a total jerk.)

The kitchen is mopped and I threw away at least three boxes of cereal and crackers that were way past their expiration date. Maybe I'll make us pancakes for breakfast, with bacon. I know, it's risky since the last time I talked about making pancakes, Brian was arrested.

I'm surprised when I can't finish my third pancake. Even more surprising is that Brian doesn't want it either.

After the last two days, I guess we aren't eating up to our usual gluttonous standards.

"Our New Year's diet is off to a great start," I say, "since our stomachs have shrunk."

He nods like he agrees. We'll see.

Sunday is my usual grocery day. I leave Brian at home watching football and head for the store. I buy lots of fruit and veggie sticks, hummus instead of blue cheese dressing, and lowfat yogurt. I don't even get the kind with 200 calories worth of fruit jam in the bottom. I also get ingredients to make a big pot of vegetable soup. We can eat a bowl for lunch each day and cut back on our sodium as well.

As I pass aisle 9, I see Fran perusing doggy toys. Are they planning another trip? I scurry to the back of the store and duck into the bathroom where she won't see me. There's no way I'm babysitting Milo again.

While I brown hamburger, I start a list of things to do first thing Monday. Top of the list is to call my insurance company—again. Between the totaled rental car and my totaled Cooper, I'm pretty sure they're going to cancel my policy and I'm going to have to use one of those shysters who advertise on the back of the phone book. Our rates will go through the roof.

I jotted down more notes for my six-part series on our adventure while Brian was taking a nap yesterday. Tomorrow, I need to see if the Atlanta or Chattanooga newspapers are interested, as well as crime magazines. My goal is to come up with enough extra income to pay our added expenses next month.

Once the soup is simmering, I check the internet to see if there's any more news about Bonnie or Clyde. There's nothing in the Chattanooga Sunday edition, not even a rehash of old news from Saturday.

At least I've got Bonnie's real name: Caitlyn Pritchett, but nothing on Clyde except that his brother's name is Bobby.

I Google Caitlyn Pritchett. The Atlanta Journal hasn't written anything with that name. I'm betting they don't know that half of the theft ring that has been hitting Atlanta is now under lock and key in Chattanooga. I call the paper and ask for the news editor. I get a recorded message; what a surprise.

I also Google Buck's, the cowboy bar, but there have been no previous incidents. At least nothing that's made the news. I don't know Dance Girl's real name so that's a dead end.

Why did I have to be so rude to Detective Napier in Chattanooga? I'd love to give him a call for an update. After my comment about learning everything I know about cops from Police Academy, I'm sure I'm on his shit list. It occurs to me that a glowing letter to the Chattanooga paper, expounding on the excellent work by the CPD, might garner me some points.

I fire off a letter-to-the-editor filled with names and dates and high praise for every cop I can remember from Friday night.

* * *

"He what?" I screech into the telephone.

My insurance agent must have yanked the phone away from her ear because it's a few seconds before she repeats what she just told me.

"Your husband neglected to check the box refusing insurance through the rental company," she says, going slower this time, "so they tacked on an insurance payment to the rental fee. They are responsible for the damage to the Toyota."

I want to drop the phone and run upstairs to shower kisses all over Brian. I'll never fuss at him again for not reading the fine print. (Okay, I probably will, but right now I can't be happier about his negligence.)

My insurance agent still isn't happy about the Cooper. I wonder if she'll slip a naughty note in our file about wrecking two cars in less than a month. At least we still have insurance for now.

Next on my Monday call list is the Chattanooga newspaper to see if they got my letter. I deliver my speech about how with all the negativity towards police departments these days, it's important to show citizens the positive side of law enforcement. The girl I talk to shows an overwhelming disinterest in my impassioned plea.

"Yeah," she says in a hum-drum monotone. "Your letter is in today's paper."

I'm in the middle of an enthusiastic 'thank you' speech when she thanks me for contacting the Chattanooga Times and hangs up.

This is fantastic news. Even if Detective Napier didn't read the letter, I'm sure someone—a neighbor, a spouse—saw the letter and called someone at the station. News like that travels fast.

I call Chattanooga PD and ask to speak to him.

"What?" he snaps.

His brusque tone might scare away a less motivated caller but I need him on my side.

"I just wanted to thank you for all your help the other day," I schmooze. "I know I was being totally unreasonable. I think the knock on my head had something to do with my belligerence."

I pause for him to say something like, 'that's okay. I've dealt with worse.' Or at least a thank you for the apology. He says nothing.

I ramble on. "It wasn't until last night that I remembered something else about Clyde. He has an accent. I heard him talking while he and Bonnie—excuse me Caitlyn—were moving. At first I thought it was Indian, or Pakistani, but now I'm wondering if it could be Middle Eastern. He definitely has the skin tone: not dark/dark, but not light. And short black hair. Oh, and he has a brother named Bobby."

"I see."

He's not budging an inch. My face temperature has shot up a good twenty degrees but I hold my tongue.

"I thought the information might give you some leverage with Caitlyn. You know, 'the police are finding out a lot about your boyfriend – without your help. If you don't speak up soon, you'll lose your bargaining chip'."

"Yeah, I know how that works."

Whew, this guy is a tough nut. I revert to my groveling thank you but he interrupts.

"So what do you want in exchange for this valuable clue?"

Am I that transparent?

I guess there's no reason to hide my motive. "I'm thinking about writing an article about the fantastic way the police handled the arrest, including an interview with Dance Girl once she wakes up. By the way, I don't remember her name."

"I don't remember telling you."

He's trying to push my buttons but I'm *not* going to cave.

"Trust me, this article is going to make you guys look like superheroes," I say. "There'll be pictures and quotes . . ."

"Wow. I always wanted to be a superhero."

I sigh. Detective Napier is not going to give me an inch. When will I learn to keep my sarcasm to myself?

"Can you at least tell me if she's under protective care? You know, like if Clyde tries to sneak in and off the only witness to the crime?"

"We got everything under control," he says.

"I'm just a little nervous. He knows I'm the one who got them busted. And he knows where I live."

Napier sighs into the phone. "Bailey Goodin."

"What?"

"Her name is Bailey Goodin."

"And she's still in a coma?"

"Yep," he says. "And no, I don't know when she's coming out of it. Now can I get back to work?"

I thank him profusely before he can hang up on me, too.

I remember when a coma used to be some kind of mysterious condition where no one knew when the patient would wake up, or even if she would. And of course there was the discussion on whether or not patients in a coma could hear you if you talked to them.

But these days, I think it's more a case of suspended animation or an 'induced' coma. Patients' nutrition, medication, and elimination are all handled through tubes and the body is at peace to heal itself. It's more humane than putting a severely injured person through all that pain, or guilt, or even anger. Then with the mere twist of a nozzle, a drug is stopped and the patient wakes up. The question is when will Bailey Goodin's doctor decide it's time for her to wake up? I'm pretty sure she's going to be pissed at being shot, and I'd like to be there to get an exclusive interview.

Detective Napier wants to be there too, and I doubt if he's going to give me a heads-up on the date and time. I need to have another source.

This is going to be tricky though. Brian's not going to be happy.

"What do you mean you're going up to Chattanooga?" he asks, his nose all squinched up, his fingers digging into the arms of his desk chair.

"I thought I'd take some flowers to that poor girl who was shot."

"Rachel?" he says, drawing my name out. "I thought Gladys had gone bye-bye."

"She did. I swear this is just greedy Rachel wanting to get the scoop on this girl so I can write a story about it and make a few bucks."

"I'll tell you how you can make a few bucks. *Don't* buy flowers, and *don't* waste gas driving two hours to Chattanooga."

I'm tempted to remind him that I have to spend money to make money but I don't think this is the right time. So how am I going to swing this? I'm sure Brian will miss his Jeep—and me—for the five hours it will take me to do this alone. I've got to get him on board.

A couple of times he's talked about checking out Savage Gulf Natural Area north of Chattanooga. Unfortunately, I'll have to suck it up and agree to go hiking in exchange for a visit to the hospital. I just hope it will be worth the effort.

* * *

I don't recall exactly when Brian became suspicious of my promises but the deal is that we go hiking *first*, then go to the hospital. When did I ever renege on an activity? Okay, there was that time when we went to the Okeefenokee and I decided not to go on the night tour. The idea of taking an airboat out into a swamp, at night, where alligators are just waiting for someone to tumble into the murky depths did not appeal to me. Besides, I really did have a headache. And that zipline in Costa Rica; have you seen how high those cables are? I'm afraid of escalators and he wanted me to zip across a canyon?

Anyway, we don't get to the hospital until after four in the afternoon. I'm tired, my hiking boots are filthy because it rained last night and the trail we took was a muddy quagmire, my hair looks like you might expect after being crunched into a knit hat all day, and my cheeks are several shades darker than rosy from the cold and wind.

I blow out my frustration and walk up to the nurses' station with a lovely bouquet of flowers courtesy of the supermarket we passed on the way. Hopefully my smile makes up for my appearance. Brian, bless his heart, leans on the counter and pours on the masculine charm.

How can he look this good after hiking? His complexion just looks healthy, not stroke-level. His zipped up hiking vest hides the extra ten pounds of gut, and his shorts show off his muscular legs.

"We're here to see Bailey Goodin," I say.

Nurse Deisel behind the counter was certainly chosen to oversee the ICU unit based on her steel-grey hair cut in a severe butch and her wrinkled puss. As soon as I speak, her nostrils flair with disapproval. "Patients in the ICU are not allowed to receive flowers." She adds a smirk at my thoughtlessness.

"Oh," I say, faking surprise. "These aren't for Bailey. They're for you and the other nurses in the ICU. To show our appreciation for how well you're taking care of our Bailey."

Her sphincter-face relaxes a little. Another nurse, cute as a button and equipped with bodacious breasts rushes to the counter and perkily parks herself in front of Brian.

(I tried to talk Brian out of wearing shorts in the dead of winter, but now I'm glad he didn't listen. Nurse Barbie is all a-quiver scoping out his manliness.)

"How sweet," she croons in a thick Southern drawl. Her eyelashes bat furiously and she angles her head to accentuate her megawatt smile.

Bingo! We have a winner. I'm not sure if it's his tousled hair or the beard stubble, but she's just a step away from having Brian's babies. It's like I've disappeared.

Nurse Deisel looks like she might try and break up this budding romance, so I sort of tilt my head for her to step to the side for a confidential inquiry. "Has Bailey's mama been here today already?"

"Yes. She left about an hour ago."

"Oh, phoo. I just missed her."

"She usually comes back after dinner." The poo-poo face comes back. "She doesn't like our cafeteria food."

I shake my head in disappointment. "That sounds just like her."

Brian is having a nice chat with Nurse Barbie. I just hope he remembers to ask the *only* thing required of him.

He pats the desk like he's wrapping up the conversation so I intervene. "Honey, would you like to go down to the cafeteria and get something to eat?" Then I turn to Nurse Deisel. "We'll come back later."

Inside the elevator, I grill Brian.

"So?"

"The doctor is going to bring Bailey out of the coma on Thursday. Probably during his morning rounds."

I grip Brian's face and plant a big wet one on him. He may be expecting more but it will have to wait until we get home and I take a shower.

CHAPTER TWENTY-FOUR

By the time we get home, it's after nine o'clock and I'm exhausted. What's interesting is that I'm not starving. I told Nurse Deisel we were going to cafeteria, which we did. What we didn't do was eat. We can't afford to eat at a good restaurant. Why would we spend money we don't have on hospital food? At least Nurse Deisel thinks we did. I may run into her again soon and I need her on my side. I took the time to peruse the menu so the next time I'm in the ICU, I can tell her how great the macaroni and cheese was.

All I want to do is take a hot bath and soak my feet. I slurp down a quick bowl of soup before I trudge upstairs. Brian is on his own.

I tried calling Napier on the drive home but the police station said he was off duty. I'll give him a call first thing in the morning. I check phone messages and emails. Still nothing from the news editor from the Atlanta Journal either.

My new morning breakfast is coffee and a bowl of fruit with yogurt, although the lowfat Greek style is so bitter I have to drizzle a little honey on it.

I carry my food up to my office, wake my computer then give Detective Napier a call. "Exciting news about Bailey, huh?"

He says nothing. I don't know if he's heard but doesn't want to talk to me, or if he's clueless. But the last thing I want to do is one-up him with information I have and he doesn't.

I rattle on. "I mean about the doctor planning to bring her out of the coma Thursday morning during his rounds."

Was that subtle enough?

He still says nothing. I try to picture his face puckering, his cheeks flaming red because I've told him something he didn't know again.

More blathering from me. "So once you've interviewed her, is there *any* chance I can have a photographer snap a quick picture of you with her? You know, the grateful survivor and the ace detective who's going to crack the case."

"Absolutely not. This woman has been through enough without some nosy reporter getting in her face as soon as she wakes up."

I should be offended by the nosy reporter jab but I've watched enough news to know that's exactly what reporters are like.

"You know some victims *want* their story in the news," I tell him. What I really mean is some victims really enjoy that fifteen minutes of fame. "Maybe you could get a fellow officer to take a picture just in case Bailey wants to see it in the paper someday."

"I'll think about it."

"Great. Thanks." I don't want to push it any farther. Especially since I need to give him a little nudge on my next agenda. "So I guess you've got two days to crack Caitlyn before Bailey wakes up and starts talking."

"Yeah. And I'm wasting time again talking to you." He hangs up.

That went well. I'm guessing within the next fifteen minutes, Detective Napier will be in Caitlyn Pritchett's face telling her that her Golden Ticket expires Thursday. If she wants to negotiate a deal with the assistant DA, she better start talking about Clyde.

While I read my emails, I dig into my fruit and yogurt. The crime magazine I submit to regularly is already interested in my six-part series on the investigation. Hot diggity.

Now an amateur might shoot an email straight back thanking them and open the dialogue on when the first part must be submitted. But I've been to a couple dog fights. I'm going to wait to see if any of the other editors I query are interested. If I'm lucky, I can drive the price-per-word up. I belt out a rebel yell and Brian suddenly appears at my door to see what the commotion is about.

"I've sold a six-part series on our investigation."

"Cool."

I don't want to jinx my chances, but his lack of enthusiasm pisses me off. "If I get another magazine interested, I could start a bidding war."

I tell him how much they might pay per word but his interest level is still flat-lining, especially since that involves cents, not dollars.

"Each part will be between 750 and 1000 words."

The old grey matter belches and sputters to life. He does that man-thing where he mentally figures out the price per word times the total number of words I will be submitting. His face explodes into a big ole' grin.

"Can you write 6000 words?"

"Sure. But I can't pad the story with bullshit. I've got to have facts."

He snaps his fingers at me. "You should call Jake. See what they found out at Bonnie and Clyde's apartment."

"How do they know about that?"

"I told them."

"You told them we were stalking Bonnie and Clyde?"

"Keisha said I should tell them everything. So I did." He looks at me. "Didn't you tell the Chattanooga police everything?"

"What was I supposed to tell them? That they lived in some apartment complex on some street in Lawrenceville?"

Mister Smug rolls his eyes at me. "They lived in the Monarch Arms apartments on Montreal Road in Tucker." He pauses for effect. "Apartment J, Building 1126."

How do guys do that? I didn't even know it was Tucker. I thought it was Lawrenceville.

So Jake has known about the apartment since Thursday. I wonder if Batesville PD has found out anything more on Bonnie or Clyde? There's no way Jake's going to tell me. I've got to go through Napier.

I snatch up my phone. One thing I have to give the detective credit for, he's still taking my calls.

The instant he answers, I blurt out: "I have the last known address of Caitlyn Pritchett."

"Yeah. We do too. Conyers."

"Conyers? I thought that area was considered Tucker."

"Conyers. Tucker. Whatever. The house is registered to Caitlyn's grandmother but we haven't caught her at home yet."

"Uhhhh," I stammer as I try to come up with a good way to tell him he's got the wrong address. There is no good way. "I'm talking about an apartment that she might have been sharing with Clyde."

I can picture the steam blowing the top off Napier's head because Batesville PD didn't give him the update.

"And how do you have that address?" he asks.

I don't want him to think I withheld information while I was in holding in Chattanooga. And I don't want to admit that Brian might be smarter than me at times. "My brother-in-law is a detective with the Batesville PD." I say, all snooty-like. I omit the 'duh' at the end.

"And what has he told you about investigating that address?"

Great. I'm in a corner again. "He was not that forthcoming."

"So you thought you'd feed me another nibble and see if I'd spill the beans, eh?"

"Look, I know you don't believe me, but I want this guy caught as badly as you do."

"Then help your brother-in-law."

I have a feeling he knows exactly what Jake thinks about me. And I'm pretty sure Napier is starting to feel the same way.

"Come on!" I cry and do my best to inflect some anguish in my voice. "All Bonnie and Clyde did in Atlanta was rob some stores. I watched that guy shoot a woman and jam her into a trunk. If you guys hadn't saved her, she'd be dead now." I take a breath to calm down before I continue. "You guys deserve this collar."

He doesn't hang up. I hope he's going through his notes from BPD to see if they shared this information. My guess is they didn't. So Napier has been wasting time tracking Caitlyn from the address on her driver's license.

"Okay," he says with a sigh. "Give me the address."

After I rattle off the name of the apartment complex and the unit number, I ask him if he needs my phone number. I don't want to push it by insisting he call me back.

"Oh, trust me," he says. "I've got your number."

* * *

When I still haven't heard back from the editor at the Journal on Wednesday, I drive to their offices and march into the lobby.

"I'd like to speak to someone about a string of area robberies that has escalated to attempted murder and kidnapping," I say to the receptionist.

She looks over the counter at me like she can't decide whether to call the editor-in-chief or security. And I'm wearing my lawyer clothes! I can't imagine what she would do if Brian walked in wearing his ratty jeans and a weathered tee shirt. Evidently they don't get a lot of walk-ins because the lobby is empty except for a man in a suit who must be waiting to sell something.

I give the receptionist a professional but reassuring smile and hand her my business card from *The Good Life*. That should impress her.

"If you'd like to have a seat," she says with a wave of her hand.

Thirty minutes later a guy named Bryce Shackleford introduces himself to me but he doesn't escort me to the inner sanctum. He wants more details, and probably wants to glance down my blouse to make sure he doesn't see any wires that might be connected to a bomb.

I give him a brief rundown on Bonnie and Clyde, with a few details of their latest smash and grab in Mansell County, and finish with the shooting and kidnapping in Chattanooga.

He's disappointed that Bailey Goodin, aka Dance Girl, wasn't killed during the crime. What can I say? Death sells. When I tell him Bailey will most likely be out of her coma on Thursday, he's even more disappointed.

"Don't worry," I reassure him, "the abduction and her nearly bleeding to death in the trunk will make great reading. And think about the uncertainty of whether she'll be brain dead or permanently paralyzed when she wakes up."

He's intrigued, but not really sold yet.

"This is Sunday edition, in-depth stuff," I assure him. "Especially her clinging to life in the ICU. You need to assign one of your best reporters for this one. It's going to be big."

Shackleford scribbles notes for a minute, but I think it's just doodling while he tries to make up his mind if he wants to check out my story. Then he picks up my card. "I see you're a writer. Why don't you want to submit this as a freelancer?"

I'm way ahead of him. "I've already sold a six-part series on the story and the magazine expects exclusivity." Doesn't that sound impressive? And it's much better than 'My brother-in-law is a douche so I can't get any info on Caitlyn from Batesville PD.' It's best that he doesn't realize how much I'll be badgering the newspaper for details once they take the story.

I do tell him that we had Bonnie and Clyde in our sights but instead of catching them, the cops arrested Brian.

"Who was the arresting officer?" he asks.

"I'd suggest you speak to either Jake Haggarty or Matthew Baker. They're both detectives in Batesville PD."

"I'll do that."

He stands. I don't know why I thought he might call BPD right away. Now I'm being dismissed.

I hold out my hand to shake. "I hope you'll keep me in the loop on this."

It's almost four o'clock when Shackleford calls me.

"Just got off the phone with Detective Baker," he says. "According to him, Caitlyn Pritchett is a small-time loser. Her dad is in jail for writing bad checks. Her mom took off when she was a kid. She was living with her grandmother until some boyfriend convinced her to live with him."

"That would be Clyde."

"Sounds like it. The grandmother never saw the guy. And get this: the apartment was rented under Caitlyn Pritchett's name only. The leasing agent never saw Clyde."

"What's this guy's deal?" I ask.

"Don't know, but it sounded like BPD is willing to let Atlanta PD or Fulton County do the groundwork on this one."

"Have you talked to either of them?"

"Not yet," Bryce says. "I've got calls out." I think he's about to hang up but then he says. "One more thing. Caitlyn Pritchett answered the phones for the realty company that had that robbery house near you listed. It's got some structural problems so it was an inactive listing, but Caitlyn had access to all that information. Including the code to the lock box on the front door, and the garage door opener."

* * *

Our old coffeemaker is sputtering and coughing so loud I almost don't hear Brian's phone ding with a text. It's from Detective Napier. *Check this morning's Chattanooga Times.* I squeal and run for the stairs.

"What's up?" Brian asks.

"I don't know."

He meanders into my office while I'm still waiting for the computer to bring up the Times.

On the front page is an article about the shooting with pictures of Caitlyn, and Bailey, and a guy named Farouk al Asad.

"Oh, my god!" I cry out. "Clyde is on a terrorist watch list."

"Holy crap!" Brian chimes in. "And that guy was pointing a gun at me."

"He saw my boobs," I whisper.

The article doesn't say anything about an arrest of Clyde/Farouk. It's mostly about the shooting, the attempted robbery, and the arrest of Caitlyn Pritchett. Napier is quoted but he never mentions me. I give him the benefit of the doubt that he did mention my name but the reporter didn't want to muddy the waters.

I figure if he's going to text me, he certainly expects me to call back for details.

When he comes on the line, I gush, "My god, you really are a superhero."

The laugh he tries to contain blurts out anyway. I don't blame him. This is a proud moment in any cop's life. He has caught a big one. Or almost.

"So you finally got her to talk," I say. "Was it the bamboo under the fingernails or did you hang her by her ankles?"

He chuckles. I'm glad he's finally getting my sarcasm. "I told her we still hadn't been able to contact her grandmother. I think she started worrying that maybe Farouk had done something to her. Like maybe her body was rotting in the basement."

"Do you think he did?"

"Nah. We finally got a hold of her Wednesday morning. She didn't have anything nice to say about Farouk even though she'd never met him. Evidently, Caitlyn met him at some bar. He was spreading around cash, had lots of cocaine. Even gave Cailtyn a gold bracelet that was stuck in the passenger seat of his car. You know, she sits down, feels something poke her butt, and pulls it out. He gives her one of those 'that old piece of junk' lines and says she can have it."

"Her grandmother told you all that?"

"No, she just said Caitlyn's new boyfriend was no good."

"And you know about Caitlyn working for the realty company."

"Yeah, for once I know more than you," he teases. "I guess she had a girlfriend who worked there and got her a job answering phones. Tried to help get her life on track."

"A lot of good that did," I say.

"Caitlyn told us the rest of the details. How her Granny tried to warn her that he was dangerous. That was her word. I think once all the drugs got out of her system, Caitlyn wised up."

"Any idea where Farouk might be?"

"Not a clue," he says, sounding disappointed. "And now the case is out of our hands."

"Why?"

"Thirty minutes after we fed his real name into the NCIC, I got a call from Homeland Security. They're taking over."

"Crap!"

"Yeah. It's better this way," he says, sounding a lot more loyal than I would. "They've got all that facial recognition technology. They've already plugged Farouk's picture in to see if he boarded an airplane or bus. They're afraid he's already left the country but at least they'll be able to see where he went. And confirm that he needs to remain on the 'watch list'."

"Well, you should still be proud that you guys gave Homeland fresh clues on this creep."

Brian has been listening to the conversation on speaker. He writes on a post-it pad. *Fingerprints?*

I nod. "So now that you've got a lead on this guy, what about fingerprints at the crime scenes, and the robbery house in Atlanta?"

"Oh, this is rich," Napier says. "Homeland sent their own crime scene techs back to the apartment in Tucker to check obscure places a cleaning crew might miss. You know, like inside a drawer, or cabinet door. Still nothing but Caitlyn's prints. Homeland has never gotten a print on Farouk. They suspect he's had his fingertips altered."

"Geez, this guy sounds like a professional criminal."

"Doesn't he? That's why Homeland put his picture out. They think more women might recognize him."

I shake my head. "I don't get his scam. What's with the women?"

"He needs a place to live but he doesn't want to be seen, doesn't want to have to show ID, so he reels in a woman to do his bidding. He gave Caitlyn some bullshit line about how he admired American women because they were so independent, wanted their own name on a lease, and utilities. Her bank account shows regular deposits of cash. Enough to pay the bills. And then of course there was the money for nice clothes, fancy restaurants."

"And since her dad had criminal tendencies, it probably wasn't too hard to convince her to become a thief too."

"You got it," Napier says.

"But why would a terrorist get caught up in crime? Why wasn't he building bombs?"

"Caitlyn says he had plenty of cash, but it wasn't nearly what they were pulling in. And of course, he didn't have any kind of bank account. She didn't know where the money was going. But Homeland is sure he's sending it back to some terrorist cell in the Middle East."

As soon as I end the call, I leap out of my chair and throw my arms around Brian.

CHAPTER TWENTY-FIVE

He kisses me with a fervor that I don't expect. My legs buckle and I drag Brian down to the floor with me. He wriggles his boxers down past his knees while I shimmy out of my panties and we have that rambunctious, bad-boy sex I've been yearning for since I hit my mid-30s. And boy, has Brian got it down now.

I'm wiping off the sweat between my breasts when Brian rolls to his knees and grabs a box of Kleenex off my desk. I stick a couple between my thighs and give one last squeeze that brings a little shiver. He flops back down next to me.

"That was unbelievable," I sigh.

"Does it make your top five?" he teases.

I roll over and kiss his neck. "I've had so many to choose from lately, I've lost count."

His arm slips around to my back and he pulls me close. He actually dozes off which is hard to believe since we just got up an hour ago.

I lay on the floor for a couple minutes while the final blush of sex fades. My body is a pool of jelly but my brain has already cranked into overdrive.

My six-part story just took a leap into the stratosphere. I might even write a book about our caper. At first I think it will be a factual account. But then I decide it could be one of those funny mystery novels; something like, 'How to Catch a Terrorist.'

By then, the authorities might even have Farouk in custody. My guess is, he's in the wind. And now that he's moved up on the watch list, it will be nearly impossible for him to come back into the country undetected.

The good thing about writing our adventure as fiction—based on a true story—is that I'll be able to embellish scenes, and make up my own ending. I don't think I'm cut out to stick to the facts.

I wriggle out from under Brian's arm and scurry downstairs to call Shackleford at the Atlanta paper without waking lover boy.

"Clyde is a terrorist," I yell when he answers. "The FBI and Homeland are all over this now."

"Uh, yeah," he says. "It's on the front page."

"Of the Chattanooga Times?"

"Of the Atlanta Journal."

Oops. I guess I should have checked first.

But he's so excited, he overlooks my blunder. "We replated around midnight, but we also sent out a new front page of the e-paper and we've been tweeting about it for hours."

Hmmm. I'm a little miffed that he didn't call me, but I'm new to his circle of confidantes. Hopefully, I'll be able to feed him another nugget of info that will reassure him I'm reliable.

While I'm in the shower, I decide I'm going to call Jake. I know it's petty, but I can't help wanting to gloat. He had the chance to catch a really bad guy and he passed just to spite me.

Unfortunately, he won't take my call at the police station. And he doesn't acknowledge my text. He probably deleted it without reading it.

Fine. I've got another idea. I go to Jackson's middle school website. I'm sure Gwen said he was playing basketball. Sure enough, the 7th and 8th grade team is playing tonight—and it's a home game.

Believe it or not, Brian is willing to go to the game with me. I guess he wants a little revenge on Jake, too. We go late, after halftime. I scan the small crowd of parents until I spot Gwen and Jake in the bleachers. Then Brian and I crawl over legs and purses to get the empty space right next to Jake. Gwen sees us pushing through and gives me a confused look. It's not like we've never been to a game before. Okay, so we haven't.

Jake glances over when I sit down but immediately turns back to the game. He's so pissed, I can almost hear his jawbone grinding.

"Hey, Jake," I say all cheery. "How's it going?"

He doesn't say a word. I follow the team up and down the court a couple times. Then without taking my eyes off the game, I say, "Farouk al Asad. Who would have guessed?"

"Screw you," he mumbles and hops to his feet. He tumbles over legs as he pushes past Gwen and the people next to her then stomps down the wooden steps. He squeezes in between a couple dads who are sitting behind the team.

Gwen whips her head in my direction to see what that was all about. I give her the big, dumb shrug, like I'm just as stumped. Brian's hand roams up my back and he massages my shoulders. After a second, I glance his way. He's grinning like a kid.

We have to stay for the rest of the game but it was worth it to rattle Jake's cage.

When we get home, we try to recreate the passion and enthusiasm we had this morning, but now that the case is over, and we've thumbed our noses at Jake, the thrill is gone.

CHAPTER TWENTY-SIX

The hairdo magazine in the waiting area is filled with impossible styles. As I flip from page to page waiting for my name to be called, I eliminate each one. 'Too much blowdrying.' "That's going to require one of those round styling brushes.' 'I'm not using gel. I'll have to wash my hair every day.'

It's not like the woman who cuts my hair will make it look anything like the picture anyway. I'm at Great Clips where I'm sure their motto is: 'Get 'em in and out in fifteen minutes or your fired.'

Our lives have gotten somewhat back to normal. Brian and I have a full schedule already for spring festivals starting March 1st.

After a couple of terse calls to the Batesville Police Department, I finally got my purse back. Since I was no longer a robbery suspect, I got a little testy with the local constabulary. In the back of my mind, I worry that I may need their assistance in the future, but right now Jake and I are still feuding.

The Chattanooga police even sent me back the tracking collar. It'll be easier to just keep it rather than try to return it to *The Good Life* office. Besides, I may need it again someday. (If Brian heard me say that, he'd have a cow.)

I haven't requested replacement credit cards yet. We got through January on the money we had in the bank. I say, let sleeping dogs use their own credit cards.

We finally got a check from the insurance company on the Cooper. Big whoop. The car was five years old so after our deductible, the amount was so small, all I could afford was a used Chevy Malibu.

Sarah promised to come by after work so we can determine the best way to handle my new haircut. As soon as I get home, though, I wash my hair, blow-dry it, and use one of those round styling brushes. It still looks like crap. I am *not* going to use gel.

When I answer the front door, I'm prepared for Sarah's gasp and 'I told you not to go there.' Instead, she's smiling so big her whole face is lit up.

"Did you see this week's *Time Magazine*?" she asks. Then she shoves a copy at me. The cover is a montage of womens' head shots. One of the women is Caitlyn Pritchett.

"Holy shit!" I snatch the magazine and start flipping through.

She's so eager, she actually has her hands clasped at her chest. "Page thirty-two."

Detective Napier was right. Once Homeland splashed Farouk's picture all over the media, other women came forward to admit they were taken in by him as well. The article is about how Farouk al Asad duped women into helping him fly under the radar. He gave one woman money to buy a car for him. Another woman bought ammunition.

Sarah reaches over the top of the magazine to flip to the next page. There at the end of the article is a small picture of me.

"Holy shit!"

"Why didn't you tell me you were going to be in *Time Magazine*," she asks.

"I didn't know!"

"How could you not know? Don't they have to get your permission?"

This is embarrassing. I got a call from some guy claiming to be with *Time Magazine*. He asked me how the whole thing started and I repeated my little ditty about 'See Something, Say Something.' Then he asked if he could use my picture from my Facebook page.

"I thought it was one of Jake's buddies pulling my chain."

I try to remember back to what all I said. I'm pretty sure I ranted about what a moron Jake was and even spelled out his name. If I'd known the reporter was legit I would have given him some better quotes. Still, being mentioned in *Time Magazine* will do wonders for my book sales—once I get it done.

"The article says the government is keeping its promise not to prosecute any woman who comes forward with a statement," Sarah says. "Well except for Caitlyn Pritchett."

Believe it or not, I actually spoke with someone from Homeland Security about their progress on the case so I knew they were letting Chattanooga prosecute Caitlyn as an accomplice to the attempted murder of Bailey Goodin. I'll be a material witness once she goes to trial. There's no big rush to run out and buy new trial clothes though. The way the justice system works, it'll be sometime next year before they even select a jury.

As far as Farouk goes, all Homeland Security has is a surveillance tape of him boarding a plane in Birmingham. They lost track of him in Charlotte. I suspect he puddle-jumped to several small airports with low security before flying out of the country. There was a flurry of activity for a couple weeks but now the investigation is at a dead end.

"How about a glass of wine?" I ask.

She shakes her head. "I can't stay. The kids are at home, doing their homework."

I take a quick glance upstairs to where Brian is working in his office. It's amazing that we have stood right here in the foyer talking about the article in *Time Magazine* and he hasn't wandered out to see what the excitement is about. But if I mentioned a key word, like 'tits' or 'potato chips', he'd be at the railing in a flash.

"I'll walk you to your car," I say, opening the closet to grab a jacket.

Once we're outside, I lament how I miss virile, aggressive Brian. I even take some of the blame. "It's hard to believe how quickly we've reverted to our boring selves."

"You might have to knock off a convenience store now and then if you want to keep the spark alive," she teases.

"Trust me, I've considered it."

"Well, don't start snooping around for trouble. You can't afford it."

I nod. "I've got a little scheme in the works for Valentine's Day this Friday but I need your help."

"A crime?"

"No. A way to get Brian's motor running. And mine." I swivel my hips. "Something sexy."

"Ooooh. I can't wait." She gets into her car and shuts the door. Then she looks up at me and rolls down the window. I know she's searching for something nice to say about the haircut. I save her the struggle. "I know. It's hideous."

* * *

You know how some clothing stores have these huge racks tightly packed with clearance items? Well, that's not the case at Victoria's Secret. There's one shabby pile of clearance lingerie in a back corner but the odds of me finding a 36B bra and matching size 9 panties are astronomical.

Sarah insisted we meet here which was crazy. She knows how poor I am. I paw through hangers of lace and satin that are on sale but it's no use.

I shake a bra and panties set at her. "How can so little fabric cost so much?"

At Penney's, I find a cute little negligee with a gathered bodice that corrals the girls nicely yet hangs almost to my knees to hide my thighs. Brian is definitely a breast man, so once he gets started on them, he won't pay much attention to anything else.

"Check this out," Sarah says, holding up a red bustier and dangling garters.

"No way."

"Come on, you'll look fantastic." She gives me the appraising eye-scan. "Are you sure you've only lost five pounds?"

Ever since the porn house case was closed, I've been hammering away on the computer, working on the rough draft of the book about our adventure. And with my fingers so busy on a keyboard, they haven't been shoveling as many cookies and chips into my mouth.

Sarah slides over to a table of panties. "You should get a matching thong."

I blow out an unladylike snort. "There's no way that's going to look sexy."

Even with my $10 off coupon, and a 15% discount for opening a Penney's charge, I still can't afford the bustier—but I buy it anyway.

As soon as I get home, I scurry upstairs and stash my purchase in my favorite hiding place: on the closet floor behind all of Brian's dress pants.

I'm on my hands and knees, making sure the hangars are all even, when Brian comes in.

"Are you cleaning?" he asks.

He scares me so bad a little fart squeaks out.

"Uh, yeah," I say as I stagger to my feet. "I was thinking of weeding out some of these pants that don't fit you anymore."

Ladies, if you want to get your husband out of the closet fast, just mention that he might have to try on pants and listen to you click your tongue if they don't fit. He'll skedaddle so fast he might trample the family dog.

I'm halfway down the stairs when Brian says, "Oh, hey, I forgot. Steve from the Wildlife Preserve in Ellijay called me. One of their black bears has given birth to an albino cub."

"No kidding."

"He's been waiting for the cub to put on a few pounds but he says I can come up Friday to take some pictures."

"Friday!? Why can't you go Saturday?"

"Because he said Friday."

"But Friday is Valentine's Day."

"Oh, cool. Why don't you come up with me? We can stop at Bubba's Bar B Que on the way back."

This isn't going like I planned. If I insist Brian change his plans, he'll be in a snit Friday night. If I have to go tromping in the wilderness to see a white bear Friday, I'll be in a snit.

"It's just that I was making plans for Friday night," I say as I climb back up the stairs. "When will you be back?" I reach into his ratty bathrobe to run my fingers down the same tee shirt he's worn for two days.

His eyebrow twitches. "When do you want me to be back?"

I put on my 'sexy smile'. "How about around eight?"

"Do I get any more clues? Are we going out for dinner?"

"I don't have all the logistics yet but I'm sure we can't afford to go out for dinner."

Besides, when Brian and I go out for dinner we always eat too much. Then we come home with our bloated bellies, collapse on the bed and watch TV until one of us slips into a coma. And there's nothing romantic about making love while you're burping garlic.

* * *

It's just as well that Brian is gone for the day. I've got a ton of things to do to get ready for our special Valentine evening, and I don't need him barging into the bathroom this afternoon while I'm all twisted up shaving my inner thighs.

I spend a good part of the afternoon chopping eggplant and tomatoes and peppers, then roasted them for a couple hours before whirling them into a tasty tapenade. I'm going to serve it hot with crackers instead of some fattening dip.

My healthy eating is starting to bug Brian. (I refuse to call it dieting.) He's been craving potato chips and chocolate chip cookies all month. Aldi's had brie on sale, Brian's favorite, so I bought a small wedge. While I was perusing the store's stellar wine selection, I discovered they had champagne, probably leftover from the boatload they bought for the New Year.

Brian can't resist Bubba's Bar B Que so I'm sure he's going to stop there on his way home. He probably won't eat much of my fare but he'll need a little something to go with the champagne. I'm not looking for sloppy drunk, just mellow and less inhibited.

Next up is the bedroom. Sarah gave me a spray bottle of blended aromatics specifically for arousal. According to the box, the jasmine will energize my passion and the orange will add a crisp, fresh note. I particularly like the part where the sandalwood will add a rugged, uplifting aroma for Brian.

At the last minute I'll spray some on our pillows, and I'm going to drape a hand towel over the back of the sofa that's been doused in the stuff.

I hop into the shower around five for the deforestation of my legs. In a brilliant move, I waxed my bikini area three days ago so all the angry red welts are gone.

Next up is my hair. Bending at the waist, I hang my head down and blow-dry to add some volume. But once I'm done, it looks like hell which is typical. I did the same thing two days ago and looked fantastic for my trip to Walgreen's. I stick my head in the sink to wet the hair and try again. Sarah offered to come over and style it but I thought that was so pathetic I turned her down. Now I wish I hadn't.

After sticking cottonballs between my toes, I polish my nails. But since I don't do this very often, I keep nicking the toes with the brush and have to scrape off the polish with my fingernail. I'm so hunched over my feet that I get a cramp in my leg and have to jump up and hobble around on my heel to walk it off.

I swear it would be a lot easier to just start a bar fight and have Brian step in to break it up. Unfortunately, adrenaline is not for sale, at least not in the United States.

An hour before Brian is due home, I put the tapenade in an ovenproof crock. I know we won't eat even half of it, but the only dish I have that will go in the oven is too big for two small servings. Presentation is everything, so I plop the whole batch in. Now the dish is almost too full but the sides will look sloppy if I take some back out. (Yes, I've seen Rachel Ray deftly wipe the sides of a serving dish. And no, I'm not going to empty the dish, wash it, and start again.) I'll just refrigerate what we don't eat and we can heat it up again tomorrow.

I get the cheese out to come to room temperature, and dunk the champagne into our ice bucket to chill. I want to have everything done before I get dressed. Tapenade dribbled on my bustier won't convey the mood I'm trying to get across.

As I'm arranging crackers around the brie it occurs to me that this is a whole lot of trouble for three minutes of pumping and a five-second explosion. I shake that negative thought out of my head and replace it with a shaggy-haired man with a glistening bare chest. Don't they say the most important sex organ is the brain?

I take one last look to be sure everything is ready. I'll light the candles once I hear the garage door go up. There are three CDs in the player on shuffle. I'm taking a different tack than the whole sexy men singing approach. That might work for me but I'm not sure about Brian. I've got some Enya and a couple yoga CDs Sarah let me borrow. We really aren't easy listening type people but I don't think The Suicide Spiders are going to cut it tonight.

I'm tempted to unplug the TV in case Brian tries to turn it on the minute he sits down. But then if the cable box is off for too long, we'll have to go through all the rigmarole of rebooting. I settle for hiding the remote.

I'm finally ready for the moment of truth. I drag the Penney's bag out from behind Brian's hanging pants and pull out the red bustier and panties. Thank goodness the buyers for Penney's understand men. The laces don't really have to be criss-crossed all the way up, and there aren't a thousand hooks that must be unhooked. There's a zipper, and it's even in the front so I don't have to dislocate a shoulder pulling it up. The girls are nicely boosted and as an added bonus, this medieval corset flattens my belly.

The panties I chose are the boy-cut style. I turn to have a look from the back. There's still a lot of cheek hanging out but I reassure myself that Brian is a breast man. He won't be ogling here. Last comes the black stockings. I have a hell of a time with the garter clasps and in a moment of panic I worry that Brian will give up in frustration and rip the stockings.

I slip on the nicest heels I have, a strappy open-toe with a two inch heel. I sure wish I'd gotten a pair of those four-inch Louboutins when I had the chance. Then I check the whole look out in the mirror. It's not as bad as I feared.

In fact, when Brian sees this he may jump right into Phase Two without nibbling on the brie in Phase One. That's okay, we can have a snack afterwards. I just have to remember to turn off the oven so the tapenade doesn't burn.

My phone dings. It's a text from Brian. *I'm in Jasper. See you at eight.*

If he's planning on seeing me at eight, he must have hit that red button on the Jeep's console that deploys the supersonic turbo jet that will blast him fifteen miles in two minutes because according to my phone, it's almost eight o'clock now.

No worries. Everything's under control.

CHAPTER TWENTY-SEVEN

I have a plan to conceal the Bustier Bomb until the right moment. When we were in San Francisco a few years back, I bought a gorgeous Chinese kimono. It wasn't at all practical, what with the droopy sleeves and the satin that stains so easily. And it's too hot for the summer, not warm enough for winter. None of that matters. With the sash tied tight, the robe hides the bustier nicely until I'm ready to reveal all.

I'm checking my look in the bedroom mirror one last time when I hear a thunk in the living room. That little stinker. He's trying to surprise me, making me think he's still driving home when he's already here. Will he have a big box of candy? I told him not to; well what I said was 'don't get me one of those humongous boxes of candy.' So maybe he got me a smaller one.

I don't hear him moving around anymore. Is he lighting the candles? Did he buy me an actual gift? Does it require assembly? Probably not or I'd hear lots of wrenches clanking and Brian swearing. It better not be a vacuum cleaner.

At the bottom of the stairs, I act real nonchalant as I walk into the living room, like I have no idea he's home. But he's not here. And I don't see a vacuum cleaner or any other gift. The candles are not burning.

Did he head straight for the kitchen when he smelled the tapenade? I have to admit, it smells delicious. I refresh the smile on my face and waltz into the kitchen. Brian must have been standing right on the other side of the wall because he pops out and grabs me from behind.

I squeal with shock and delight. We're both thinking the same thing: kinky sex. Wait until he sees what I'm wearing.

He clamps a hand on my mouth while his other arm pulls me close to his chest. Be still my beating heart. I've got to remember to turn off the dip before we scamper upstairs.

His mouth nestles up close to my ear, and he whispers. "You bitch. I will make you and your husband pay for what you did."

My heart goes into a seizure. This is not Brian. And the Middle Eastern accent is a dead giveaway. It's Farouk. I try to scream but his hand is clamped on my mouth; I can barely breathe through my nose let alone cry out.

I wriggle back and forth but he's got me in a tight hold. I try to remember the videos I've watched on YouTube, and the defensive moves they use on crime shows but the only signal I'm getting from my brain is *panic*.

"You whore," he growls at me. "You daughter of a filthy dog."

Whore?

I put my weight on my left leg and stomp down hard with my right foot. I miss. I shift and try my left foot and make contact with his shoe. I put all my weight on my heel and grind. He cries out and lets go.

The momentum sends me flying across the room, off balance. I bang into the stove where I see the salt and pepper shakers. I grab the pepper, my hands trembling as I wrench the lid off. He's hobbling towards me when I turn around.

I take a deep breath and toss the whole container of pepper into his face. He gasps and reels back. I drop to my knees to avoid the pepper cloud and crawl towards the door to the garage. He blindly grabs my foot, and I reach out to hang on to something. It turns out to be the bottom drawer of our cabinets.

As he drags me back, the drawer opens. It's the junk drawer full of kitchen gadgets I never uses. I grab the rolling pin just as he lunges on top of me. Swinging wildly behind my head, I manage to smack him once but there's little force to the blow.

He snarls in anger as he grabs my wrists to keep me from taking another swing. Then I guess he manages to sit up because my back takes the brunt of his weight. He braces a knee against my arm and wrenches the rolling pin away. I squeeze my eyes closed, waiting for him to bludgeon me to death.

Instead, he pulls my hands behind her back, and handcuffs me. I buck and squirm but it's no use. He's got me.

"A dog collar?" he screams as he wraps a fist around my hair and pulls hard. "You ruined me with a dog collar?"

Then he slams my face into the floor. There's an explosion of pain. I don't actually hear the crunch but I'm sure he has broken my nose. My ears ring, and all of these white spirals of light zoom across my eyes.

Farouk drives his knee into my back and pushes off to stand. Then he grabs me by the handcuffs and pulls up. I scramble to get my knees on the floor before he pulls my arms out of their sockets. My head swims with dizziness, either from the bang on the head or the excruciating pain in my shoulders. By the time I can blink away the tears, he's unwinding the ball of cook's twine that has been in the bottom drawer for over three years. Unbelievable. I never trussed the first turkey and now he's going to tie me up with it.

Who knew there was so much twine? He lashes me to a kitchen chair at the shoulders and around my waist. I'm not going anywhere.

It won't do any good, but I scream anyway. He shoves one of my good dish towels into my mouth and ties it in place with more twine.

Now that he has me incapacitated, he leans against the counter and pants. It looks like he's in pain. He bends and gingerly removes his shoe. His foot is bleeding where I stomped on it.

How can he even tell I'm smiling with this bulky towel in my mouth? Evidently he does though because he slaps me. Hard. My nose erupts in pain again. I can feel the oozing blood soak into the towel. At least it isn't dripping all over my Japanese kimono and fancy bustier.

He turns to the sink, raises his leg, and puts his foot under the faucet to run cold water on the wound. He sighs with relief.

"Why did you decide to destroy my life?" he asks without turning around. "My beautiful Caitlyn is in jail." His voice gets louder. "My cousin Badi is dead. The police almost apprehended me." He spins around to glare at me. "Who in the hell do you think you are?"

I'm wondering that myself.

He blots his foot with the matching hand towel. Well, now they're both ruined.

With lots of hissing and groaning, he puts his shoe back on. It hurts so bad he screams and yanks a knife out of the block on the counter. I've been nagging Brian for months to sharpen those things. Will that dull blade hurt even more when he stabs me with it? Or will he have to poke me several times just to break the skin?

I'm pretty sure he won't be able to stab me in the heart. This bustier is like a Kevlar vest. Instead, he holds the knife to my throat. "Where is your fatherless husband?"

I mumble big long sentences through the towel in my mouth until he finally unties the twine and yanks the towel free. Now that I'm able, I'm not sure what to say.

"I thought your cousin's name was Bobby." Brilliant diversion, huh?

"How do you know Badi?"

"I heard you and Caitlyn talking about him."

"Did I say that he was a filthy rodent who dared to betray me?"

"Uh, no," I say. "But Caitlyn was pretty mad that he wasn't helping you move out of your apartment."

Farouk hesitates as he thinks back. The knife recedes as he straightens up. Then his face caves like something sad has occurred to him.

"He was dead. He had stolen pages from my notebook, codes to bank accounts." Farouk is gazing over my head, remembering. "I demanded he return the pages. He said he did not have them. But I knew he did. I killed him."

Farouk's eyes zero in on mine now. "I killed him!" he screams. "And then I read in the *Time Magazine* that you had my notebook." He gets right in my face. "You took pictures." I try to lean away but he just gets closer. And he screams at the top of his lungs, "You will give me back those pages!"

Tears gush from my eyes. I don't have his pages. I'm going to die tonight.

"Where is your husband?!" he yells, and presses the blade against my neck again.

I try to think. There must be a way out of this. But what? If I say Brian's coming home soon, I'm sure Farouk will wait. The question is whether Brian will figure out what's going on or walk right into a trap? I'm pretty sure he'll walk into a trap.

When I don't answer, Farouk presses the blade harder against my throat.

"He's out of town," I yelp. "For two days."

I don't know why I'm being a hero. But after all I've put Brian through, the least I can do is spare him being stabbed to death in his own house.

Farouk gets this creepy smile on his face. "Is that so? What you are saying is that for two days I may enjoy your company?" He leans closer to whisper in my ear. "With my darling Caitlyn in prison, I have become a lonely man."

Dear lord, has he seen what I'm wearing under this robe? I'm in big trouble.

"That won't work," I say. "My brother-in-law is a cop and he's coming first thing in the morning to clean out our gutters."

"That is shit from a camel. You are lying." He grips a fistful of my hair again and yanks my head back. I think he's a little disappointed that he has not done any damage to my throat.

He throws the knife on the counter and grabs the serrated bread knife. Damn! There's no point on that knife but if he decides to saw off my head, I'm sure he'll succeed eventually.

"I believe your husband is coming home tonight. And I am going to be right here when he walks in that door. He will watch as I kill you."

With that, he hops up on the counter. I straighten my neck and all the blood that has been pooling up in my sinuses gushes out in a steady stream. That does it for the kimono.

I cross my fingers that Brian has a flat tire, or a truck full of chickens overturns on the highway. While I frantically scan my kitchen for a magical voice-activated emergency phone or one of those pull chains you see in retirement homes, I see smoke curling out of the oven. My tapenade is burning. How can that be? I was just warming it up. I must have turned up the dial when I grabbed the pepper earlier.

Great, now Brian and I will both die and our house will burn down and there won't be any evidence that Farouk was even here.

"Listen," I say. "While we're waiting, would you mind taking my dip out of the oven?"

He glances over to see the smoke but does nothing.

"Suit yourself," I say. "But if the smoke gets bad enough the alarm will go off and the fire department will be called."

I have a plan.

Farouk finally slides off the counter making sure not to put any weight on his gouged foot. When he bends to pull the dip out, I'm going to give him a good shove just like Hansel and Gretel did to the wicked witch. If I'm lucky, he'll tumble into the oven, sustain some third degree burns, possibly be knocked unconscious, and maybe even die of smoke inhalation.

He picks up the pot holders. I brace my legs and grip the sides of the chair. He opens the oven. I raise up on wobbly legs, my body contorted into an awkward S shape by the chair. Then I charge. But he doesn't immediately bend to get the dip. He steps to the side and fans the potholders to blow the smoke away. So now I'm barreling towards the gaping maw of my open oven, my hands tied behind my back.

Instead of lamenting my imminent demise, I'm obsessed with all the dip I piled into the dish bubbling over, dripping onto the oven floor, and burning. Who's going to clean up this mess after I'm gone? Brian certainly won't. Maybe he'll remarry and this is the first thing she'll see. My dirty oven. She'll insist he buy her a new one, which he certainly will not be able to afford.

One dripping blob actually ignites with the added oxygen from the open door. The billowing cloud of reality snaps me out of my thoughts. I'm about to burn my own face off.

Farouk hears me grunt with panic and turns to watch me put on the brakes. I don't know why I thought this would work. He has the audacity to smile.

I get myself stopped just before I tumble headfirst into the oven. But as I plop back down on the chair, it wobbles a couple times. I'm going to fall sideways and break my neck.

It's a miracle that the chair settles upright.

"You are not a very smart lady," he says, wagging a finger at me.

Then he reaches into the oven, pulls out the baking dish and sets it on the counter.

"Hey! Hey! Don't do that," I screech. "Set it on the stove."

He must have been nagged as a child because he immediately slides it over onto the stove and even turns off the oven. I'd praise him for being a good boy but I really don't think it will improve our relationship.

I go back to bleeding on my kimono while he paces. At one point he takes a closer look at the wooden block of knives on the counter. Is he thinking of sharpening one?

The aroma of the tapenade distracts him after about thirty seconds. He glances over at the plate of crackers, picks up one and drags it through the roasted eggplant and tomatoes. This is Mediterranean fare. We might have a bonding moment yet.

But then the dope pops the whole cracker into his mouth. Immediately, he begins with the huffing and blowing because the dip is scalding hot. He dashes to the sink and spits it out.

He's running cold water and sucking it into his mouth when out of the corner of my eye, I detect movement.

Brian rushes up behind Farouk and beans him on the head with a shovel. Farouk bangs his chin on the counter before slumping to the floor.

We both stare at his lifeless body for a couple seconds. Then Brian turns to me and I scream. "Get the keys to the handcuffs!"

"Are you okay?" Brian asks.

"I'm fine. Let's just get him tied up."

Brian kneels beside Farouk and digs into his pockets. He finds the key, unlocks the cuffs and slaps them on Farouk. The instant I'm untied, I jump up and throw my arms around Brian.

We both babble at the same time, me chattering about how scared I was, and him reassuring me everything is okay now.

When I stop shaking, I pull away to wipe the tears from my eyes. He bares his teeth in a grimace.

"What?"

He circles a finger hand around his mouth. I turn to the kitchen window which reflects my image. The lower half of my face is covered in blood.

"Ice," he says and turns away to the refrigerator. I lean over the sink and splash water. The red blood swirling down the drain makes me queasy so I grab one of my ruined towels and sit to blot the rest of the blood off.

Brian hands me a Ziploc bag full of ice and I hold it on my throbbing nose. My hand shakes.

"How did you know he was here?" I ask.

"I saw the light on in the kitchen when I pulled into the driveway," he says. "I thought you were sneaking a late night snack so I figured I'd catch you in the act." He gives me the classic husband shrug, the non-verbal apology in case he says something that irritates me. "I came up on the deck with my phone out. I was going to take of a picture through the kitchen window of you feeding your face. He was sitting on the counter."

I burst out laughing. "Did you see me try to push him into the oven?"

Brian laughs, too. "Yeah. It would have worked if he hadn't moved."

"Right?" I actually giggle. "What made you think of the shovel?"

He puffs his chest out. "I asked myself 'What would Jack Reacher do?' And I remembered in one of the books I read, how people can't concentrate on anything for very long. They're vigilant for a short while but then their mind and attention start to wander. I went out to the shed, got the shovel and just waited." He snorts out a laugh. "Who knew the bozo was going to eat that hot dip."

I chuckle with him even though he does the same thing all the time.

Farouk groans and his head lolls to the side.

261

"Let's call the police," I say. "I can't wait to see Jake's face."

Brian takes the towel from me and gently wipes my chin. "Yeah. He's going to love looking at yours, too."

CHAPTER TWENTY-EIGHT

Before the police arrive, Brian hauls out his camera bag and shoots pictures of Farouk, front, side, closeup, and long shots with the disheveled kitchen. At one point, Farouk snarls at Brian and curses but I doubt if anything will come of his hex. He also takes pictures of my bloody face before I get it all cleaned up.

While Brian is snapping pictures, I grab my phone to call to Shackleford at the AJC. He heard about the disturbance on the police band; he's got a reporter on the way.

"How about I give you guys an exclusive interview?" I say.

Yes, I've got a soft spot for print media. And it's always good to know someone in the media.

"Fantastic!" Shackleford says. "His name's Adam Whitaker. I'll text him and tell him you're available."

Within minutes of our 911 call, Hamilton Farms is swarming with police cars, both city and county, plus sheriff's deputies who didn't have anything else to do, all of their blue lights reflecting off surrounding homes. At the first sound of sirens, neighbors come pouring out to see what's happening. At least this time Brian isn't being arrested.

Two uniformed cops come to the front door, their hands on their guns. I pull away the baggie of ice on my face and see by their expressions that they think this is a domestic disturbance. When one of them makes a move to restrain Brian, he shakes his head.

"Take it easy, boys," he says, his hands out front in a non-threatening manner. "I'm not the suspect." He turns slowly to lead them to the kitchen. "He's back here."

I stand at the doorway while Brian formally introduces the cops to Farouk al Asad, bound and gagged to our kitchen chair. One of the cops makes the official arrest by taking off the handcuffs we put on Farouk and slapping on his own.

"An ambulance is on the way, ma'am," the other officer says. "If you'll just wait in the living room for a moment, we'll get this guy out of here."

Right on cue, we hear another wail in the distance. I head back to the living room to wait.

The ambulance whoops its siren to get people out of the way but they still have to park down at Paul and Linda Cook's house.

Television station vans careen into the subdivision close behind. Crews leap from their vehicles and scramble to get set up. The police must understand this delay because it's a couple minutes before Farouk is marched out the front door, captured in the blazing lights of TV cameras.

The paramedics slow down when they see Farouk on our front sidewalk but one of the officers waves them off and points a thumb at the house. They rattle through the front door with their stretcher and their bags.

Again, Brian and I get the sideways glances. Domestic abuse must run rampant in this area.

Brian raises his hand in one of those 'stop right there' moves. "I'm the husband. You just passed the assailant."

"Ma'am," one of the paramedics says as he motions for me to get on the stretcher.

"I'm fine," I tell him. And I don't want him whisking me out to the ambulance before I get my interview with the AJC. "But let's take this into the kitchen. If you stir up my nose again, I'd rather bleed on the kitchen floor. It already needs mopping."

I'm sitting on a kitchen chair while a paramedic shines a light in my eyes. I catch a glimpse of Detective Baker as he slips in.

"Well," he says as he surveys the mess. "It looks like you got your man, Mrs. Sanders."

The paramedic turns off his flashlight and I twist around to face Baker.

"Whoa!" Baker says, taking a step closer to get a better look at the damage. "Looks like he got you."

I go for the cliché. "You can't make an omelet without breaking some eggs."

He comes back with his own. "If you're gonna lie down with dogs you're gonna get fleas."

The other paramedic wants to get my blood pressure so I open my robe and pull out a bare arm before I remember I'm still wearing the bustier and stockings. Eyebrows go haywire. Detective Baker coughs and politely backs out of the room. Brian gawps like a fish. He reaches for his camera but decides against it.

Another glance at my reflection in the kitchen window shows blood has run down into my cleavage. I look like Elvira, Mistress of the Dark, after a chainsaw massacre. No wonder Brian wants to get pictures.

"Later," I say.

Baker signals for Brian to join him in the living room. I get another bug-eyed stare from Brian before he leaves. Is he wishing he'd passed on the albino bear?

"And when you're done with her," Baker says to the paramedics, "I need you to check out the suspect's jaw, maybe take him to the emergency room for a head x-ray."

"You should take a look at his foot, too," I say.

None of us wants this turkey to get off on the technicality of receiving improper medical attention.

Once it is determined that my nose is not broken, the guy prescribes ice—lots and lots of ice. I show him the bag in my hand, then hold it back on my face.

The paramedics pack up their bags and hustle away. And now that they're gone, Baker wants my side of the story. The interview is brief. We all know the minute the feds step in the local jurisdiction is kaput.

The AJC reporter swaggers up the sidewalk and proudly shows his credentials to the cop at the front door. I can hear the other reporters grousing and grumbling. Whitaker turns for one last victorious moment before he steps inside.

Our interview goes pretty much as expected. Other than giving an exhaustive account of my harrowing experience, I also make sure to mention that I'm a journalist with *The Good Life*, I brag on Brian's photographic credentials, and with what I consider great restraint, I do NOT further malign Jake Haggarty. I hope he appreciates that.

About ten minutes into the interview, Baker decides to placate the rest of the news hounds and goes out front. Brian tags along to give a brief statement. I don't know what he's saying, but he gestures back towards the house at one point. No doubt it's something about his courageous wife, or the savagery of al Asad, or possibly an inquiry on how best to clean our oven. Then in a moment of impeccable timing, a helicopter flies overhead, its searchlight sweeping, its rotor blades tousling Brian's hair. It's a perfect sound bite.

As expected, Homeland Security arrives and whisks Farouk away. The crowd outside disburses. A lone police car sits outside our house until the cop is sure no one is going to disturb us before he leaves, too.

It's quiet for the first time in hours.

"Thank god," I groan as I tug at the bustier. "I need to get out of this thing and take a shower."

"Hang on!" Brian says as he snatches up his camera. "How about just a few more shots. Without the robe."

He's a naughty boy.

I let him take a few art house meets horror house shots before I trudge upstairs. While I'm soaking sore muscles and washing off blood, Brian sets up a tripod in our bedroom.

"What's this?" I ask as I dry my hair with a towel.

"I thought I'd get a couple shots of you convalescing."

It's not a bad idea. I dig out the nice nightgown I save for vacations and slip it on. Unfortunately, my fancy Japanese kimono is ruined so I can't wear it. I climb into bed while Brian sets the timer on the camera. Then he pulls a chair close, sits by my side, and takes my hand. He has to take several pictures before I'm satisfied with one.

"Honey," he says finally. "You've been beat up. There's nothing you can do about it."

"But my hair looks awful!"

We try to sleep in but it's no use. By eight o'clock the sun is blazing through the gaps in our blinds. Brian rolls out of bed and ambles into the bathroom. I turn on the TV to see if we're on the news. The instant I hear him step into the shower, the front door bell rings.

My back screams when I try to sit up, and my legs are not the least bit interested in supporting my weight. I trudge down the stairs, clinging to the handrail for support.

"What are you doing out of bed?" Sarah says when I finally open the front door. "I thought you were dying."

"It looks worse than it is."

"Where's Brian? Why isn't he waiting you on hand and foot?"

"He's in the shower."

"Well this ought to brighten your day." She hands me our Saturday paper.

I'm on the front page, above the fold in all of my black and blue glory. The newspaper used the picture of me in bed with Brian at my side. How touching. The caption reads: *Terrorist Captured by Locals.*

At first, I consider keeping her out of my kitchen. We went to bed last night and left the whole mess. But she is my best friend. And she may be able to offer some suggestions on how to get blood out of grout. Besides, I need coffee.

"Oh, my god!" she howls when she sees the black splotches of dried blood on the counter and floor. The brie I set out last night has crusted over, the tapenade is a goner.

I groan and flop onto a chair. "Maybe we should just move."

"Don't worry about a thing," she says. "I'll have this place cleaned up in a jiffy."

Then she slings a plastic grocery bag up onto the counter and pulls out a plastic container of cut up fruit. She's also brought a pack of those horrible bagel thins. I wait, but she does not produce any cream cheese.

CHAPTER TWENTY-NINE

All of the hubbub from the capture of Farouk al Asad has died down. The bruises on my face went through a colorful array of dark blue, a freakish purple, and finally a sickly yellow-green reminiscent of what you'd see in a tissue if you had a bad cold.

My neighbors no longer stop me during my walk to discuss the latest news on al Asad. He's locked up and it will be months, maybe years, before he goes to trial.

Bailey Goodin recovered completely from the two gunshot wounds to the back. I went up to visit her in Chattanooga a couple times. She gave me some good background material for my book. She even swore she was through drinking but I'll give that resolution another month before she's back shooting tequila and chasing it with Red Bull.

Brian and I just got back from New York where we covered the city's annual St. Patrick's Day parade. Two years ago, we did Boston since they have the largest population of Irish, and they were the first to hold a parade. Last year it was Chicago, just because we wanted to see how they were able to die their river green. I tried to talk Ray into sending us to Dublin for the festivities there but he didn't buy my authenticity speech.

I'm emptying the dishwasher when Brian comes in with today's mail. He lays the bills on the counter and hands me this week's copy of the Mansell Messenger.

Because we live way out in the suburbs, we subscribe to a little neighborhood newspaper, too. It's the only way to get the health inspections for local restaurants, and I love to read their 'rant' column filled with important issues of the day, like: *I just drove past a road crew fixing a pothole on Oakley Road. Since when does it take for (sic) men to patch one hole?*

"Take a look at this," Brian says.

There's a picture of a tow truck dragging a car out of a small pond.

"That looks like Arbor Estates."

"It is."

Arbor Estates is a pretentious subdivision I pass every time I go to Target. When it was first built, it included a guardhouse at the entrance, but hard times have hit even the rich because they no longer pay a security guy to man the building. Instead they put in an electronic gate that requires a code.

The subdivision is set off the road about 100 yards to accommodate the two retention ponds that catch the run-off from storms. The designer added spraying fountains in the middle of each pond to make them look elegant. The drive into the subdivision passes between the two ponds and acts like sort of a dam to keep them separated.

I read the headline: *Freak drowning ruled accident.* The opening paragraph says some woman drove her car off this raised drive and down into the left pond. By the time rescuers arrived, she was a goner.

"How could someone drown in a shallow pond like that?" I ask. "How deep do you think they are?"

"I don't know. Five feet?"

I look at the picture again, visualizing a woman careening off the road at five in the morning. The paper doesn't say anything about her alcohol level but I assume they checked.

The distance from the gate to the pond is maybe twenty feet. How does someone go from idling while a gate opens, to a high enough speed to lose control and run off the road?

"So her car was barely submerged in the pond," I mutter.

"I guess."

"But she doesn't try to get out?"

"Maybe she panicked," Brian says. "They say the water pressure against a car door can be pretty powerful until the water seeps inside enough to equalize."

"So she can't roll a window down and swim out?"

"If she had power windows, they wouldn't work."

"And she just sits in the car watching the water rise and doesn't do anything."

"Suppose she tried the door at first but it wouldn't open. She gets all hysterical, she doesn't understand the physics of force, so she just gives up."

I skim the rest of the story. "Didn't she have a cell phone?"

"It doesn't say."

"Her name is Deborah Wiley. Why does that sound familiar?"

Brian taps at the article. "It says she was a newspaper carrier."

"Oh, my god! She's *our* newspaper carrier. She always sticks a Christmas card into our paper in December so we'll give her some money."

"Maybe you can use this for one of your mystery short stories," Brian says.

The call of the refrigerator lures him away. He opens the door and stands searching.

I'm tempted to tell him dinner is in an hour but that's just a waste of breath. Instead, I go back to studying the picture of the car. Maybe she was epileptic, or she had some other kind of seizure. But wouldn't the coroner have found that out in an autopsy? If they tested her alcohol level they surely tested for drugs, too.

"I don't know. It sounds a little fishy to me," I say.

Brian snorts because he thinks I'm making a pun.

"We should look into this," I say.

"You don't need to look into anything." He yanks the newspaper away so I can't look at it anymore. "Just use your imagination and dream something up."

271

I get a bit snippy. "I want to drive by there and see exactly where she was when she ran off the road."

"No."

"I promise I won't even get out of the car."

"NO."

I grab my purse that's hanging off the back of a kitchen chair. "Ten minutes, tops."

"Gladys!" he yells, but I'm already in the garage.

TURN THE PAGE FOR A PREVIEW OF

A TALE OF MORAL CORRUPTION

By Marsha Cornelius

CHAPTER ONE

"It's a boy."

Merriam's mouth sagged at the corners when she made her announcement yesterday, like she was reporting a cockroach sighting in the break room. She reminded us that Navin's paternity leave starts today; we'll all need to pick up the slack while he's out.

Of course, we knew it was a boy months ago when Navin started parading around the office with that artificial womb strapped to his belly. His wife Lanelle is president of Jarvis Corporation, so naturally, they paid for the deluxe womb with the clear walls where everyone can see the little darling.

Like the pompous show-off he is, Navin didn't drape the womb with a coverlet. Oh, no, he wanted to draw attention to his miniscule contribution to the process. At the beginning of the pregnancy, he kept insisting that the genital tubercle on the fetus was a glans clitoridis. He caught me in the break room one morning, and actually juggled the womb until the little fetus rolled over. Then using a stylus, Navin proudly poked at a tiny nub. "See? It's a girl!"

But once the tubercle continued to extend, Navin could no longer carry his false hope around with the unborn child. The appendage was definitely phallic. After that, Navin adopted the privacy coverlet that most expectant parents wear.

Andrew says there was a time, long ago, when those three words—'It's a boy'—meant more than even the words 'I love you.'

He says the birth of a boy was heralded as a major event, bringing untold pride and joy to parents and the community. Evidently, a boy held the mystical guarantee of the continuation of a family's lineage.

When I was young, I imagined my mother crying tears of disappointment when she heard the news that her first-born was going to be a boy. Back then, the artificial womb was still experimental, and too expensive for my mother's salary as a young orthopedic surgeon. She didn't get the disheartening news until I was nearly 20 weeks along. I visualized my father hanging his head in shame at not being able to carry out the simple task of creating a girl child.

My mother said they tried all the usual tricks to produce a girl, but it just didn't work out that way. Always the martyr, she lamented my father's cursed Y chromosome that screwed everything up, and shamed us both in the process. But my dad has never acted like he was disappointed. In fact, he and I are a lot closer than he is with my sister Jillian.

According to Andrew, all children were given the father's surname, and that is how families were recorded generation after generation.

I don't know how Andrew remembers all this trivia. He and I went to the same schools but I don't recall seeing all this stuff about how revered male children were. All I've ever read was how men screwed up the world so bad that women took away their ability to make any kind of business or political decisions.

My grandmother says that if a woman is responsible enough to nurture a child from birth to adulthood, she can certainly nurture a business. She says all men ever did was cheat and steal from each other.

When I ask my father about this role reversal, he seems reticent to discuss the matter. Notice how I used 'reticent'? Andrew says I need to improve my vocabulary, to raise my score on the Approved Partner Registry.

I've been on the APR for over a year now. The board won't consider men until they're twenty-five years old, and then the open enrollment is only once a year. The first two times I applied, I was rejected. It's that questionnaire! They ask the same thing twice, only they put a little twist in the second time to see if you slip up. Like on one question, I strongly agreed that I preferred work that is routine, which was the right answer. But then on the question where it asked if I considered myself creative, someone who comes up with new ideas, I disagreed and got penalized.

But aren't those kind of the same question?

Andrew says I was just trying to answer the way I thought they wanted me to. But what does he know? He's never taken those stupid tests. He's never had to sweat it out, waiting for the results. I know, I shouldn't be so hard on him. He's not on the APR and his chances of getting on are slim. He has Erb's Palsy.

The brachial plexus muscle in Andrew's shoulder was damaged during childbirth. That kind of accident rarely happens these days, but his mother and father were in some third-world country as part of a humanitarian effort to help people recovering from an earthquake. His mother had assured everyone she'd be back in plenty of time for delivery, but then the country was hit with a second quake and they were stranded.

She went into premature labor at some godforsaken outpost. A midwife was sent for, but Andrew's father panicked. The baby was coming. Some hidden instinct to take charge overwhelmed him. He pulled Andrew's head to the side as he tugged to free him from the birth canal and the muscle in his shoulder tore.

Now his left arm hangs useless at his side, and it's definitely smaller than his right. He always wears long-sleeved shirts, even in the summer, to hide the deformity. Funny how just a moment's panic during those few seconds of childbirth can determine your whole life.

Back in the U.S., his mother's insurance paid to try and correct the damage, but the surgeon did a crappy job. Too bad

Andrew wasn't born a girl. His mother would have insisted on a top surgeon, for sure.

So of course, he'll never be a candidate for the APR. Only attractive men with above average IQs, and strong compatibility traits are accepted. I mean, I'm pretty good looking, but I still had a hard time getting in.

My supervisor, Merriam, once told me I was a knock-out. She said if she weren't already married, she'd take some of that Mason magic. That's sexual harassment, but I'm not going to report her. I appreciate the compliment.

My best friend Ben took the APR test the day he turned 25 and aced it. Within a week, he was getting all kinds of requests from women, and last year he got married. I try not to be jealous but come on, he had three different women interested in him. He's going to call me any day now to say he and his new wife are launching a pregnancy, and I'll have to be all positive and supportive.

I grab a nutrition bar as I pass through my kitchen, rip away the end of the wrapper, and gnaw off a bite. The dry nuts and oats get stuck in my throat and I can hardly swallow. How do some guys have all the luck? Even Oliver has a steady girlfriend from the APR. I can remember in high school when the three of us did everything together. I always thought we'd get married and have kids and hang out in somebody's backyard cooking burgers while our wives huddled to talk about work. Now the only friend I have left is Andrew.

I stuff the rest of my tasteless nutrition bar in my pocket, then lock the front door with the Universal Identification chip embedded in my wrist. Nearly everyone uses these now. It's the law.

I've heard horror stories of people's UI chips being cut right out of their arms, stolen by unsavory individuals. But I think that's just urban legend. What good would it do to steal someone's UI chip? There's way too much information stored in those for anyone to assume another's identity. A UI has everything from your DNA to your credit history in there. And with retinal scanners everywhere, it's impossible to try and impersonate someone else.

It's still dark outside, but not as cold as it was last month. The weather service says it will rain today, but thankfully it hasn't started. I've got my umbrella just in case.

I can't afford an automobile on my salary, so I take the train to work. Cars are discouraged anyway; they cause traffic congestion, and some of the older models still use a fuel that pollutes the air.

The transit line runs right next to our neighborhood, so it's no big deal to walk the three blocks to the MARTA station.

The homes in our area are older; they aren't wired for all the electronics so I have to actually turn on the lights when I walk from the living room to the kitchen. And the climate control gauge has to be manually set, but at least the system filters and humidifies the air.

Most women on their way to the top of the corporate ladder aren't interested in these older homes, but mine will do until I get settled with someone.

There are a few single-income families scattered around the neighborhood. The husband stays home with the kids while the wife works long hours to get ahead. They don't stick around long though. Once the money starts rolling in, they move to the suburbs with the fully-automated homes.

Right up the block is a new family that moved in a couple months ago. I slow down to look at the playset in their side yard with the tiny slide and brightly-colored plastic swing. Toys are scattered around the front yard; there's a playpen on the large covered porch where the dad sits at a small desk. I think he's writing a book.

A gust of wind blows a pinwheel stuck in the grass; it's red and blue and green blades whirl around. It reminds me of a movie I saw when I was young. A father is helping his daughter with a science project on wind power. They have the mechanics all set up, but then the little brother comes toddling along and messes it up.

The daughter is crying, and the little boy is crying, but the father takes them both in his arms and soothes them. I love that scene, with the kids on the dad's lap. He knows just what to say to make it all better. And he doesn't get mad at the little boy. He loves his son as much as his daughter.

Ever since I saw that movie, I've wanted to be a father like that. I want to teach a child to catch a ball and draw a picture and read a book. We'll make sandwiches for lunch, spreading the peanut butter across the bread and over our thumbs. We'll pretend we're explorers and wade through a creek in our boots looking for salamanders and unusual rocks.

My roommate Damon doesn't care if he ever gets into a relationship, much less married. He's on the road all week, setting up and demonstrating 3D copiers. Most companies just send a video demonstration of their equipment, but Damon's company claims that by sending a live rep, they answer more questions, and get fewer complaints and service calls. They must be right because they're the top seller of 3D copiers in the country.

On the weekends, Damon is happy hitting the bars with his buddies to watch sports. Or they hang around the house, drinking beers and playing video games. I don't have a lot in common with Damon, but that's okay. We aren't supposed to judge others.

I've been sharing the house with him for a couple years now. When I first graduated from Georgia State my dad wanted me to move back home—'to save money' he said—but I really think he was looking for an ally against my mom and my Grandma Lisa. That lasted about six months before I had to get out on my own.

The house Damon advertised fit the bill; it was on the metro line, and the rent was reasonable. Once I'd moved in, I asked him if he was on the registry. He looked at me like I was crazy.

"Why would I want a woman bossing me around all the time," he said. "Or expecting me to change dirty diapers, and wipe snotty noses."

He said he was registered with the escort service and as soon as he found a woman who wanted to fuck a couple times a month, he was taking his name off. That kind of talk can get a guy in real trouble, but Damon doesn't seem to care. He acts cocky like that whenever he's around his friends and me. In the two years I've known him, I've never seen him with a woman to know how he behaves around them.

Getting into the escort service is pretty easy compared to the registry. You just enter some information online and you're in. But with the registry, you have to actually go into one of their offices. I guess they had too many inaccurate registrations, where a man misrepresented himself. Now you have to prove that you're not a troll.

And you have to take the tests at the center instead of online at home. I heard there was a lot of cheating; guys helping each other with the answers. I know I would have asked Andrew to help me if I'd had the chance.

I've never told anyone this, but I had some 'performance' issues as well. Two different women reported me to the registry and I was classified as PME: A premature ejaculator. How embarrassing is that?

During high school, sex wasn't even an option for most guys. Solexa was just coming on the market and a lot of parents put their boys on the drug before they got their first wisp of underarm hair. Those pills did a great job of suppressing the libido, but they didn't do much for a guy's confidence. Once I got accepted at Georgia State, my mother decided to wean me off the stuff.

Unfortunately, the college girls were just like they were in high school, so driven to excel that they didn't pay much attention to guys. The few girls who weren't on the fast track didn't appeal to me, so I was a virgin when I got on the APR. What did those women expect? I had no experience.

Nevertheless, I had to take remedial training with a surrogate for two months. And believe me, having sex with a surrogate is not as much fun as you might think be. It's like she's evaluating everything you do, timing you, trying to get you to slip up.

Thank goodness I passed the course, and got the PME removed from my profile, but I'm constantly worried that someone will find out.

My counselor assures me that a PME classification is sometimes preferred. Lots of women aren't interested in sex, they just want to get pregnant, so a man who can get in and get out quickly is a benefit. But I've masturbated enough to know how good an orgasm feels. I want the fireworks, and I want to be married to a woman who wants them, too.

A raindrop hits my cheek, then another on my forehead. Here it comes. I dash the last half a block to the MARTA station. Once under the overhanging roof, I skid to a stop, swipe my UI, and step through the security scanner.

Downstairs, a crowd waits on the platform for the next train to downtown Atlanta. I don't have to be at work until 8:30, but there's always a good mix of women on the 7:23—the early birds who like to be at their desk before eight—so I try to catch it every morning. Maybe I'll get noticed.

Our station is far enough out of the city that I usually find a place to sit, but if a woman gets on, I always give up my seat. It's a show of respect. And I never know when a woman might strike up a conversation just because I'm polite. It's happened a couple times already. And of course, they ask if I'm on the registry. I don't get many hits on my profile, but it's all about playing the numbers.

Someday I'll get lucky. I don't mean to sound conceited, but honestly? There isn't a day goes by that a woman won't turn her head to get a second look at me, or pause just a moment longer when she's scanning the crowd of faces.

They're not allowed to say anything. There are strict laws about sexual harassment, and they are rigidly enforced. But that doesn't stop women from looking. I see it in their gaze, the twitch of a brow, the slight parting of their lips. They're fantasizing about me.

Even now while I make my way to an empty seat on the train, a woman gives me one of those up and down inspections, like she's checking out the whole package. She turns to whisper something to the woman seated beside her, and she gives me the once over, too.

I don't care. I like the attention. I want to get married and live in a nice house instead of our rundown rental. What's wrong with that?

As soon as I was hired at Campbell and Fetter, I signed up to volunteer at the company's daycare on the first floor. My assignment is three year-olds. Inexperienced men are prohibited from handling infants under a year, but evidently, once babies are out of diapers, and are mobile, men can be trusted to monitor these children. Basically, I follow little tykes around, making sure they don't conk each other on the head, or trip and fall on sharp objects.

There's this little kid, Evan. He's really shy. The first time I noticed him, he was off in a corner playing by himself. We're supposed to encourage the children to be active, so I had started the song 'Watch Me' and there were maybe ten kids all jumping around. As we flew past Evan, flapping our arms like birds, I called to him to come on and join us, but he wouldn't. So after the song, I flew over to him, perched on one of those tiny chairs, tucked my arms up, and peeped at him until he finally smiled.

He's such a cute little dude, with his wispy red hair poking out all around his head. I've kind of made him my special project. Whenever I see him, I fold in my arms, flap my elbows and peep. He makes his own little wings and peeps back.

He doesn't talk though. Deana, one of the supervisors, says he's a slow learner. Maybe. I think he just doesn't have anything to say yet.

Today I brought a stone I found once in Michigan. It's called a Petosky stone. When it's dry, it just looks boring and gray. But when it's wet, you can see all the little segments that used to be living coral. Evan's too young to understand what a fossil is, but I think he'll be surprised to see how different a plain rock can look when it's wet.

I'm working from three o'clock to eight today. It's one of my favorite shifts because most of the children are picked up by six. Then the rest of the kids are fed supper, and sometimes we watch a movie.

Evan's mom almost always works late, so he and I can hang out for some quality 'man time.' If there's a movie, we'll make the sound effects, like a door creaking open, or a dog barking. Evan's really good at animal sounds.

My building is on the same block as the train station, which is good this morning because as we all ride the escalator up to street level, I can hear the rain coming down. The pace of the crowd slows at the exit, like we're all assessing the situation, judging if we can walk without getting too wet, or if this calls for a mad dash.

Then umbrellas pop open, almost in unison, and the crowd disperses. I'd offer a dry spot under my umbrella, but all the women have their own.

I guess that's the whole problem: women don't need men anymore.

My grandfather says there was a time when a woman would intentionally act helpless just so a man would come to her aid; like she'd forget her umbrella, so a man would offer the use of his. It was all part of a master plan to find a husband.

In the olden days, a man wanted a female companion, 'a pretty little thing on his arm', my grandfather says, like he was showing off an exotic bird or rare flower.

But it's not like that anymore.

If a woman wants a companion, she usually chooses another woman. They think alike, they see things from the same perspective, they're on the same wave-length. Women aren't interested in listening to men talk about themselves, and they don't want us hanging around all the time.

I've heard different theories on how everything changed. My grandfather says this role reversal started once the majority of Congress was female. Grandma Lisa says that education reform is responsible. Teachers were trained to encourage girls as well as boys to excel in school. My mom insists that advertising restrictions stopped women from being viewed as sex objects and portrayed them as strong and independent.

Personally? I think women gained their greatest freedom when the artificial womb was invented.

It's probably a little of each of these things. All I know for sure is that men once ruled the world, and now they don't.

A Tale of Moral Corruption *may be purchased*
at your favorite bookstore

TURN THE PAGE FOR A PREVIEW OF

LOSING IT ALL

By Marsha Cornelius

FEBRUARY, 1984

CHAPTER ONE

Pain's a bitch.

The doctor at the VA called it phantom pain, nerve trauma that would eventually go away. Yeah, right. Frank was twelve years and counting.

This morning, he woke to a cold, sluggish fog that had his foot throbbing before he even stood. His only relief was to shift his weight to his toes and keep pressure off the heel. Of course, the gimp-walk didn't do much for his appearance. People already shied away from his long hair and shaggy beard. The shuffling limp and tortured expression convinced onlookers that he was a derelict.

They should have seen him twelve years ago at the VA. The pain was so intense all he could do was lie in bed, groaning and thrashing, his hospital gown soaked in sweat. Once he was up and around, he'd rolled down the hallway in his wheelchair, ranting at other Vietnam veterans with missing legs and arms. His rage seemed to ease his pain, but like a drug, he needed more. So he started ramming into other wheelchairs, then chasing after those who could walk, bruising their ankles with his metal foot-plates.

On his feet, Frank was a regular fighting machine, wielding a crutch like a club, or throwing sucker punches when least expected. It never occurred to him that those guys were battling their own pain.

In desperation, he pinned a doctor to the wall with his own clipboard, threatening to decapitate him if he didn't up Frank's morphine dosage. An orderly put him out on the street.

Then the pain really took hold. The dribble of morphine still in his system wore off while he slouched in the back of a city bus headed for downtown Atlanta. When he threw up in the aisle, the driver tossed him off. Unable to stand, much less walk, Frank crawled into an alleyway and passed out.

A wino rummaging through a trashcan woke him. Frank offered the bum some dough for his bottle of Thunderbird, and slugged the wine down in one long gulp. From there it was all downhill.

Frank shook off the memories, and tipped his face up to feel the warm afternoon sun. The day felt more like April than February. And now that the morning fog had burned off, his foot had stopped pulsing. He eased a little more weight onto his right heel and strolled down Argonne Avenue a good hour ahead of the city's garbage trucks.

A crumpled drink can lay in the gutter. Frank shook the dead leaves off before dropping the can into the black garbage bag slung over his shoulder. This would be a good day to hit Piedmont Park. The Midtown crowd had probably flocked there for lunch, clutching their brown bags and sodas.

Frank paused at a cardboard box of junk next to a garbage can. Digging past chipped dishes and frayed towels, Frank found a pair of Converse sneakers splattered with green paint. Elevens. He sat on the curb and tried the left one on. Perfect. Ripping off a corner of the box, he folded the cardboard and wedged it into the heel of the right shoe to fill the space where half of his foot was missing.

He'd had a pair of shoes like these in high school. Chuck Taylor All Stars. He thought he was a real all-star back then, playing basketball, dating one of the cheerleaders. *Candy.* They were so naïve, thinking that their love was the only force in the universe. Then Nixon came up with the lottery.

The night Frank found out he was number sixteen in the draft, he and Candy crawled into the back of his '59 Impala to grind their hips against each other in desperation. She cried the whole time. If he had known how soon he'd be sweltering in that Godforsaken jungle, or how long he'd lay helpless in that dirt pit waiting to die, he might have bawled right along with her.

With his thumb and index finger, he pinched away the sting in his eyes, then tossed his old shoes into the cardboard box.

Across the street, a staircase lay beached on its side in the front yard of an old Victorian in the middle of renovation. A worker stepped out to the porch and tossed an armload of rotting two-by-fours onto a rubbish heap of chipped drywall, old carpet, rusted pipe, and Little Debbie snack boxes. Frank made a mental note to run by the Piggly Wiggly for a grocery cart.

At Tenth Street, Frank waited at the light to cross into Piedmont Park. A cab pulled up in front of Taco Mac, down half a block. A smartly dressed woman stepped out of the cab, brushed her skirt smooth and slung her purse over her shoulder.

From out of nowhere, a kid barreled toward the woman, snatched the purse, and tucked it under his arm like a football. Caught off guard, the woman managed to clamp a fist around the strap as it raked down her arm. The kid gave a hard yank; the woman staggered to stay on her feet. Then one of her high heels wobbled and she dropped to her knees. She screamed, still clinging to the purse strap.

Frank expected the cab driver to come to her rescue. When the jerk drove away instead, Frank scanned the front of the restaurant, waiting for someone to come tearing out. No one did. He watched the woman's stockings peel away from her knees as the kid dragged her along the concrete.

Crap.

"Hey!" Frank yelled as he drew up to his full six-two height, and took a step toward the ruckus. "Let go!"

He hoped his tough guy act would either scare the kid or freak out the woman, but they both clung to that purse like pit bulls. Just as Frank broke into a run to rescue the woman, the kid flicked open a knife and cut the strap. The woman tumbled forward. The kid lurched into Frank, and the impact knocked his sack of drink cans loose. They clanged to the sidewalk.

For a split second, the kid cringed at the noise, but then his arm started slashing through the air and Frank couldn't get out of the way fast enough. The first swipe of the knife barely grazed Frank's green Army jacket, but the back swing caught him on the chin. The contact with flesh seemed to bolster the kid's confidence. He lunged at Frank, aiming for his gut.

With his forearm, Frank knocked the kid's hand to the side then drove a fist into the punk's soft belly, doubling him over. The stupid kid never saw it coming. Probably figured Frank for just another stumbling wino.

While the kid gasped for breath, Frank raised both arms to finish the punk off with a Bobo Brazil elbow drop, but the rumble of voices distracted him.

A crowd had gathered around the woman. A man helped her to her feet, while a girl handed the woman a tissue to dab her bloody knees. Another woman gaped at Frank in horror, like *he* was the bad guy. Somebody suggested calling the police, and suddenly everyone was looking at Frank.

Oh sure. It's always the homeless guy.

Instead of the body slam, Frank jerked the knife out of the kid's hand. "Drop the purse."

The kid let the bag fall before dashing to the corner and out of sight.

When Frank hobbled toward the six or so people huddled around the woman, they gasped and took a collective step back. The tissue girl actually screamed. Geez, did they think he was suddenly going to turn into a psycho killer? Did they not just see him take the knife away from that punk? He let the weapon clank to the sidewalk.

Holding out the purse, he waited for the woman to take it. When she didn't, he tossed it at her feet. What had he expected? Gratitude?

A siren screamed over on Peachtree. Oh, no. He wasn't going to spend the night in the Atlanta jail. Some guys appreciated the warm meal and dry bed even if it meant getting knocked around, but not Frank.

Like Quasimodo, he lumbered across the street, through a stand of trees, and into Piedmont Park.

Frank stood over a drinking fountain in the park and splashed water on his chin. Blood drained through the ends of his beard. An old codger edged his way toward a trash barrel nearby.

"That you, Frank?"

Frank glanced up. "Hey, Ben."

"What happened?"

The old man stepped closer, his eyes jittering in their sockets.

"Nothing," Frank mumbled.

Ben's eyes focused long enough to peer into the garbage. With a toothless grin, he pulled a half-eaten burger out of a fast-food bag and shoved it into his mouth.

Frank watched him for a second. "Got a napkin in there?"

The old man fished one out and Frank pressed it against his cut.

At the can bank, the other fellas had already heard about the purse snatching. Big Bob thought Frank had been arrested. Fred G's version of the story had the woman attacking Frank; the kid wasn't even in the mix. Other guys paced and licked their dry lips, anxious for their turn at the can bank.

Frank understood their anticipation: that first drink of the day. He'd floated in a drug and booze induced state of bliss the whole time he was in Saigon. It wasn't until they heaved his swollen, aching body onto a transport plane headed for the States that he started to come down. Then there was hell to pay. He shook. He puked. He slapped at imaginary stinging ants that crawled inside his shirt.

Once he got to the VA, the angels of mercy hooked him up to a morphine drip to take his mind off the chunk of foot they'd removed. Days later, when he finally took a piss on his own, he noticed his withered, purple cock, and saw lingering traces of blood in his urine. Damn whores.

Now that the sun had gone down, the night air regained its bite. Frank zipped his jacket up to his raw chin. The front wheel of his grocery cart squeaked as he pushed a load of rotten lumber toward his favorite convenience store. A hooker stood under a street lamp, displaying her wares to drivers that passed. When she saw Frank, she relaxed her pose.

"Evening, Frank," Diamond called, boosting her double Ds in a tight sweater.

"Hey, Diamond." Frank parked his buggy against the lamppost. "How you doing?"

"Glittering, honey." She fluffed her Afro with silver fingernails.

"I see that."

"Got some sugar for you." She cocked a leg out and ran her hand up her fishnet stocking.

"I'll pass tonight. Thanks."

Those fingernails had raked a good chunk of flesh off Frank's forearm the first time he met Diamond all those years ago. His GI cut had grown just shaggy enough that she thought he was an Emory student on his way to the Plaza Theater. But when she offered to suck his dick, he flashed-back on those whores in Saigon, and took a swing at Diamond with the pint of Sloe gin he'd been guzzling. He grazed the side of her head, and she came after him, her arms whirling like a windmill.

Frank had tried to retreat but somehow Diamond got a fistful of his hair. Her shiny silver high-heel drew back, and when Frank saw her knee rise up toward his crotch, he cried out, fell to the sidewalk, and curled into a fetal position, clutching his jewels.

She could have laughed at him, or taken advantage of his sniveling by kicking him with said silver shoe. But she knelt and helped him to his feet. "Come here, Sugar. Why don't you tell Diamond all about it?"

Between slurps of gin, he told her about the horrors of Vietnam, and how he'd been compensating ever since with drugs and alcohol.

"Watch my stuff?" he asked Diamond as he reached for the door handle.

She swiveled her hips. "Like you be watchin' mine."

Inside the deserted convenience store, a clerk perched on a stool watching a small black and white TV. A little old lady in a commercial stepped up to a counter and grumbled, "Where's the beef?" The clerk laughed and tried to mimic the phrase in his heavy accent. He grinned and nodded at Frank for approval.

"Not bad," Frank told him.

"Marlboros, Mr. Frank?" the clerk asked.

"You got it." Frank pulled a fist full of coins and chinked them on the counter. He barely had enough, what with losing his cans in the purse incident.

One of the front wheels on Frank's cart started to shimmy as he cut through the parking lot of the Omni arena. At the railroad tracks, he grunted as he lifted the front wheels over each rail. From the top of a small rise beyond an abandoned warehouse, he saw the flickering light of a campfire. Home.

Four shacks stood in a half-circle around the fire, each constructed from scraps of plywood, corrugated metal, and plastic, held together with bent nails and rope. Wood slapped against wood as he rumbled down the weed-tangled slope.

"Jesus, Frank." Del relaxed his guard and sat down on an overturned milk crate. "We could hear you clear back at the Omni."

Randall left the fading campfire to check out Frank's load. "What you got?"

"Firewood." Frank handed him some of the shorter pieces. "Looks like I'm right on time."

A smirk wrinkled Randall's face. "Heard about the purse snatcher."

"Is that the one where the cops kicked my butt?"

Randall's grin widened, exposing a missing tooth. "No, the one where the woman pulled a gun out of the purse after you returned it, and shot you."

They shared a laugh as they stacked wood on dying embers.

Del grumbled. "When you gonna learn to keep outta other people's business?"

Frank ignored the comment. Instead, he sat on his own milk crate, pulled a sandwich out of his pocket and took a bite. "Where's Shorty?" He tossed the wrapper into the fire and watched the plastic shrivel before it burst into flames.

"Gone," Randall said.

"Where to?" Frank asked.

"Roswell. Gonna look for a *job*." Del spat out the word.

"No kidding." Frank reached into another pocket for an apple and took a big bite, juice dribbling into his beard. He sucked the drips.

"I figure he just got too old to drift," Randall said.

"That's bullshit," Del said in a gravely voice. "I'm sixty and I ain't about to give up."

"Yeah, but he was a suit, remember?" Randall said.

Once he'd eaten the apple, Frank twizzled the stem between his fingers. "I think he got tired."

"Tired of what?" Del asked. "Cruising from Techwood to Courtland and back every day?"

"No. Tired of being cold, tired of being hungry—"

Randall nodded. "Tired of being scared."

"Scared? What the hell did he have to be scared of?" Del grumbled.

"It's not like it used to be." Randall tipped his head toward the skyline. "Those young guys, they're mad. They don't like being homeless. Think everybody owes 'em something."

"It's getting scary all right," Frank said as he pulled out his Marlboros and flipped up the lid. "Want one?"

Del rose on bandy legs and reached across Randall to snatch a cigarette. He lit it off a piece of burning wood, and inhaled deeply. His cough started slow, but picked up steam until he doubled over, gasping for air. With his hands on his knees, he hacked a blob of mucus onto the dirt.

Once his coughing jag passed, Del managed a couple more puffs before he carefully stubbed out the cigarette and slipped it into his pocket. Then he stood close to the fire, warming his wiry body one last time before heading for his shelter. His hand pushed aside a sheet of heavy plastic, and he crawled between two pieces of plywood that leaned on each other. A groan escaped as he dropped to the ground.

Randall tilted his head back and studied the stars as he blew out smoke. "You suppose we ought to keep Shorty's place open for a while? In case he comes back?"

"I doubt he will," Frank flicked an ash. "That charity center up in Roswell . . . I hear they got a men's dorm, free food."

"Why would they do that?"

"I guess they don't want anybody roaming the streets."

Del's cough started up again, rose an octave as it grew more intense, and ended with a shrill gasp for air that echoed through the night. Randall took one last drag from his cigarette and tossed it in the fire before he crawled into his own lean-to. He pulled a bent stop sign across the entrance.

Frank flicked his own cigarette into the fire, his fingers tense. Pain jack-hammered his heel. He hobbled to his shack and stretched out on an old sleeping bag. It was always the quiet of night that brought out the worst in his pain.

First he tried a song. "Well she was just seventeen," he sang through clenched teeth, "you know what I mean." Halfway through the tune, Del hollered at him to shut up.

Years ago, when Randall had seen how much pain Frank was in, he'd suggested thinking of an old girlfriend. Said masturbation was an excellent way to relieve pain. Supposedly, Randall worked at some mental hospital back in the fifties. He'd fought for years to improve the treatment of patients, but a sadistic staff and filthy conditions finally fried his brain. He just walked out the door one day, and had drifted ever since. Frank found it ironic that when the government deinstitutionalized tons of patients in the late sixties, Randall had his hands full with those same schizos who now wandered the streets.

Frank told him it was too painful to jerk off, so Randall came up with the idea of reciting a poem or a song. If that didn't take his mind off the pain, Frank could run through a difficult task in his head. After a couple slow, deep breaths, he mentally pulled the carburetor out of his '59 Impala and cleaned the choke plate and fuel intake until he fell asleep.

CHAPTER TWO

A metal cash box clutched to her chest, Chloe slipped into her checkout lane at Foodtown, a pitiful excuse for a grocery store, with rusty stains on the floor tiles, and the rancid odor of old meat. She slid the box into her drawer and turned on the light.

In the next lane over, Jennifer popped her gum as she swiped food items across her scanner. "You're late again."

"Sorry." Chloe gave a weak smile. Just because she worked in a rundown part of town didn't mean she shouldn't look her best. It took time to find just the right shade of eyeshadow to coordinate with her lavender blouse from K-Mart. Chloe wasn't the type to just smear a quick coat of lipstick on her mouth. She outlined her lips with a deeper shade, like she'd seen in the magazines. And after what she had paid to get her hair colored, she wanted to make sure it was teased and sprayed to look just like Lucy Ewing on Dallas.

Jennifer's Foodtown smock was unbuttoned enough to show a peek of the red bra she wore. Chloe bristled as a construction worker buying a sub sandwich and a quart of beer bent in for a closer look. His hands were filthy. Was he going to wash those hands before he ate?

Flattered, Jennifer puffed out her chest and grinned at him! Sure, Duane loved to see Chloe dressed in short skirts and low-cut blouses. But not the whole world.

Once the construction worker left, Jennifer leaned against her register, and dug something out of her teeth with a polished fingernail. "So, what's your excuse today?"

Chloe reached under the counter for a bottle of glass cleaner and spritzed her scanner. "You know how my niece Staci has been babysitting for me? Well, she was late because she had to stay after school to meet with a teacher."

"Yeah, right." Jennifer snorted a laugh. "You believe anything, Chloe. That's why you're in deep shit."

Chloe glared at her. "I do not."

"Right. Your husband took off, and you think he's looking for a better job in Chattanooga."

"He is!" Chloe felt the heat rising up her neck. "He should be back any day now."

"Back my ass." Jennifer's glossy red lips curled into a sneer. "It's been three months."

"He's training for a career," Chloe repeated what she had been told. "Not just a job."

Jennifer wasn't buying it. "Wake up. He hasn't even called you. And as close as Chattanooga is, surely he could get away to come home some weekend."

Chloe's bottom lip quivered as she swirled her paper towel around the glass.

Duane had been in such a rush, he'd tossed shirts into his suitcase without even folding them. Chloe had tried to slow him down by buttoning every button on a white dress shirt so she could fold it properly.

Her lip had quivered then, too. "When will you be back?"

"Christ Almighty, Chloe, we've been over this a thousand times." Duane slapped his hands to his sides like he was fussing out Ethan over spilled milk. But he wouldn't look her in the eye. He just stomped back to the closet for pants.

If she hadn't pulled the freshly-folded shirts out of the suitcase, Duane would have flopped his pants right down on top of them. She remembered how he'd bared his teeth when he jabbed a finger at her. "You're the one who complained I never stick with a job. This is my chance for a real career and now you're nagging me about it."

Just because he was right, didn't make it easier.

"I'm afraid . . ."

"Look . . ." He pulled fifty dollars out of his pocket. "It's a five-day course and then they place us with a rep so we can meet the customers. If I'm lucky I'll get a territory around here, find us an apartment and be back in a couple weeks, tops."

"What if . . ." She choked on her questions. What if he didn't come back in two weeks? What if somebody called about the bills and the rent? What if she ran out of money?

Duane slammed the suitcase lid shut and clicked the latches into place. "Stop worrying. Don't I always take care of things?"

An elderly woman pushed her shopping cart toward Chloe's lane but Jennifer flagged her down. "You better bring that over here. She's having a moment."

Tears that welled up in Chloe's eyes threatened to damage her make-up. She blotted with the corner of a clean paper towel.

Once Jennifer ripped the receipt out and handed it to the woman, she hissed at Chloe. "For God's sake, get it together. Do you want to get fired?"

"I can't help it," Chloe said as she shook her head. "I'm in deep trouble. My rent's past due and they keep sending me eviction letters. I got the electric bill, the car payment's due . . ."

"Car payment?" Jennifer screeched. "You don't even have the friggin' car!"

"I know." Chloe dabbed at another tear.

Before the bus even came to a stop, Chloe's stomach tightened. She hated to walk along Shallowford Road late at night. Who knew what kind of perverts were in the cars that drove by? Sometimes a driver tooted his horn, and even slowed down. She gripped her coat tight to her chest and ducked her head into her collar as she got off the bus. For the first few steps, she tried to keep the bus between her and the street, but after half a block, it sped away in a cloud of exhaust.

The walk through the apartment complex frightened Chloe even more. She could hear people yell from inside, and once she was sure she'd heard a gun fire. Why had Duane ever signed a lease here?

Chloe dashed up the sidewalk, fumbling to get her key in the door. Safe inside, she collapsed in a chair. Her heart pounded. Sweat beaded under her bangs. She took a deep breath and closed her eyes, but when she heard that first faint moan, her eyes flew open wide. Katie! Ethan! She was out of her chair like she was on fire.

Inside the tiny bedroom, Ethan lay fast asleep, his mouth wide open but silent. In the next bed, Katie was curled around her purple bunny, Mr. Rabbit.

The next moan sounded more like a cry, coming from Chloe's bedroom.

The light from the hallway cast a beam that widened as she opened the door. Like a spotlight, it shined on her niece, Staci, naked astride her boyfriend. The girl was bouncing like Duane had on that mechanical bull at Dooley's.

With a yelp, Staci turned toward the light, and scrambled for the sheet.

"Staci!" Chloe slammed the door and fell against the wall. Dear God, she was only fifteen. Still a child. How could they do that? And in Chloe's bed.

Staci shuffled out, barefoot but dressed, with Chad right behind. They both looked tousled but not the least bit embarrassed. Staci took one look at the scowl on Chloe's face and turned to her boyfriend. "Go on, I'll be out in a minute."

He patted her on the butt and winked. Who did he think he was? Didn't they have laws against twenty-year-old men preying on young girls? Chloe waited for the front door to close before she exploded. "What on earth is going on?"

"Don't act so shocked. We've been going together for a year."

"How could you bring him here, with the children right in the next room?"

Staci dropped her shoes to the floor. "Oh, like you and Duane never got it on."

Chloe's face flushed. "I don't mean that. What if Chad decided to . . . try something with Katie?"

She was only ten when her stepfather, Cal slipped into the bedroom Chloe shared with her sister Sherry. Still groggy from sleep, Chloe was confused to find Cal kneeling beside the bed. Under the sheet, his hand crept up her bare leg. He held a finger to his lips to shush her before he slipped his fingers into her panties. Her knees jerked together, and she tried to roll away, but he leaned a forearm against her throat. He had her pinned down, her air cut off.

When he finally finished with a shudder and pulled away his hand, Chloe glanced over at Sherry. She lay turned to the wall, her knees curled tight against her chest, her whole body quaking.

"Bullshit!" Staci's eyes flashed. "Chad would never do that."

Chloe's voice rose. "How do you know? Sometimes men get wild ideas and they do things . . ."

"Chad's not a pervert. He loves kids." Staci grinned and glanced down at her belly. "In fact, he's going to be a daddy himself in a few months."

"What?" Chloe's lips went numb. Her heart pounded so fast it made the tips of her fingers tingle.

"I'm pregnant. We're going to get married."

"You can't be." Chloe pressed cold fingers against her throat as her mind raced. "You . . . oh, God, your mother . . . maybe you're wrong."

Staci patted her little paunch. "No. We went to the doctor today. That's why I was late, 'cause I was late." She giggled.

Chloe staggered to the kitchen and sank into a chair. "Your mother's going to kill me. She trusted me. I told her you'd do better in school if you were here doing your homework instead of off with that boy."

Wasn't there some saying about history repeating itself? Here Staci had gone and got herself into the same mess Sherry had fifteen years ago. After all the screaming and fighting between Sherry and Walter, why would Staci get into the same fix?

"Oh, screw her, and screw Daddy." Staci opened the refrigerator and grabbed two RC Colas. She opened one. "All they do is bitch and complain. I'm sick of it, and so's Chad. We're going to Jackson. His older sister said we can stay in her basement."

Chloe's fingers massaged the Formica on the table.

"Oh, sweetheart, you're so young. I know you think you love Chad, but . . ."

"I do." Staci slipped her feet into her shoes. "And he loves me. We're leaving and that's final."

"What if it doesn't work out? You'll be clear over in Mississippi, alone with a little baby."

"Oh, that's rich coming from you. Just because Duane ran off don't mean Chad will."

Staci stomped out, and the door banged shut. Chloe sat with her face cradled in her hands, her fingers pressed against her eyelids.

Did Chad really love Staci, or was he just a smooth talker like Duane? Chloe slowly shook her head as she wandered into the bedroom. What a fool she'd been.

She yanked the sheets off her bed, and the smell of sex filled the air. She held her breath as she wadded the tainted linens into a ball.

Why hadn't she seen this coming? If Staci went to Mississippi, she would lose her free babysitter, and when Sherry found out—Chloe could hear her sister already.

Walter may have married Sherry, but he never let her forget how she'd ruined his life. One of his favorite jabs was, "no daughter of mine is gonna get knocked up." Then he'd raise an eyebrow and glare at Sherry. (Like he didn't have anything to do with the making of Staci.)

Sherry had dropped out of high school her junior year and never got around to graduating, so her dream was that her only child would at least get her high school diploma.

Now both of their dreams were about to get blown away like a puff of smoke.

Chloe sighed to loosen the tightness in her throat. Her temples pulsed, her stomach boiled. All she wanted to do was crawl under her covers and hope it would all go away in the morning.

Instead, she stomped the sheets into the laundry basket, then headed to the kitchen to get her own RC from the refrigerator. She took a long drink. The caffeine from the soda eased her headache, and the sugar settled her stomach.

With her back against the kitchen counter, she re-evaluated the situation. Surely, once the shock wore off, Sherry would want Staci and the baby near her, not clear over in Mississippi.

She took another drink, and let her train of thought run free.

Staci and Chad could stay in Atlanta. Staci could still babysit Ethan and Katie while she tended her own baby. Chloe could work more hours if Staci wasn't in school.

Chloe had just gotten to the point where she could get a nicer apartment when the telephone rang.

She jumped. "Hello?"

"Chloe? Is that you?"

Her stomach clenched, and she felt a sudden stab over her left eye.

"Hi, Sherry."

"If you're home, where's Staci?"

"She . . ." Chloe pressed against the pain in her forehead. "She and Chad left a little while ago."

"What?" Sherry shrieked, and Chloe cringed against the attack that was coming. "I knew it! That goddamn loser! Twenty years-old and sniffing around my daughter."

Chloe could hear Walter in the background. "What the hell's going on?"

"It's Staci," Sherry said.

Walter came on the line. "Listen here, you little tramp, you're only fifteen years-old which means I still own your ass."

"Walter, it's me, Chloe."

"Chloe! Where's Staci?" he asked.

"I'm not sure."

Chloe lay sprawled facedown on the bed, her pillow pulled over her head. She hadn't slept a wink last night, and now Katie had climbed onto the bed to snuggle. Through one eye, Chloe watched her daughter pop her thumb into her mouth and stare at the ceiling.

Ethan followed right behind. "Mama, I'm hungry. When are you gonna to get up?"

Chloe's hand tightened on the pillow. She never wanted to get up again. What she wanted was for Duane to come home and pay the rent and let her quit her job so it wouldn't matter that Staci was running off and Walter had cussed her out.

"Mama," Ethan said louder. "Katie and me are hungry. Aren't we, Katie? When are you gonna get up?" He tugged at the sheets.

"In a minute, Ethan. Go watch <u>Sesame Street</u>." Chloe turned her face under the pillow.

"<u>Sesame Street</u>'s over, Mama. It's time for breakfast." He came around the bed and shook her arm, then moved up to her shoulder. "Come on, Mama."

"All right, all right."

Chloe shuffled to the kitchen and poured cereal into two bowls. How did other women do it? Every morning, she watched single mothers in the apartment complex go to work. They paid for day care, and food, and rent. And they had money left over to buy their children Cabbage Patch dolls and those cute Jelly shoes. Some of the women even owned cars!

She sat on the tiny vanity in the bathroom with her feet in the sink, and leaned close to the mirror to pluck stray hairs from her eyebrows. She turned her head as she applied her foundation, feathering the makeup down her chin and onto her neck. Then with eyes open wide, she brushed on the mascara, using a curler to add curve to her lashes. And a couple poses with puckered lips, she moved on to her hair, teasing, spraying, fluffing and more spraying. She picked through her tubes of lipstick, choosing a shade called Pink Panther to match her blouse. Back in her bedroom, she sorted through her jewelry box to find just the right dangly earrings to match her nail polish.

Evelyn, the store manager, never once looked up all the while Chloe explained how she'd lost her babysitter and could no longer work at Foodtown. She just ripped the check from her big black book and handed it to Chloe. "Turn in your smock and name badge before you go."

The bank teller gave Chloe a funny look when her fingers clung to that last paycheck. And the apartment manager got real huffy when Chloe stopped by to pay her back rent.

"It's about time," he snapped. "I was just about to add you to my list of evictions for the sheriff's department."

"I think that pays me up." Chloe nodded at the check.

"Remington Properties don't put up with deadbeats, Mrs. Roberts. We expect our renters to pay in a timely manner."

She got huffy. "I'm not a deadbeat." She knew the instant she turned to herd the children out of the office, that the manager had his eyes on her backside.

As they walked back to their apartment, Chloe's head throbbed. How had her life gotten so fouled up? When she met Duane, she thought all her problems were over. She hated her job and Duane told her to quit. He wanted a sexpot for a wife, and she'd been one. Why couldn't he keep up his end of the bargain?

All she wanted was a husband who provided for her and the children. Was that asking too much?

They were on the sidewalk when Chloe noticed a man sitting on the stoop. Her mind kicked into panic mode. Something had happened to Duane. He was dead. He was in a hospital. God forbid, he was in jail.

CPSIA information can be obtained
at www.ICGtesting.com
Printed in the USA
FFOW03n0120291017
41594FF

The man stood up and stubbed out a cigarette. He hadn't shaved and his hair needed washing.

"You know a Duane Roberts?" he asked.

"Yes, he's my husband."

"You got a 1980 Toyota Corolla?"

"My husband does."

Katie whined and gripped Chloe's leg.

"And where could I find him?" the man asked.

"I don't know." She ignored his eyes as she fidgeted with her door key.

He yanked his sunglasses off and unzipped his jacket. As he reached into his breast pocket, a wave of body odor escaped. He pulled out some folded papers and gave them an official snap. "I'm here to repossess the car."

"I don't have it. My husband does and I don't know . . ."

"He runned away," Ethan said.

"Ethan, hush."

"That's not my problem. I'm here to get a car or . . ." the man opened the document, ". . . seven hundred and forty three dollars."

Chloe choked after repeating the seven. Then she blinked furiously at the tears that sprang to her eyes.

"Look lady," he growled at her. "I do this every day, so let me give you a tip. Cryin' don't work. I've even had women offer me of piece of ass. All I want is the car or the money."

Horrified, Chloe pushed past him. Her hand trembled as she unlocked the door. And when the filthy man leaned close, she yelped.

"I don't give up," he hissed at her. "I'm going to get that car, or the money—guaranteed."

She slammed the door in his face.

Losing It All may be purchased at your favorite bookstore